A Chain of Lakes Series Novel

The Color
of Truth

Stacy Monson

*Maxine,
Look to God for
your truth.
Blessings,
Stacy*

His Image Publications

Plymouth, Minnesota

ISBN: 978-0-9861245-6-3 (print)
ISBN: 978-0-9861245-7-0 (ebook)

To those who don't seem to measure up, who have screwed up, who can't keep up—God speaks truth into your life because He knows who you really are. He knit you together in your mother's womb, whispered your name, and numbered the days of your life and the hairs on your head. He longs to reveal the truth to you—you are His Beloved, just as you are.

In you, Lord my God, I put my trust. I trust in you; do not let me be put to shame, nor let my enemies triumph over me. No one who hopes in you will ever be put to shame, but shame will come on those who are treacherous without cause. Show me your ways, Lord, teach me your paths. Guide me in your truth and teach me, for you are God my Savior, and my hope is in you all day long.
Psalm 25:1-5

– 1 –

"Do you know who did this to you?" The man's question came down a long tunnel, echoing through her throbbing head.

Marti Gustafson turned her face from the questions he'd been asking since he entered the claustrophobic ER room. Of course she knew. The memory sent her heart into overdrive. An icy liquid blazed against her cheek and she sucked in a sharp breath, lifting a hand in protest. *Why won't they leave me alone?*

"I know it stings, honey," soothed a female voice. "It will take the edge off the pain." A gentle hand brushed her forehead; the touch was soft, cool. Safe. "Take slow breaths. There you go. I'll be back in a few minutes. Push the button if you need me."

"Miss." The man again, gently persistent. "Once you tell us who did this, we can get him locked up."

With both eyes swollen shut, she couldn't see her questioner. No doubt he wore a black uniform, cop hat in hand, shiny badge glinting in the light. Maybe he thought he could help, but he'd only make it worse.

"Doesn't matter," she croaked. Moving her lips sent fire across her face. "He's gone."

"They're never gone for long. If we can put him away for a while, it'll send a clear message. Was he your boyfriend?"

"No!" The emphatic word shot through her ribs and she flinched. Not that Eddy hadn't suggested it. Numerous times. She'd protected herself with a knife, the only thing she could thank her father for, but the one time she hadn't kept it handy—

"A relative?"

"A mistake." The biggest of her life. A deep sigh stung her split lip and she ran her tongue over it carefully, tasting antiseptic, salt, and blood.

"I'll let you rest," the man said quietly. "We can talk later. My name is Detective Ben Evans. I'll leave my card here so you can call me."

The door to her left opened and closed, his purposeful footsteps fading down the hall. Silence, the first she'd had in months. She relaxed into the bed, her head aching. Even in her tiny Uptown Minneapolis apartment there'd been constant noise, deep voices, ringing phones at all hours. She'd slept facing the locked and barred bedroom door, knife in hand, since Eddy took advantage of her kindness and commandeered her life.

All she'd ever wanted was a quiet life. No drama, no excitement. Just her and Katie. A tear trickled along her temple. She'd take another beating if it meant Eddy would stay away from her younger sister.

When she'd received the landlord's complaint letter, she hadn't considered Eddy's reaction before showing it to him. She should have. Awash in relief that she would finally be free of him, she'd told him he had to leave or the cops would show up. *Stupid, stupid, stupid.* She shivered beneath the lightweight blanket, the memory as clear and cold as the ER.

His cool, polished persona had transformed in an instant, and he'd slammed her against the wall, her toes barely touching the kitchen floor. "You called the cops?"

"No!" she'd squeaked, clawing at his forearm against her neck. "*They* will. Eddy, I…can't breathe."

He stepped back and she collapsed to the worn linoleum, a hand at her neck as she wheezed in a breath.

"I've watched you talking with the lady in the office downstairs." The controlled image returned, vibrating with the energy of a rattlesnake. "Have you mentioned me?"

"Of course not."

He cocked his head of thick dark hair, the gold chain at his neck catching the overhead light. "Then how would she know I'm here?"

"You're hard to miss with your expensive suits. And there are cameras everywhere." She pushed to her feet, every nerve screaming an alert.

"Tell them I'm your cousin, and I'm here for a visit."

"They know you're not." She started toward her bedroom where her knife hid under the mattress, legs wobbling like jelly.

The click of Eddy's expensive boots followed, and she fought the urge to run.

"I suggest you make them believe it, Martha. If trouble comes, you'll go down first."

"Why don't you go live off someone else?" she threw over her shoulder. Because no one was as big a fool as her. She prayed he couldn't hear the thrashing under her ribs. A few more steps—

"Looking for this?"

She turned slightly. Her pearl handled knife dangled from his long, manicured fingers. She'd seen him turn that smile on "clients" who couldn't pay; her gut clenched. All these months she'd kept her mouth shut, head down, staying out of his way. Now she was the sole focus of his wrath.

"I didn't get to where I am today without understanding human nature. I picked you because you're easy to manipulate, Martha." His chuckle lacked humor, the glint in his black eyes unmistakable from where he stood in the doorway. "You're not hard to look at either."

She set her shoulders against an icy shiver and thrust out a hand. "Give me that, Eddy. It's from my dad."

Darkness edged his short laugh. "He's in jail, sweetheart. Same place you'll be if you turn on me."

Facing him, she scrounged deep for courage. "I won't if you get out of my apartment. I want my life back."

His was the face of a lion studying its next meal. He was toying with her, as if he could smell her fear. "We could have ruled the world together, Martha. We still can be if you lighten up."

Nausea edged the panic that kept her rooted in place. "I don't want to be 'together,' Eddy. Give me my knife. Then you can pack your stuff, and I'll forget you were ever here."

"Perhaps I should pay Katherine a visit. I'm sure she'd be more welcoming to a…friendship."

She swayed as the world fell away from her feet. "You stay away from her! She's a child."

His chuckle was as sharp as the blade in his hand. "Oh, but haven't you noticed? She's grown into a lovely young woman. I've always preferred blondes, you know."

Bile stung her throat. *Enough! This nightmare ends right now.* "I'm warning you, Eddy. If you go near her, I *will* call the cops."

He considered the knife. "I guess you're right, Martha. This does belong to you."

The knife whizzed toward her.

She shrieked and ducked, then lunged toward where it stuck in the wall over her bed. His arms around her waist sent her to the floor, and she kicked hard, connecting with some part of him hard enough for him to grunt and curse.

She was in the fight of her life. *For* her life. And for Katie's. He would *not* win. Her blouse ripped and she screamed, clawing at him. His fist connected with her face. She tasted blood. In the distance, she heard pounding. She pummeled and kicked, her strength ebbing.

"Help…" It was the last thing she remembered as the apartment door crashed open.

The cool of the ER pulled her back, and the shuddering intensified. She burrowed under the blanket, clutching the flimsy sheet to her chest. She'd survived—this time.

What if he meant it? What if he went after Katie? Her pulse rate tripled, and she pushed up on an elbow, ribs screaming in protest. "Katie!" She used the icy bed rail to ease upright, then paused, woozy and panting as an alarm chimed behind her.

"Marti, what can I get for you?" The nurse's voice, a gentle hand on her shoulder. The alarm stopped.

"I need…to get to Katie." She tried to force her eyes open. The door was to her left. If she could just—

"Honey, you're in no shape to even stand up. I'm sure she's fine."

"No!" She wrapped an arm across her chest, swaying. "He said he'd go there."

"We'll send a police officer to check on her, all right? Let's get you back on the pillow."

"But I have to..." The little strength she'd found slipped away, and she let the nurse resettle her.

Cool fingers stroked her forehead. "We'll make sure Katie is safe."

"Where's...my phone?" She'd had it on her. Hadn't she?

"It's right here."

The familiar device was pressed into her hand, and Marti pulled it under the covers, curling around it. The photos of Eddy's business were her only insurance against him. "I need to...Katie..." The protest trailed off her lips into swirling darkness that inched closer. The fiery pain around her eyes waned and she drifted under the nurse's butterfly touch.

Images faded in and out. Beautiful Katie—green eyes sparkling, long blonde hair swept up into a crazy ponytail as they laughed together over ice cream. Marti had done all she could to protect her—from their mother, from the men who came and went. From Eddy. She reached for her baby sister, but she was so tired, her arms like lead. Darkness beckoned. A little rest now and she'd get back to building their future.

– 2 –

Sam Evans lifted the handle, and the whine of his table saw dwindled. He blew sawdust from the dark wood and nodded. Clean, even. Precise. Setting the board on the growing stack, he selected another and glanced across the spacious workroom at his cousin. Safety glasses pushed up on his forehead, Jimmy frowned at the dresser he'd assembled. While Sam liked things precise, Jimmy was downright fanatical, which explained his thriving woodworking business.

As the blade bit into the fragrant cedar, he kept a tight hold on the 2x6. The tenth board this morning. The ninth perfect cut. He'd settled into the shop easily enough, apparently better suited to working with wood than impressionable youth. When he "left" his job at the Teen Center, Jimmy had badgered him to join the team at North Country Woodworking. Once he'd run out of excuses, he'd agreed. These months of working with his hands had allowed him time to decompress.

He studied the fresh cut. He sure missed the teens. Sharing life, wrestling with issues, eating doughnuts. He'd learned far more from their hard-earned wisdom than he'd ever taught them. His bumpy road had been nothing compared to what many of them lived through every day. If he'd kept his focus—

His back pocket vibrated, and he set the board on the stack before retrieving his phone. "Hello?"

"Sam Evans!" a familiar voice said. "Richard Ellis here."

"Richard? Seriously?"

"Ah, when have I ever been serious?"

Sam laughed, pushing his safety goggles up on his head, and leaned back against the workbench. "Good point. You cracked up at a funeral."

"Not my finest moment, I'll admit. Evans, you're a hard man to track down."

The result of keeping a low profile and minding his own business. It had been over a year since they'd talked. "Just staying out of trouble. Why were you looking for me?"

"I have a job for you."

"Thanks, but I have one."

"I heard you're working with your cousin. I'm sure Jimmy's glad to have you, but that's not your calling, or at least, not the whole thing."

Sam rubbed his face. "I don't have a calling, Rich, so this job is fine."

"I need a burger. How about we meet at Ike's at one?"

He'd been fired from his supposed calling. And he was good at woodworking. Really good.

"I know what you're capable of, Sam, and it's not hiding in a woodworking shop."

"Who says I'm hiding?"

"Aren't you?"

He didn't bite. Richard had mentored him into the counseling job he'd loved, then fired him from it. So much for a calling. He pinched the bridge of his nose, ignoring the rush of memories.

"Ike's, downtown," Richard said. "One o'clock. I'll buy if you'll come with an open mind."

Dropping his head back, Sam stared at the metal framework of the ceiling. He'd been open to everything at one time. A lot of doors had slammed shut since. "Fine. If you're buying, I'll eat. I may even listen."

Over burgers and fries, they caught up on the past year. Richard's life had followed the path Sam thought his own would—happily married, kids, a dog, even a house with a picket fence. While he'd never cared about the picket fence, he still yearned for the family Jillian had given to someone else.

Richard pushed his empty plate to the side, settled back in his chair and folded long arms. Two inches taller than Sam's six foot-two, he was as thin as ever. "So tell me what you've been doing the past year."

"Since you fired me?" It had been twelve long months of trying to get his head on straight. He took a swig of ice water.

Acknowledging the sarcasm, Richard dipped his head. "After you were cleared, I'd have hired you back in a heartbeat if the center hadn't closed. You know that."

"After I was cleared, they told me to get on with my life." He drew a breath to calm the anger that still flared when he thought of how everything had spiraled out of control. He'd managed to build a respectable life after his rocky teen years, only to have it blown to bits by the tornado of events. "I started working with Jimmy and became a craftsman."

"You always had a creative streak."

Sam tossed his napkin on the rest of his fries, and leaned back, balancing on the chair's back legs. "So why me? And why now?"

"Because you're also creative working with people."

"And that's why you fired me." Which wasn't entirely true, although that supposed creativity had nearly landed him in jail.

"You know I had to when the charges were filed. But you were cleared, Sam. You can let that go."

Sam dropped the chair to the ground and folded his arms, frowning out the window. "Sure. My career, my marriage, my reputation. Yup. Working on letting all of that go. Doesn't leave much."

When Richard remained silent, Sam turned his attention back.

Dark eyes behind wire-rimmed frames rested patiently on him. "To answer your other question of why now, the program is taking off. It's going to benefit a whole lot of people, Sam, especially those who want to move forward. At least hear me out."

He'd forgotten how relentless Richard could be. "Fine. Gimme the details."

Richard propped his elbows on the table. "About six months ago, I started with a new venture called GPS, an offshoot of River House."

Too bad the House hadn't been hiring when he'd suddenly become jobless. "With the Teen Center closed, River House is vital to the neighborhood. What's the offshoot about?"

"GPS, Gathering Place Services, is for people who don't fit at River House. They might be past 18, or they need a different focus. We offer one-on-ones and classes on interviewing, resume writing, computer skills, and job hunting. We're also offering GED prep courses. That's where we need help. We have more registrations than we expected, so we need another teacher."

An unexpected brawl brewed in Sam's chest between a longing to do youth work again and an itching desire to run out of the restaurant. "After what happened with Andrew and Shareen, and then the accusation, I'm done with ministry, Rich."

"No, you're not. It's in your blood, Sam. It's who you are."

"More coffee, gentlemen? A piece of pie? Our special today is Key Lime." The waitress beamed at them expectantly.

"Just the check, thanks." Richard gave her a brief smile.

The silence at their table was covered by the low hum of conversation, bursts of laughter, the clank of silverware against plates. Sam's knee bounced double time to the rock beat pulsing in the background.

"Working with my hands has always been rewarding for me," he said. "I enjoy making things. And if I screw up, I get to start over. Nobody suffers. I gave it my best shot, Rich, but I think it's pretty clear I wasn't meant for that work. I don't want to mess up anyone else's life."

"Wow." Richard sank back. "I wouldn't have believed Sam Evans excelled at pity parties."

"I don't!" People looked their way and he leaned forward, voice lowered. "It's fact, Rich. Kids died because I wasn't there for them."

The waitress brought their check, waiting while Richard fished out several twenties, allowing Sam a moment to absorb the rush of pain. Richard had stood beside him at two funerals within weeks of each other. *But he went home to his wife and kids, while I went home to an empty house to dismantle the nursery, and wait for the divorce to finalize.* Then the accusation unhinged what was left of his life.

He pushed his chair back, ready to escape the smell of grease and the pounding in his temples.

"If what happened to Andrew and Shareen was your fault, then it's doubly mine," Richard said.

"You were running the center, not counseling," Sam countered. "I wasn't there for them. I was wrapped up in my own issues, trying to figure out how I'd let my marriage fall apart. I should have been able to focus on both."

"People make choices, Sam. You know that. And teens make incredibly stupid choices on occasion. I doubt it would have mattered if you were getting divorced or happily married with ten kids."

How many times had he reminded himself of that? "I know."

"You might not like this, but—" Richard waited for Sam's attention. "I never thought you and Jillian were a good match. She didn't get your work, what you were trying to do for the community. Life was always about her."

Sam's eyebrows rose at the uncharacteristic judgment. He'd heard that sentiment from others, but never Richard. "You're not the first to say that. I heard it a lot from Lizzy and the girls."

"Sisters know things," Richard said with a wry smile, then sobered. "Sam, you did the best you could. She chose to look elsewhere. You can't carry the blame around forever."

He had no clue how to let go. It had become a second skin.

"So, let's get back to the job opportunity. GPS is growing so fast, we already need help. I don't have time to convince you that your life's not over, and that God does indeed still have a plan for you. You already know that."

The words stung. Richard had to be surprised to find him wallowing in muck. *He* certainly was.

"The choice is yours, Sam. You can stick with woodworking. Nothing at all wrong with that. Or you can help the community by taking over one or two of the GED classes."

"It's not a secret that I didn't excel in school, Rich. I'm not qualified to teach." Nor to give guidance or encouragement to people. He wasn't qualified to do anything except turn slats of wood into something useful.

"The curriculum is easy to follow."

"Then you shouldn't have trouble finding someone else. I'm not your guy."

"Actually, you are. Who better to teach it than someone who went that route and got their GED? And since I'm in charge, I get to pick my staff."

"What's your job?"

"Boss guy." Richard grinned. "Kurt and his wife Vanessa started the program, but they needed to focus on running River House. They heard about me because, well, you know how amazing I am, and now I'm happy to be working with them."

The corners of Sam's mouth twitched. Richard hadn't changed. He envied that.

"So, what do you say? You and I make a great team." Richard raised an eyebrow. "We're doing exciting work at GPS, Evans. You can make it even better."

"I appreciate you thinking—"

"Knowing."

"I appreciate you thinking you know I might be able to help, but—"

"But you'll take the next few days to consider this one-of-a-kind offer and let me know your decision." Richard stood and held out his hand.

Sam pushed to his feet, fear and frustration tangled in his chest, then shook his hand. His meal churned as they headed out into the sunshine. The truth was, Sam Evans had lost his nerve.

– 3 –

Marti savored the chocolate shake. While her ribs still protested if she coughed or breathed too deeply, she no longer flinched with every breath. The ice cream tasted like heaven after two days of clear liquids.

"Knock, knock." A petite, pregnant blonde stood in the hospital room doorway with a potted plant and a warm smile. "Hi. I'm Vanessa Wagner. I volunteer here at the hospital. Are you up to having a visitor?"

Marti managed a tiny nod and set the cup aside.

"This is for you." Vanessa set the plant on the window ledge. The green brought a welcome burst of color to the sterile room. "It's a philodendron. Requires pretty much no upkeep and will keep on growing until you're sick of it." She pulled a chair next to the bed. "How are you feeling?"

"'kay." *For a punching bag.*

"You look like you're doing well for what you've been through."

Marti's cheeks burned under the bruises. Did everyone know what happened?

"I'm a victim's advocate," Vanessa said gently. "When women are brought in after a domestic dispute, I help them sort through their options."

"Not...domestic," Marti managed, her jaw protesting. She'd spoken few words since being wheeled into the room. "Not boyfriend."

Vanessa's brow wrinkled. "Oh, I'm sorry. I must have misunderstood. I thought they said you were living together."

She shivered. "Not together." The effort to form words brought a sting to her eyes; humiliation soured the ice cream she'd eaten. "Never."

"I see. Well, I'm here to help. If you need legal advice, want to change your living situation, or maybe need some meals while you're recuperating, I can get things lined up."

Marti studied her through slitted eyes. What would this perfect, beautiful girl know about real life? She'd do her volunteer duty and return to her happy life with her baby and husband.

Vanessa set a hand lightly on Marti's arm. "No matter what your story is, Marti, there are people who can help you heal and move toward a better future. I've had some rough patches," she said, lifting the edge of her skirt to reveal the prosthesis that was her right leg. "I lost every member of my family. Because of my injury, I couldn't work so I lost my home. But some wonderful people helped me get back on my feet. They can help you too."

For one crazy moment, Marti believed the passion in her words, that everything would work out. No one had offered help in…forever. Then she took a breath and reality raged back in bolts of pain. She crossed an arm gently across her ribs. When she'd called in sick yesterday, the restaurant had fired her. No doubt the dry-cleaning job would end the same. She'd have to start over. Again.

"Do you think he'll come back?" Vanessa asked.

The question jarred her heart into a staccato pattern. Would he? "I don't think so." She wet her swollen bottom lip. She'd get a new lock when she got back to the apartment to be sure.

"Is he still living at your place?"

"Manager said he had to go." Eddy's fist flashed before her. She flinched. "That's why he…left. I'll be okay."

"Marti, at the very least I can see he injured your arm, hurt your ribs, and gave you two black eyes. Hon, you won't be okay if he comes back."

She hadn't allowed those thoughts to surface. If the neighbor hadn't broken down the door and said he'd called the police— A breath inched out and she pulled the blanket higher. She'd let Eddy take over her life. What happened to the strong, independent girl who'd been on her own for ten years? *When did I lose my backbone?* She eased her chin up. "He caught me off-guard."

"Do you have family in the area?"

"A younger sister, Katie. We're going to live together."

"Good for you. I took care of my younger brother and sister after our mom died." Her peaceful smile became wistful. "I'll bet she idolizes you."

"I hope not. She deserves better." Closing her eyes, Marti rested her head against the pillow. She was determined to give Katie the best life possible, but it still wouldn't be enough.

The young woman stood. "You need to rest. I'll leave my card here so you know how to find me. Marti, I want you to believe me when I say I'm here to help. Whatever you or Katie need, we can figure it out. Okay?"

The compassion in her blue eyes soothed and stung Marti's heart. Maybe in a different life they could have been friends. "Thank you."

Vanessa squeezed her hand. "You're welcome. Let's talk soon."

In the quiet, Marti brushed away a stray tear. She'd be okay. She had to be. She pressed the nurse button, hoping it was time for a pain pill.

Nose wrinkled, Sam dumped the remnants of yesterday's coffee into his kitchen sink. Even he had limits. Two days since the lunch conversation with Richard, and he was still restless and irritable. It had taken a year, but he'd finally come to grips with leaving youth ministry. Or so he thought. The job offer had cracked open the door he'd slammed on his past.

He started a new pot of coffee, then stared out his townhome window, letting the dark roast aroma seep into his pores. Not that long ago, he'd thought he had everything he wanted. A beautiful, if high-strung, wife with a baby on the way. A job helping troubled kids like he'd been at one time. He'd discovered he was pretty decent at listening to and encouraging kids, and at sharing his faith. Life had been good…until God dismantled it piece by piece, person by person.

The ring of the phone yanked him from memories he'd rather avoid. He checked caller ID and let it go to voicemail, too cranky for a chat with his mother. He poured a fresh cup of coffee and played her message.

"Hello, dear. I'm calling about your cousin's wedding next month. Now,

I know you don't like going to these things alone." *An understatement.* "I'm sure Betty's daughter would be happy to go with you. As friends, of course."

His mother's middle name had never been subtle.

"You remember her, the tall blonde? You met her last summer at the barbeque. Betty said she's not interested in dating anyone seriously right now."

He rolled his eyes and sipped loudly, as if he could drown out her suggestion.

"Anyway. Your sister said they aren't taking the kids so..."

Her voice faded as the invite taped to his refrigerator mocked him. For eight years, he'd had a wife to take to family events. Now he didn't even have a date. His mother tried not to interfere, but the whole divorce mess had hit her hard. She wouldn't be happy until he found someone new, and that wouldn't happen anytime soon. He'd stay single rather than go through that again.

He clicked off the message and glanced at the clock. A long run with his brothers would help him focus on something other than the family event he planned to avoid, and the job offer he couldn't.

"About time you showed up." Joey grinned from where he lounged on the park bench that afternoon.

"And you've been here all of thirty seconds," Sam replied. "I watched you park."

His youngest brother bounded to his feet and punched Sam's shoulder. "Why aren't you the cop instead of Ben? You're always spying on people."

"Only the ones who need to be watched. And that's been you from day one." He stretched his hamstrings to prepare for their run, eager to get started.

Joey laughed. "Just trying to keep up with the pack. Speaking of cops, here he is now."

Sam hadn't seen their middle brother for several weeks, far too long without at least a check-in. "Hey, Ben. Glad you finally surfaced."

Ben returned his hug. "Glad to be surfaced. It's been a long couple of weeks."

"Working on a new case?"

"Nah." Crossing his ankles, he reached for his toes and released a long breath, then straightened, his face flushed. "Same drug case that's been on the docket for two years."

The same case Sam had hounded him daily about after Andrew and Shareen died. *Eddy*. The name made him taste metal. If the rat had been put away years ago, the kids might still be alive. Putting him in jail wouldn't solve everything, but it would make a dent in local drug dealing, at least until the next scumbag stepped in.

"We're close to bringing him in, Sam. I talked to a girl in the ER we think he beat up. I've got a feeling she could be our star witness. I'll talk to her again when she's released."

"How about we run and talk?" Joey suggested, hands on his hips. "I'm aging as we stand here. Pretty soon I'll be old and decrepit like you two."

They started at a light jog, Sam flanked by his brothers. No matter how old they got, he still needed to make sure they were fine. He glanced between them. Joey shared an animated story that made the ever-serious Ben smile. As the front man of a band finally getting noticed, Joey had found the perfect outlet for his excessive energy.

The conversation moved to the band's next show, and he needled Sam for missing the last two. "You'd better be there. No excuse other than being dead is acceptable."

"And even then, you'd better have a note from your doctor," Ben added.

Sam laughed and picked up their pace. This Sunday afternoon run with his brothers was the highlight of his week. As the eldest by two minutes over Lizzy, he'd always felt responsible for their four younger siblings. Probably because their police officer father had browbeat it into him.

"Anybody hear anything about Lauren's new job?" Ben asked, wiping his forehead.

"She texted yesterday to say she made it through her first week and loved it," Sam said. Their middle sister was an amazing social worker. He lengthened his stride as they followed the curve of Lake Calhoun. Joey's groan made him smile.

"The other place must've been pretty bad for her to quit," Joey panted. "She never admits defeat."

Sam cringed. Unlike him. He let his mind wander as his brothers talked. Their father, Officer Lionel Evans, had thirty years on the force before heart attacks cut his career and then his life short. Even on his deathbed, he'd given a parting shot at Sam's choice of ministry over law enforcement.

"You're in charge now." The once commanding voice managed only a raspy whisper. "Act like it. Don't let the church ruin everything I've built for this family. It's time to step up."

"Sam, watch it!"

He snapped to the present in time to see doggie leftovers just underfoot. His shoe made a direct hit and he slipped, flailing to stay upright. Regaining his balance, he glared at his brothers, doubled over at the side of the path. "You could have warned me a little earlier."

"We did," Ben said, catching his breath, "but you were out in space somewhere."

Sam rubbed his shoe in the grass, eyes watering from the odor. "Whatever."

Joey elbowed Ben. "Too bad we didn't catch that on camera. It would have gone viral in seconds. Squeaky clean counselor dances in dog doo."

Sam returned to the run, ramping the speed again, his brothers trailing him. That little incident too clearly illustrated his relationship with their dad. His stupid choices in high school had created a chasm they'd never been able to breach. Stepping in dog doo now reminded him how far he'd slipped in his job as the Evans family first born. It stunk.

The next morning Sam tried, with little success, to focus on his job. While Richard's unexpected appearance had been a welcome event, his job offer wasn't. The idea kept poking at him, disrupting his concentration, even ruining a cup of coffee from the Java Depot on his way into work.

He finished planing the board, flipped it over, and adjusted the volume on his earbuds. Some loud rock music should drown out the persistent thoughts. A light sweat touched his face. What was he so afraid of? Teaching a GED class wouldn't require anything more than presenting facts. He could do that. He wasn't a total loser.

The board wobbled, shearing off too much of the edge. "Great. Now you can do it again. Idiot." He jerked the board off the equipment and turned to set it on the growing pile of mistakes, then jumped. Jimmy stood behind him, arms folded. Sam yanked his earphones out. "Don't do that!"

"Do what, stand here? I have been for five minutes, which you normally would have noticed."

Sam grimaced and set the board aside. "Sorry. A lot on my mind. You need something?"

"My employee back in the game. What's going on?"

"Nothing. Well, I had lunch with my former boss and he offered me a job." He held up a hand when Jimmy's eyebrows lifted. "Sort of. Teaching a GED prep class."

"Phew." Jimmy made an exaggerated swipe of his forehead, and they shared a laugh. "You didn't jump at the chance?"

He shrugged. "I don't know that I want to get back into all that."

"All what? Teaching?"

"Working with young people. Any people." The woodshop kept him plenty busy and out of anyone's problems.

Jimmy's eyebrow lifted. "Yeah, you do, because that's who you are. Working here has been a stop-gap measure. I've known that all along."

"That's news to me."

"Sam, you went through the wringer. You needed a place to get your head on straight, and I'm glad you came here to do it. But I've never expected you to stay forever. Not full-time, anyway."

Sam scowled. Why did other people think they knew him better than he did? "Well, you're going to have to fire me because I'm not leaving."

Chuckling, Jimmy clapped a hand on Sam's shoulder. "There's no way I'll fire you, Sammy. But don't use me as an excuse not to get back into the game of life, got it? Otherwise I *will* fire you. Now get back to work."

His cousin strode to his office whistling off-key. A smile curving the corners of his mouth, Sam selected a new board. Jimmy might be bossy, but he was as solid as the wood in Sam's hands. It was comforting to have family in his corner.

− 4 −

As the wheelchair glided between the sliding doors, Marti lifted a hand to block the sting of welcome sunlight. She squinted still-swollen eyes and took a careful breath. After four days in the sterile solitude of the hospital room, she'd never take fresh air for granted again.

"Here we are." The cheery attendant stopped the chair beside the taxi. "Your chariot ride home."

If she weren't battling a headache, Marti would have rolled her eyes. *That's hardly Prince Charming in the driver's seat.*

The girl opened the back door and tossed the plastic drawstring bag of hospital souvenirs onto the seat. Toothbrush and paste, comb, lotion, bright red socks with non-stick stuff on the bottom. Katie would get a kick out of the goodies.

Marti accepted help as she slid onto the seat, holding her breath until she was settled, then set the plant on her lap. When the attendant reached for the seatbelt, Marti waved her off. Nothing would touch her ribcage.

"Well, take it easy, Marti." She handed the driver money supplied by the social worker.

The cab pulled away from the curb, and Marti lowered the window. The gentle breeze revived her battered soul. Lilacs with a touch of exhaust from the bus ahead of them. Her first to-do—find a new job. Katie would age out of foster care at the end of summer and she needed to be ready for her.

"You hab ackceedent?"

The driver's accented question broke into her thoughts. She met his dark-eyed gaze in the rearview mirror. "What?"

"Your face. You hab ackceedent."

"Oh. I...fell down the stairs." *Okay, buy makeup before looking for a job.*

"Big stairs."

Apparently sarcasm was universal. She turned her attention back to the window. She'd have to sound more convincing next time, maybe blame a car accident. Too bad she hadn't protected her face better, but Eddy's attack had surprised her. She set her jaw. It wouldn't happen again.

Minutes later she contemplated the front steps of her apartment building as the cab drove away. *Were there always this many?* She'd lived here a year, the longest anywhere since getting kicked out at fifteen. Hopefully it wouldn't cost the whole damage deposit to fix the mess from Eddy's attack.

Grasping the railing, she took one excruciating step at a time. Sweat trickled down her back as she pulled open the front door with the last of her fading energy. She wobbled into the lobby, anxious to get to the apartment to rest. Who'd have thought a cab ride could be so exhausting?

Fern, the building manager, stood in the office doorway. No smile, no welcome home or glad you're okay. Just the crook of a finger as she turned back to her office. The perpetually puckered manager would no doubt scold her for last week's event.

Marti followed and sank onto a chair at the table, a hand over the throbbing in her ribs. Fern pulled a folder from a pile on her desk and sat across the table. Marti forced the corners of her mouth up.

Fern didn't return the feeble smile, her expression more rigid than usual. "Martha, we have to discuss your lease."

She hated her given name, except when her grandparents used it. "Yes. It's time to renew already." A whole year in one place deserved a pat on the—

"We won't be renewing it."

"What?" She straightened, flames spiking up her spine. "Why?"

"When you signed your lease last year, we discussed that it would only be you living in the apartment."

"It is." Until Eddy charmed his way in, and then used photos of Katie to keep her quiet.

Fern folded gnarled hands on the folder. "How do you explain the man living there these past four months? The one who did this to you?"

"He wasn't living here. He…" If she explained, she'd end up in jail. "He showed up sometimes. We didn't—" Heat crawled up her neck. "He wasn't my boyfriend. Ever."

"If he didn't live with you, why did he come and go at all hours?" Fern's lowered brow gave her a bulldog look. "May I remind you, our security cameras run 24/7."

Air vanished from Marti's lungs. Everything was on tape. Eddy and his "business partners." The exchange of packages, backpacks, and envelopes. And her in the middle of it. How could she have been so stupid?

"He needed…he said there were too many people at his house for him to get work done." That had been his story at first. "He came for the quiet."

Fern's thin lips pinched. Marti tried to keep her eyes wide and innocent, difficult to do when they couldn't open all the way. "He didn't live with me. I didn't even like him." *Shut up!*

"Why did you let him use our property for his business dealings? Why didn't he rent an office somewhere?"

"I…I didn't ask. I only knew him from the restaurant where we worked." Truth blurred at the edges. "I didn't think it hurt anything for him to come and go as long as he didn't live here."

"You knew it wasn't permitted in your lease."

The photos he'd shown her a month after he started coming flashed before her like one of those flipbooks Katie loved. Marti greeting several of his "associates" at the door with a smile. Accepting envelopes in exchange for packages. Katie with her foster family, Eddy in the background casually displaying a gun under his jacket. Katie at her bakery job, Eddy outside admiring the window display. Gun showing. She'd wised up too late.

"Martha?"

She crashed back to the stuffy office. A drop of sweat trickled behind her ear. "I know he won't come back after the…the…"

Leaning forward, she clutched the plant to her chest. "I promise I won't ever have company again. Please. This is the best place I've ever lived."

Begging had a sharp tang to it, like the taste after Eddy split her lip. "I'll sign a two-year lease, if you want. I don't…have anywhere else to go."

Pucker-faced Fern played judge and jury, her pen hovering over the lease agreement. Marti waited, the throbbing behind her eyes making her nauseous.

Finally, the woman shook her head. "I'm sorry about your troubles, Martha. But I have no choice in the matter." She marked a perfect black X in a box at the bottom, turned the paper around and held out a pen. "Since tomorrow is the end of the month, you have 24 hours to vacate the premises. And, of course, the damage deposit will not be returned to you."

Marti bit down on her trembling lip and scribbled her signature. With as much dignity as her aching body would allow, she gathered her belongings and left the office.

Homeless yet again.

Sam relaxed at the corner table beside the front windows of the coffee shop, relishing a fresh cappuccino. The Java Depot had become his favorite spot to sit and watch the world go by, to ponder the crooked path his life had taken, and wonder what might have been if he'd made different choices.

He set the beverage aside and shaded part of the sketch for his next project. A baby cradle. He'd researched design ideas, then had to wrestle his emotions under control. He should be making a cradle for his own baby, the one Jillian now raised with someone else.

Bells jangled as the coffee shop door opened, and a group of high school kids jostled in, their energy and chatter charging the atmosphere. He missed that.

"Hey, Pastor Sam!" A blonde girl waved from the middle of the pack.

He smiled and nodded at her, then at the other girls who giggled and waved. Pastor Sam. The nickname had stuck after Richard said it once in jest. When the kids started using it, he'd taken it very seriously. Faith had been important to him then.

He finished shading the drawing, a bit too heavily. There. At least that gave him something to work from.

"Pastor Sam?" The blonde stood beside his table, an uncertain smile on her face. "Can I ask a favor?"

"Sure, Kelsey. What do you need?" He motioned to a chair.

She slid into it, clutching an iced drink, and glanced over her shoulder at the friends clustered across the room. "There's a kid we know at school. Justin. We think he's into some bad stuff, but he won't listen to us."

A warning bell tolled in the back of his mind. "What kind of stuff?"

"We're pretty sure it's drugs. Like maybe he's running them for somebody. These nasty looking guys have been hanging around Faith Church after our Wednesday night event, waiting for him."

Her eyebrows pinched upward. Sam's stomach tightened.

"Justin goes off with them and we don't see him for days. The last time I saw him, he looked rough, like he got beat up. And he was real jumpy."

"Have you talked to the pastors at the church? Or whoever's running the Wednesday night event?" *Anyone but me.*

"Sort of, but they're super busy with so many kids. They told the guys to stop hanging around the church, so now they wait down the block. We called the cops, but that didn't do anything."

The squeak of the straw she slid in and out of her cup grated on Sam's heightened nerves.

"If you talked to him, I know you could convince him to stop."

The idea of giving advice sent an icy blast through him. His counsel hadn't helped Andrew or Shareen. "I'm not sure what I can do, Kelsey. I think talking to the people at Faith would be better for him."

Her slumping shoulders were a kick to his gut. She picked at a crack in the wood table. "They said they would try but…" She pushed to her feet. "Okay. Well, see ya."

"Kelsey, wait. If you bring Justin by the woodshop, I can talk to him." He slid a business card across the table, then folded his arms against the urge to snatch it back. "I don't know if it will help, but I can try."

Her brow relaxed. "Yeah, okay. I'll see what he says. Thanks."

She returned to her group, and he drained his cup. What could he actually do for the kid? Talking wouldn't help much if he were in deep with a drug ring. No doubt it was that Eddy again, building his empire at the expense of yet another kid.

He crushed the empty cup. He'd tried for months to get the scum arrested. Hounded Ben to do more, canvassed nearly all of Uptown looking for people to testify. Fear kept decent people from stepping forward. He needed the satisfaction of seeing the gutter rat in jail, but so far the man had eluded them all.

Chairs scraped against the wood floor, and the kids filed out of the shop, the bells jangling a harsh reminder of the failure he'd become. Or maybe always had been. He returned his attention to the sketch. It was safer for everyone if he stuck to woodworking.

– 5 –

Marti unlocked the apartment door and inched it open, prepared to flee if Eddy materialized. Like she'd get very far. Heavy, stifling silence greeted her and her shoulders lowered. She flipped on the light, locked the door behind her, and stepped back into her nightmare. The makings of dinner, a can of soup and a saucepan, still waited on the counter. Unopened mail on the ledge. An empty wine glass on the coffee table. She shuddered. Eddy's.

She set the plant on the kitchen table and lowered onto a chair, sweat trickling down her back. How she'd loved this little apartment. Though sparsely furnished, she'd cherished the peace and privacy. If only she'd kept it that way. Her sweet haven reeked of stale cologne, and even now pulsed with evil.

"If only" had become her mantra. If only she'd told Eddy no. If only she hadn't taken the job at the restaurant. If only she and Katie had been raised by people who'd actually cared about them. Too tired to stop the taunts, she rested her head on her folded arms. Her mistakes and missteps were too numerous to count, but too costly to ignore. She'd always been strong, stubborn, and focused. Dropping her guard had cost her nearly everything.

She sat up slowly, carefully, and lifted her chin. Enough. Time to leave the ugly memories of this place behind. She stood, holding onto the table until the wooziness passed, then shuffled toward the bedroom, dreading the scene that awaited. In her nightmares, she still heard the crash of the bedside table, glass breaking, her screams and his curses.

"Oh…" There was no blood, no sign of a struggle. The room smelled fresh, the carpet recently cleaned. Her meager belongings were piled neatly on the bed. Someone—surely not Fern—had put the room back in order. Nothing looked amiss.

Her legs wobbled and she leaned against the wall, tears burning. An act of kindness amidst the chaos of her life. She forced her emotions to steady, and went to the closet, pulling out a backpack and her grandmother's worn fabric bag. What should she take into the unknown? What could she even carry?

On the dresser sat a small wooden box, the first item she'd made by herself, with direction from Gramps. She ran her fingers lightly over the inlaid top, a smile lifting a corner of her mouth. How she'd loved working beside him, dreaming of being a craftsman like him, making old wood come alive again.

When he died, right after her 14th birthday, her world changed forever. She and Katie never returned to the farm. They saw their beloved Grandy only once more, at Gramps's funeral. The safety and unconditional love Marti experienced with them was now a distant memory.

Sitting on the edge of the bed, she removed the memory card from her cell phone and studied it. Such a small thing to hold the weight of her future, her life. She slid it into a tiny drawstring bag, and put the bag inside the wooden box, then tucked it deep into Grandy's bag. The only time Eddy had stepped out of the apartment without locking his briefcase, she'd leaped into action, taking as many photos as she could.

She pressed a hand against her chest, feeling anew the terror of those short minutes as she scrambled through his papers. They were all she had to keep him away from Katie. And from herself. She glanced behind her at the wall. Only a small mark where the knife had been. The knife itself was nowhere to be seen. Maybe the police took it. She shivered, feeling exposed without it. She'd have to buy a new one.

She packed some clothes, meager toiletries, and photos of her with Katie, and the two of them with their grandparents. Trailing her fingers across familiar faces, a shuddering sigh slumped her shoulders. "I'm sorry, Grandy," she whispered. "I know this isn't what you'd hoped for me, or for Katie. I'm doing the best I can."

Blinking away the sting of tears, she stuffed the backpack with a small pillow, a jacket, and extra socks, then tugged it over a shoulder, wincing as it bumped against her spine. She tucked a sleeping bag under her arm, gathered the fabric bag and the plant, and left the apartment without looking back. Letting the door swing shut behind her, the slam echoed down the empty hallway. *Another ending.*

"Another beginning," she announced. She'd had lots of practice, her life a patchwork of beginnings and endings, like the colorful quilt she'd snuggled under when Grandy had tucked her into bed at the farm. Gramps's encouragement echoed in her heart. "You can do whatever you set your mind to, Martha Joy. I know you can." During their woodworking lessons, he'd taught her how to persevere, to never give up. She wouldn't give up now either.

She set the plant at her neighbor's door, and touched the leaves, remembering Vanessa's warm smile, then limped away. The elevator creaked and shuddered to the ground floor one last time. At the back of the building, she rounded the corner and stopped by the downspout, setting the bag at her feet before lowering gingerly to her knees. She swiped her forehead and rested a moment, watching a maintenance worker move a buzzing grass trimmer along the building.

Removing the cement piece under the aluminum spout, she lifted a coffee can from the hole, pulled off the plastic lid, and stared. A single dollar bill lay crumpled at the bottom of the otherwise empty can. Her pulse whooshed through her ears, drowning out the world as her trembling fingers curled around the bill. *But...* Even on minimum wage, she'd put a little aside each paycheck, sneaking out at night to hide it in this safe place. She'd counted it last week.

Eyes squeezed shut, she forced her fuzzy brain to retrace her last visit. About 2:00 a.m. on Wednesday. She'd tiptoed out of the apartment, a twenty-dollar bill clutched in her fist, Eddy snoring on the couch, locked briefcase beside him.

Under a bright moon, amidst the song of crickets, she'd paused long enough to count her precious savings. Four hundred dollars! The largest safety net she'd ever had. She'd danced her way back to the apartment, Eddy still snoring when she slipped back in.

She dropped back on her rear, tears trickling down her cheeks, and looked up at her apartment window. He hadn't been sleeping after all. A year's worth of saving for Katie, gone. One measly dollar to her name. She pounded the ground with a fist. "One lousy break. Is that so much to ask?"

Shoulders already aching from the tug of the backpack, she dropped her head into her hands. *What's the point? I can't do this anymore.*

"Lady? You okay?"

She was slow to lift her head. The maintenance worker's eyes widened. "Did you fall?"

She wiped her cheeks, then took the hand he offered and got carefully to her feet. "I'm okay."

He squinted at her. "Maybe you need to see a doctor for..." he waved a hand toward her face, "all that?"

"I will. Thank you." Grandy's bag in hand, she trudged away as the grass trimmer buzzed to life again. The sweet ringtone she'd picked for Katie sang from her pocket. No money meant no more minutes for her prepaid phone. The minutes she'd added last week wouldn't last long.

She forced a smile to her voice. "Hey, Kat."

"Hi, Marti. I miss you."

"I miss you too, sweet girl. What have you been doing?" She stopped in the shade of a maple tree and rested against the trunk.

"We baked cookies today. Chocolate chip."

"Mmm. Our favorite."

Katie giggled. "Yup. I saved some for you. Can you come over?"

Marti blinked up at the clear sky to keep the tears back. Katie would freak if she saw the bruises. "I'm afraid not today, hon." A few more days and she'd be presentable. "How about Saturday?"

"Saturday?" Katie wailed. "But that's like a whole week away."

The ache in her chest wasn't from Eddy's blows. "I know, sweetie, but I've been sick." Not a total lie since she'd had a fever the first day in the hospital. "I want to be sure I'm all better before we spend the day together. Do you think you can save my cookies until them?"

Katie sniffed. "Maybe. I'll try."

"Well, if you eat them all, we'll make more. So tell me what else is going on."

"I made a new friend. His name is Tim, and he's super nice. He's cute too."

A warning bell rang in the back of her mind. Nice, cute guys weren't interested in girls like Katie. Sweet-natured, beautiful, and far too trusting, it never took people long to figure out she was also a bit slower than other teenage girls. "Where did you meet him?"

"At the park. He's really, really nice. We talk a lot. Aunt Gloria said he's nice too."

Hardly an endorsement. "Aunt" Gloria's track record wasn't great; Buster was either her third or fourth husband. "How often have you seen Tim?"

"A few times. He helped bake cookies today. Aunt Gloria is taking us to a movie tomorrow night." An unfamiliar note rang in Katie's voice, something shy and hopeful.

"She's going with you, right?" The bell got louder. After Katie had been placed with Gloria five years ago, Marti had struggled to trust the foster care mother, although Kat always seemed well-cared for.

"Yup, but she let me pick the movie. I picked one about penguins. Tim wants to see it too."

At the $2 theater. Of course. Gloria kept every cent she could from the money she got as a foster parent. *Well, I'll be there too, to check this guy out, and make sure Gloria goes in with them.* Even if she had to do it from the shadows where she could hide her bruises.

"That sounds really fun, sweetie. Hey, I've gotta run. I'll see you Saturday morning, okay? We can go to Minnehaha Falls, and eat cookies, and do whatever you want."

"Okay. I miss you. Bye, Marti."

Marti clicked off the call and held the phone over her heart. *This* was why she would start over again, however many times she had to. Katie deserved the best life possible, and Marti would find a way to provide it.

This was just a little set-back.

Before Sam had finished crafting his "thanks, but no thanks" response, Richard called. "Evans, I'm sending up a flare."

He leaned back in his chair at the Java Depot. "Wait. I need to get this recorded. The always-capable Richard Ellis is asking for help."

"Screaming for it, actually."

"Wow. What's got you begging at my doorstep?"

"This morning we got three more applicants for the GED class. I don't want to turn anyone away who wants to get their life on track, but we'll have to unless we can add a second class. Maybe even a third, at this rate. Cue the screaming."

Sam chuckled despite the cold knot forming in his stomach.

"It's amazing how word has already gotten out about the work we're doing. There's one young woman who came out of an abusive relationship and now wants to counsel others..."

As the story unfolded, Sam had the ridiculous urge to stick his fingers in his ears. Face after familiar face from his years at the teen center plowed through his mind, their stories similar in so many ways. People needing a break, a hand up. A place from which to launch into a better future.

"How can we not help her, Sam? And the others like her? Problem is, with all the other stuff I need to do, I don't have enough hours in the day."

Did he really have a choice? "Hmm. Sounds more like pleading, with an edge of hysteria."

"Call it what you want. I'll admit I'm desperate. So what do you think? Would you do it temporarily? When the class is done, you're free to stay on or not. I'll be cool with whatever decision you make."

He could help out, at least for a couple of months. Sam rubbed his forehead. And really, he couldn't hurt anyone by teaching a class, and sharing facts. No opinions, no wise words to send students spiraling down the wrong path.

"Sam?"

"Yeah. I'd say you definitely have a problem."

"Thanks, Captain Obvious."

"What kind of friend would I be if I didn't help out?"

Richard whooped. "Man, you're a life-saver. Did I mention classes won't start for another week? Right now we'll have a morning and an evening class.

You can take either one. How about we barbeque tonight at our house and we can go over the curriculum? Next Monday you can come by and meet the GPS staff."

Sam pinched the bridge of his nose. He'd gone from no to yes in one minute flat. "Shoot me a text with the time and your address. And clear it with your wife this time, will ya?" Back when he'd worked at the Teen Center, he'd surprised Amy more than once when Richard extended an invite she didn't know about.

He clicked off the call and shook his head. "If you remember, God, the plan was for you to direct me to a job *outside* of ministry, not try sneaking me in the back door. I'll do this for now, for Richard, but I could use some help not screwing up any more lives."

That might be a tall order even for God.

– 6 –

Marti shivered in the early evening breeze where she leaned against a tree in the movie theater parking lot. Each day she was a little less sore, a little stronger, her fuzzy brain clearing. Unfortunately, the reflection in the shelter's bathroom mirror reminded her more healing was needed.

Given her injuries, the shelter had put her at the front of the line for the first two nights, but she'd slept poorly. The place terrified her. It took hours before she relaxed enough to doze off, belongings clutched to her chest. She preferred a protected corner somewhere outside.

She shifted against the tree, watching cars trickle into the parking lot, waiting for Gloria's rusted sedan. Staying hidden from Katie doubled the ache in her ribs. Saturday couldn't come fast enough. Gloria's car rattled into the lot and squeaked to a stop. Marti slid behind the tree and watched. Gloria and her round, balding husband got out first. A slender young man with a mop of dark hair climbed from the backseat, then held out a hand for Katie. The simple gesture pinged Marti's heart.

The group headed toward the theater, and Marti followed, hanging back to stay out of sight. Katie's beautiful face lit with a smile as she looked up at the young man. He leaned close and said something. Her sparkling laughter knocked Marti's breath away. Who was this guy? He had to see Katie wasn't like other girls her age. How dare he take advantage of that?

Pausing behind a column near the front doors, she waited for the group to pass by. As they did, she whistled quietly, and Gloria glanced over, then startled. She spoke to her husband and waited until he led the kids into the theater before approaching.

"What in the world happened to you this time?"

"A little accident. It looks worse than it feels." Doubtful. "Who's Tim? Where did he come from? And why is he hanging around Katie?"

Gloria held up a hand to stop the barrage. "Calm down. He's fine. He's a kid she met at the park."

"But what do you know about him? Is he part of a gang? Why did he pick Katie?" Unease had become her constant companion since the beating.

"Give me some credit, Marti." Annoyance edged Gloria's words as she pulled a cigarette from her purse. "Katie's been with us for five years. She's as much my daughter as she is your sister."

Hardly. Marti curled her swollen fingers. She'd fought the placement as hard as she could. "You're supposed to keep her safe and not let just anyone start hanging around her."

Gloria released a long stream of smoke before responding. "From the looks of you, I doubt you can keep yourself safe, let alone Katie." Two fingers holding the cigarette gestured toward Marti's face. "Who did that to you?"

"I did it to myself." In a roundabout way. "I want to know about Tim and if you're keeping an eye on him."

"We're a licensed foster home, Martha." Disdain filled the words. "It's my job to keep an eye on Katie, not everyone who crosses her path. Tim seems to be a nice young man who is very respectful of her. He makes her laugh, talks with her on the phone, does fun things with her. Which is more than I can say for you lately. You haven't seen her in almost two weeks."

The barb went deep. "And I'm sure you can see why. The last thing I want to do is scare her."

"Which that look will definitely do." She studied Marti through a plume of smoke. "Are you still in your apartment or did you have to move again?"

"Where I'm living right now doesn't matter," Marti shot back.

"If you want Katie released to your custody it does. Since she's a vulnerable adult, her caregiver is required to have a safe, stable living environment. I'm doubting you can provide that."

The hard words were a punch to her gut. Having a home could be the deciding factor when the time came for Katie to be released into her care.

"If we're done here, I'd like to get in to see the movie." Gloria had never been warm and fuzzy, at least not to Marti. She tossed her cigarette into the gutter. "You might want to see someone to make sure the damage isn't permanent."

"It's not." Marti stood tall, shoulders back. "I told Katie I'll see her on Saturday, if not before. I plan on taking her out for the day." As far from Gloria as possible.

"We'll see you on Saturday then." Gloria started toward the doors. "Hopefully nothing else will happen to you in the meantime."

People jostled past Marti where she stood rooted to the sidewalk. The world around her pulsed with energy as her shoulders slowly drooped. Her future with Katie seemed suddenly questionable, as if someone were inching it out of reach. And that someone was short, squat, and smoked incessantly.

You watch, Gloria. I'll be ready for Katie by the end of summer. Her sister's birthday would be a day to celebrate a new life for both of them.

Man, it's like being back in school again. Settled at his favorite corner table in the Java Depot, sipping a dark roast, Sam leaned back and released a breath. Algebra. Social Studies. General Math. Writing. Reading Comprehension. How had he ever managed to pass this on his own?

And he was supposed to stand up front and teach this to adults, no problem. Right now it felt like a big problem. *Maybe I should tell Richard something came up.* He wouldn't have to know the real reason, that he'd chickened out.

"Whatsa matter, Evans? You chicken?" The memory leaped off the pages of his past, taunting him even now. "C'mon, man. It's not like people die the first time. It's barely enough to give you a buzz."

He'd been an impressionable fourteen-year-old, eager to fit in, tired of trying to please his father. The guys had been right—he'd barely gotten a buzz from it. Unfortunately, he was braver the next time. Or dumber. It had been a long, bumpy ride down that slippery slope. And a tough climb back up.

Just be.

He straightened, frowning. *Be what? A chicken? A better man?* He'd spent his whole life trying to "man up," as his father repeatedly ordered. He'd never known what that actually meant, but figured it had to do with not wearing his faith on his sleeve.

He'd tried to do what he thought God had called him to do—work with people who were floundering, the way he had for so long. Not having a gun holstered at his hip hadn't made his work any less important.

Just be.

The simple directive seared into his heart now, igniting something he'd thought long gone, something still smoldering beneath the collapse of life as he'd known it. With the curriculum spread before him, the spark sputtered into a tiny flame. Richard had sought him out for this opportunity, to be an encourager to people who needed a hand up. Or a kick in the rear. He'd specialized in rear-kicking for the past year.

A wry smile formed. Time to kick someone else's. He drew a deep breath and pulled Lesson 1 in front of him. He'd man up, all right. Too bad Officer Lionel Evans wasn't around to watch.

– 7 –

Exhausted, Marti dropped onto the metal bench near the edge of Lake Calhoun, watching six ducklings skim across the water as they chased after their mother in the waning sunlight. The corners of her mouth lifted, then drooped. She'd paddled hard today too, chasing the elusive job. No one was hiring, or if they were, she'd messed up the application so much she looked stupid.

Why could she read fine sometimes, but other times the letters floated up and down? Or worse, totally disappeared? Maybe she'd been dropped on her head as a baby. Or left too long in the bathtub. *Why doesn't being good with my hands count? Or being a hard worker? I can build a dresser without help. I just don't read well.* The beauty of the summer evening faded into an old memory.

"I told you Camel *lights*." Her mother had snatched the carton out of her hands and thrown it on the chipped counter. "I can't smoke these. They're disgusting."

"They're all disgusting," Marti muttered.

Her mother's hand made a stinging impression on her cheek.

"Did you call me disgusting? Your own mother?"

Marti kept her eyes from watering thanks to years of practice. "I said cigarettes are disgusting."

"You're too good for smoking, that it? With all those fancy clothes, you think you're better'n us."

Marti glanced down at her torn jeans and oversized blouse from Goodwill. Fancy all right.

Her mother ripped open the offensive carton, pulled out a cigarette and lit it with trembling fingers. "But you ain't smart enough to graduate high school, are ya? And you're too stupid to read so I don't get why you think you're so much better'n the rest of us."

Jaw clenched, Marti lifted her chin against the sharp words, holding back a cough. As usual, the apartment air clouded with smoke. This couldn't be healthy for little Katie. "I don't have time for school. I have to *work* so Katie has food and clothes. And you get your cigarettes."

Her mother shoved wiry, unkempt hair from her haggard face and glared at Marti. "What's that supposed to mean? I work. I'm stuck here takin' care of her because you were too stupid to watch her."

As always, the cruel words cut deep into her soul. "Does it make you feel better to remind me? I live with it every day."

"Good." Large tears had rolled down her cheeks, and she dropped her face into tobacco stained hands. The same tired routine. "My poor baby Katherine. You ruined my perfect baby. You don't deserve to forget. Ever."

The pain of those hateful, alcohol-laced words still colored her life today, twelve years later. The memory had come out of nowhere, slipping out of the box she'd stuffed it in after her mother's death five years ago. She wiped her face on her sleeve and stood, folding her arms against the breeze.

She would make sure their so-called mother wasn't right. She'd find a new job, save up more money, and be ready when Katie left foster care. *Kat needs me. I have to try harder. Slow down and read the applications more carefully.*

Renewed energy hastened her steps as she covered the last few blocks to the alley. The rain had stopped early in the day, something to be grateful for. Her corner behind the coffee shop would have dried out by now. Maybe she'd even sleep better tonight. Trying to sleep in the rain stunk.

She moved quickly down the alley. Behind the large green dumpster was a nicely hidden niche by the Java Depot backdoor. She'd found a number of these out-of-the-way spots around Uptown over the years, since being kicked out of their dingy apartment as a teen. Perfect for an overnight or two. This was her favorite. Maybe because the coffee aroma masked the stench of garbage. Or because Jason and his wife had always been kind to her when she stopped in on free sample days. For whatever reason, she felt safe tucked back here.

Using a tree branch, she swept damp leaves out the corner, thankful for the sleeping bag that cushioned the cement but also wrapped her in warmth. Ignoring the rumble of her stomach, she burrowed in and looked up at the darkening sky.

Only a few stars shone through the haze of high clouds and city lights, but millions more twinkled out of sight, gathered in the forms of a bear, a fish, and other mysterious creatures. She smiled, remembering Grandy's arms around her as she described the constellations. On many warm summer nights, they'd snuggled together under a beautiful quilt on the front porch where Grandy told stories about the stars in the black sky, and the carpet of sparkling lights that led to God's throne room.

Wrapped in warm memories, Marti snuggled in deeper. As a child, she'd gone to sleep dreaming of a throne room where she and Katie were princesses. She still remembered those dreams, full of sunshine and laughter. The throne room was a happy place where parents took care of their kids, no one took drugs, and dads were never in jail. Katie kept up with all the kids…

"Marti?" The surprised male voice didn't belong in the throne room. "Marti! Wake up. What are you doing here?"

Reluctantly, Marti let the vision fade, prodded awake by something. Who dared poke a princess? Forcing her eyes open, she found Jason, the coffee shop owner, looming over her, a confused frown on his bearded face. She blinked, trying to clear her mind.

"Did you sleep here all night?"

She bolted upright. *What time is it?* Her phone should have woken her before anyone arrived. *Dead battery.* "My…roommate had company."

"You don't have a roommate." He helped her up, his frown deepening when she winced. "Unless that guy you mentioned is living with you?"

"No!" Seemed to be the popular idea. She focused on rolling up her sleeping bag.

Jason unlocked the back door and held it open for her. "You'd better come in and tell me what's going on."

"Thanks, but I have to go—"

"It's six a.m. Nothing's open this early." He swept his arm toward the coffee shop. "C'mon. I'll get you a coffee and you can clean up."

She wavered between humiliation and hunger, then preceded him into the building, head lowered. She needed to use the bathroom anyway before starting another day of job hunting. Scurrying to the ladies' room, she locked the door and sagged against it, face flaming.

Of course Jason opened the coffee shop the one morning her phone didn't work, Jason who caught her sleeping behind his store. Why not Ibrahim, like usual?

She stared at her disheveled appearance, a tangled mess of dark hair framing her ghostly face. Leaning toward the mirror, she studied the bruises. Most of the black and blue had faded, leaving an ugly yellow tint around her eyes. If only the memory of that night would fade as well.

A splash of cold water on her face slapped her fully awake. She patted her skin dry with a paper towel, pulled a new stick of cover-up out of her backpack and applied a light coat, ignoring the sting of shame. Once she had a job, she'd figure out how to repay the store where she'd gotten the make-up. She wasn't a thief. Not usually.

Taming her thick hair wasn't easy, but she wrestled it into a respectable braid. She brushed her teeth, returned everything to her backpack, then drew a deep breath and opened the door, determined to slip out while Jason wasn't looking.

"Your coffee's getting cold."

She pivoted halfway to the front door and ambled to the table where he'd set a steaming mug and a breakfast sandwich. Though her mouth watered, she declined. "Thanks, Jason, but I really need to get going. Lots to do today."

"Eat. You're too skinny."

Thanks. Her stomach growled. Traitor.

Leaning back against the counter, he folded beefy arms. "You don't have any money, do you?"

"Of course! I just...I have things to do." The bluster lacked energy and she sank down at the table, lips pressed together. The backpack thudded to the floor beside her. "Eddy stole it," she admitted.

Jason grunted as he swung a chair around and straddled it, arms resting on the back. "No surprise there. Why were you hanging around with him in the first place?"

"I wasn't. Not by choice." She wrapped her hands around the mug, drawing strength from its warmth. "We met at the restaurant and got to talking. He said he needed a quiet place to work. I stupidly said he could use my apartment sometimes."

"And he moved in."

"Yeah. Well, not—" Heat blazed across her face. "Not with benefits."

Dark eyes studied her from beneath bushy brows. His gruff demeanor hid a big heart, but he still scared her. Most men did.

"And as thanks, he did that to you."

She dipped her head. Quite a parting gift.

"So why are you sleeping behind my shop? Did he take over your apartment?"

"No." Shame coursed through her. He didn't need all the details. She sipped the coffee.

"Do you still have the restaurant job?" When she remained silent, he released a noisy breath. "Marti, I can't help you if you don't tell me what's going on. And if Lorna finds out I didn't do everything I could for you, I'll be dead."

She'd gotten to know his wife over the past year when she'd stopped by on free coffee days. Like Jason, she was kind beneath the bluster. "So don't tell her."

"I won't have to." His eyebrows wiggled. "She knows all. Now eat before that gets any colder."

A lump grew in her throat. He'd always been nice to her, as he would a stray cat that needed a pat on the head and an occasional saucer of milk. He returned to setting up for the morning, and she devoured the sandwich, enjoying the silence.

This coffee shop had become one of her favorite haunts over the past year. Brightly lit by large front windows and antique light fixtures, the rich aroma of coffee and baked goods welcomed a constant stream of customers. Few left without a Java Depot bag of treats. She loved Sample Day—free coffee and a chance to try one of their new goodies.

Nature photographs in rustic wood frames filled the sand-colored walls, adding a sense of the outdoors to this Uptown shop. The local lakes captured at sunset and sunrise, wildflowers crowded along meandering streams, the silhouette of a fisherman at the end of a dock. The peaceful ambiance invited guests to sit awhile and enjoy their favorite blends, as traffic rushed past the windows.

Jason slid a tray heavy with freshly baked items into the glass display case. Marti smiled. One time last winter, Lorna, his wife, had explained how he created new treats. Cookies, breads, sweet rolls, luscious desserts. "An artist in the kitchen," she'd declared. Marti had agreed with a nod, her mouth filled with one of those creations.

Rustic tables and chairs with wrought-iron detail filled the large space. Marti ran her fingers across the tabletop. Oak and mahogany, the padded seats a woodsy green fabric, the floors scuffed barn wood. But while the front of the shop was comfortably rustic, the barista area behind the counter was high-tech, roomy and spotless. A half-wall separated the baristas from the stainless work stations of the soup and sandwich makers.

Bittersweet memories of Grandy in her kitchen crowded her mind. Marti finished her coffee and gathered her belongings. Time to head out before she burst into tears.

"Can you clean?" Jason asked.

Her head lifted. "What?"

"Can you clean?" he repeated from behind the counter. "I need someone to clean this place. Top to bottom. I told Lorna I'd get it done, but I haven't had time. If you do it, I won't have to sleep on the couch because she's mad at me. I figure it'll take at least a week to do it right. And the storeroom needs cleaning and organizing. That'll take another week. I'll pay you the going rate. Unless you have some place else to be?"

She heard the challenge in his words. "Okay," she managed, over the knot in her throat. He was offering her a job? "When should I start?"

"Right now. Work on the storeroom first. Wipe it all down. Rearrange however you want. And I'll need an inventory of everything. Take your time. I'd rather it's done well than fast."

"Okay," she repeated. "But could I, um, ask a favor?"

"Go ahead."

"Would you, maybe, call me Gus while I'm here?"

He moved past her to turn on a set of lights. "Any particular reason?"

She shrugged, trailing her fingers over the back of the chair. It seemed like a good idea to stay as hidden as possible—while working in plain sight.

He flipped on another set, illuminating the shop with a warm glow, and headed toward the front door. "Thanks for stepping up to help, *Gus*. This will make Lorna happy, which will make *me* happy."

Dazed by his offer, she watched him greet the first customers with booming laughter and a handshake. Stepping around the front counter, she pushed through the swinging doors, and went down the hall to the storeroom. Meager belongings piled in the corner, she plugged in her phone and then perused the room, hands on her hips. Maybe he felt sorry for her, but the room really did need work. Shelves overloaded with product, items scattered here and there. A smile shot through her as she rolled up her sleeves. *I'll show him what clean looks like.*

— 8 —

Parked in front of the address Richard had given him, Sam studied the house. The wooden sign posted in the yard stated "GPS." Situated between two larger homes, the simple grey house, with dormer windows and a white porch, was the smallest on the block, but the most nicely landscaped. Rich said Kurt and Vanessa had been stunned to learn the house had been donated to them, and saw it as a sign from God to start GPS. Richard's invitation could be a sign. Or a fluke.

One step at a time, Evans. Knees wobbling like a teenager at his first job, he crossed the street and went up the steps. A sign taped over the doorbell declared no ringing or knocking allowed. He pulled open the screen door and stepped in.

The main room, with neutral walls and gleaming woodwork, smelled of candles and coffee. A long oak table and chairs sat off to the side. Two couches and a rocker gathered by the picture window. Bookshelves filled the walls at either side of a gas fireplace, filled with a mix of tattered and new books, photos, an old CD player, and several remotes.

A young woman with spiky black hair smiled at him from a desk at the far end of the room. Huge hoop earrings brushed shoulders decorated with colorful tattoos. "Hi. Welcome to GPS. I'll bet you're Pastor Sam."

He held back a snort as he crossed the room to shake her hand. "Just Sam." The title hadn't fit before, and it certainly didn't now.

"Okay, Just Sam. I'm Just Tiffani with an i. I'll let Richard know you're here. There's coffee over there, if you'd like some." She waved toward a counter at the side of the room as she came around the desk. "This is a self-serve joint. Be right back."

She disappeared toward the back of the house, and he stood still, uncertain how quickly she'd return. Maybe coffee would settle his nerves. He poured a cup and added a sugar packet, then wandered toward the large photo above the fireplace.

Smiling faces on the human pyramid glowed with fun. Six people on the bottom, then five, four, three, and two. A petite blonde woman balanced on top, a fist thrust upward in celebration. A mix of men, women, age, color, and size. He could almost hear their laughter, feel the sunshine as it spilled over them. It had been too long since he'd been part of a group like that.

"We got that picture in, like, one shot." Tiffani stood beside him, looking up at the photo. She pointed at the bottom row. "There's me with the blue hair."

Sam chuckled. "Certainly makes you stand out from the crowd."

"I dyed it in memory of Razzie, a friend of mine. Anyway, Rich is on the phone. He'll be right out."

"Thanks." Sam lowered into a chair by the window and sipped his coffee.

"Sam!" Richard emerged moments later from an office off the main room. In jeans and a cotton shirt, a smile filled his face. "I'm pumped you showed up today."

"You doubted I would?" They shook hands with a hearty grip.

"I never count my chickens."

"You have chickens?" Tiffani asked. She looked from one to the other. "You're both, like, super tall. How do you know each other?"

"We met in the tall guy section of a bookstore," Richard said.

Her dark eyes went wide. "There's a section only for tall guys?"

Sam laughed. "No. We became friends when we both realized how bad we are at golf. He can't putt and my drive stinks."

"Bad golfers need to stick together," Richard said, slapping him on the back.

Tiffani's eyebrows remained pinched upward so Sam added, "We used to work together."

"Ohh." She lifted hands with neon pink nails and shook her head, a purple stripe of hair along one side. "Chickens. Golfers. That's enough info for me."

Richard handed Sam a folder. "Here's some initial info for you. Monday mornings we have staff meetings for GPS and River House to review what's planned for the week. This week we're meeting here. I'll give you a tour afterwards. Then we can have lunch and talk about how we want to run the classes."

Sam nodded, glancing through the papers in the folder. Meeting agendas. Employee paperwork. Brochures. He tugged at the collar of his dress shirt. Starting over again. Maybe this wasn't such a great idea.

"Evans, this will be better than old times." Richard's voice broke through the blitz of nerves. "We're older and wiser."

Older, definitely. "If you say so."

"Have I ever been wrong?" Richard asked, then held up a hand. "Don't answer that. Now, we have a couple of minutes before the GPS staff meeting. Did Tiffani point out the bathroom?"

After a much-needed stop, Sam emerged to meet the enthusiastic GPS staff as they wandered into the room. Red-headed Kiera Theisen had a firm handshake. "As the image consultant, I help people discover and bring out their best self for interviews," she explained. "Everyone has far more God-given potential than they're aware of."

"Don't get her started." The dark-haired man next to her greeted Sam with a laugh. "My lovely wife has a soapbox and she's not afraid to use it. Glad to meet you, Sam. I'm Peter Theisen. I teach songwriting and an intro to basic music production for people interested in a career in the music industry."

Sam squashed the awe that bubbled up. He'd heard Peter's songs on the radio. His wife was stunning. A young man stepped up next. With the build of a wrestler, short black hair going every direction, he looked about the age of the clientele.

He stuck out a meaty hand. "Parker Johnson. I head up the computer skills area. We start with the basics, and then I'm available to troubleshoot once they get a job."

Richard and Tiffani rounded out the team that settled at the meeting table. After Tiffani led with a prayer, Kiera reported a sharp rise in registrations for her "One of Me" image class. Peter had a tour of the Simmons Music Productions studio set for Thursday, including several kids from River House. Parker asked to be included in the tour before reporting on his ongoing web design class.

Like a wild game of tennis, Sam's attention bounced from one person to the next as he scribbled notes. To have had access to such creative programming at the Teen Center would have been amazing. What a difference GPS could make in the community. A growing energy chased away doubts that had plagued him since that first lunch with Richard.

The screen door opened and people filed in carrying donuts and a Java Depot coffee box. The room filled with laughter and teasing as the GPS staff greeted the River House staff with hugs and handshakes. Their genuine affection and respect for each other sparked a flash of envy in Sam. There had been that same chemistry at the Teen Center. The envy faded. That had ended poorly.

With River House right across the street, the programs shared resources and staff. Sam lost track of names. He'd heard plenty, however, about Kurt Wagner. Meeting him now, he could see why the community loved him. Perpetually smiling and energetic, the humility in his words and actions was striking.

"Man, I'm so glad to finally meet you, Sam," he said. With shaggy dark hair, dressed in jeans and a black T-shirt, he stood a half-foot shorter than Sam but still a presence to look up to. "Rich has talked about you nonstop. I started to think he made you up."

"I'm sure he made most of it up." Laughter met Sam's assurance. "It's great to meet you, Kurt. I've heard a lot about you and River House."

"Good stuff, I hope. Thanks for jumping in to help us with the classes. Have you met my wife, Vanessa?"

Sam shook the pretty blonde's hand. Quite pregnant, she couldn't be much over five foot. Her skirt revealed a prosthesis where her right leg should have been. "Vanessa, it's a pleasure."

Deep blue eyes sparkled up at him. "Welcome to our team, Sam. Thanks for joining us."

Kurt put an arm around her and pulled her close. "She might be small," he warned Sam with a wink, "but don't let that fool you. She's a task-master."

"Well, someone needs to be," she shot back before rising to press a kiss to his cheek. "Since you're too nice, it falls to me. Okay everyone, let's get started."

Kurt grinned at Sam and mouthed, "See?" before following her to the couch.

Sam took a seat next to Tiffani and studied the couple as the meeting progressed. They obviously adored each other. Mutual respect showed in how they deferred to each other to answer questions, asked for the other's opinion, and listened. They seemed to really listen to each other.

He flinched. So wrapped up in his work at the Teen Center, he hadn't noticed Jillian pulling away. An image flashed before him. Jill, round tummy poking out of her raincoat, suitcases in hand, regret on her face. He'd watched his future walk out of the house and climb into another man's car.

A burst of laughter dissolved the image. He forced a smile and returned his focus to his new coworkers. This was his chance to start fresh, and help others do the same. Working beside these people and learning from them was an added bonus.

When the meeting broke up, Richard gave him a tour of the house. The upstairs expansion had two small bedrooms turned into meeting rooms, a half-bath, and a room filled with clothing and accessories set up like a store. The main floor had been expanded to include a spacious kitchen, two larger meeting rooms, and an open-format office area.

"And that, my friend," Richard pointed to a metal desk in the corner, "is your work space. The GPS design is that we spend more time out in the community than holed up in an office. Whenever possible, we meet people in coffee shops or places where they're comfortable, hold classes in public meeting spaces, and generally have a presence *out there*, not only in here."

Sam nodded. *Great.* He'd be back in the public eye again. He perked up when they reached the basement with a wide-open woodworking space. Now *here* he'd be comfortable. "What have you done down here so far?"

"Not much," Richard admitted. "We're hoping you have some thoughts."

Ideas lit his brain like fireworks. "How about offering basic construction and woodworking skills? We could talk about different trades and what jobs are available. And we could do a field trip to Jimmy's to see how a shop like his runs. He loves showing off his place," he added with a chuckle.

The room had several workbenches, and a wide array of tools ready for use. "Man, this is great stuff. Looks brand new. Hey, we could have guest speakers come in, local experts who could share their experience, how they got to where they are, what type of education or training is required."

Richard slapped him on the back. "And this is why we need you here. How about we keep this conversation going over lunch?"

Upstairs in the kitchen, he paused. "Sam, thanks for jumping in, at least for now. I'm thinking it's a God-thing."

A God-thing? "Let's get these classes rollin'."

– 9 –

Eggs, bacon, toast, and coffee at the local cafe—the best breakfast Marti had enjoyed in a long time, thanks to the money Jason insisted she take yesterday. Payment for her first days of work. Marti washed up in the restroom, and smoothed as many wrinkles as she could from her clothes. She might be a thief but she didn't have to look the part. On jellied legs, she walked two blocks to the convenience store, drawing a deep breath before passing through the door. She checked the price of the concealer, then stood in line at the front register, hands clasped to keep them still.

As a tiny old woman counted out change with crooked fingers, Marti glanced around the store. Cameras in every corner stared back at her. Did they recognize her? Were the police already on their way? What if they figured out her connection with Eddy? She'd go to jail forever. The trembling intensified, and she steadied herself against the counter.

A young couple stepped into line behind her, followed by a bearded man. When a police officer stood behind him, Marti's lungs emptied. She couldn't make her confession with an audience, especially a cop. The officer's radio crackled, followed by indistinct voices. They'd ID'd her. Any minute he'd throw cuffs on her.

"I…I forgot something. Go ahead," she stammered to the couple, and scurried away. Pretending to look at magazines, she watched the line inch forward. The officer added a candy bar to the items he held, and laughed with the bearded man.

Marti wandered the aisles, waiting for the line at the register to finish. Sweat slid down her back one fiery droplet at a time. Finally it quieted at the front, and she watched the officer leave the store without looking for her.

Could she admit out loud that she'd stolen something? If she went to jail, what would happen to Katie? Would Gloria get to keep her? Resolve stiffened her spine and she marched to the register.

The teenage gum-popping cashier waited. When she stood silent before him, unable to speak over the hammering in her chest, he lifted a pierced eyebrow. "Need something?"

"Yes. I…" The words stuck. *Can't do it. Not if it will affect Katie.* She snatched up a pack of gum and plopped it in front of him.

He swiped it over the scanner. "Eighty-seven cents."

She handed him a ten-dollar bill. **No change.** She started and glanced around. The impression seemed to have come from inside her. But she'd get plenty of— *Oh!* She stuffed the gum into her pocket and hurried away.

"Hey! Your change."

She paused at the door. "Keep it. It's for an item I forgot to pay for a few days ago."

He frowned, her money in his upraised hand. "What item?"

"Concealer. In cosmetics." With that pseudo-confession, she scooted out of the store and race walked down the block. Slipping around the corner, she dropped against the wall to catch her breath. If the kid called security, that candy bar cop would be after her in a blink.

She peeked back around the corner. Nobody— A hand closed around her arm and she squealed, spinning around with a fist raised.

"Whoa!" Ibrahim jumped back, hands raised and eyes wide.

"Oh, my gosh." She pressed the fist to her chest. "Don't ever do that again!"

"Trust me, I won't." He gave a toothy grin. "Hiding from the cops?"

"Would I be standing here if I was?"

"If you thought you'd ditched them." He started walking. "Heading to work?"

"Actually, yes, I am." She fell into step beside him.

The morning sun warmed her back as they walked in companionable silence. She'd more than paid for the makeup, in a backward sort of way. She wouldn't go to jail. Katie wouldn't have to stay with Gloria forever. And she'd never steal another thing in her life. As long as no one connected her to Eddy, she was free to start over. Free! What a wonderful concept.

She returned to the storeroom more peaceful than she'd felt in a long time. Yesterday she'd sorted through unopened boxes and separated items into categories. Today she'd start cleaning—right after Ibrahim gave her another lesson on the register.

Giddy with excitement, she joined him at the register and greeted each customer, watching him enter their orders. She'd sketched the screen on a napkin and stuck it on a clipboard so she could practice entering each order along with him. She couldn't read every button but she'd already memorized half of the screen. Another lesson or two, and she'd be good to go if Jason ever needed her up front. A long shot, but her best, and only, option for a job. She'd be ready.

When two teenagers stepped up to the register, Ibrahim moved back and motioned for Marti. She stood frozen until he raised a dark eyebrow in challenge.

"Good morning, ladies," she said with a bright smile, hoping they couldn't see her heart pounding under the black apron. "What can I get you this morning?"

They rattled off simple drink orders. While Ibrahim watched, she easily entered the orders and gave the girls their change. As they moved toward the pickup counter, she did a happy dance.

He laughed. "I said you could do it, didn't I?"

"You did," she agreed, "but it's nice to have the first one done. Thanks for teaching me."

"You learn quickly."

Her smile faded. "For someone who reads like a third grader."

"We've had lots of people who couldn't figure it out, and they could read fine. You caught on fast 'cause you're smart." The door bells jangled, and he grinned. "So now you can do these next few."

Wha—? No one had ever called her smart. Ever. She snapped her mouth closed. His praise buoyed her as she entered several more orders, even correcting her own mistake. Finally, with Jason due any minute, she left Ibrahim at the register and moved around the shop collecting empty plates and cups, humming softly as she weaved around occupied tables.

Her first customers, the teenage girls, giggled over their phones. *No doubt about boys.* She'd had a crush or two before quitting high school. She sighed at the distant hope of going on an actual date someday. Or having girlfriends to giggle with.

A well-dressed business woman, red hair ensnared in a bun, frowned at her tablet, swiping through screens. *Unhappy boss.* Plenty of experience working with them over the years. Or maybe her bun was too tight.

At the corner table, a man studied papers spread before him. Thick blond hair, athletic build. His smiling thanks as she removed his empty plate sent a tingle along her arms. *Maybe a teacher?* No doubt the girls in his class spent their time mooning over him. She hid a smile as she cleared a nearby table. She would have.

Bypassing the storeroom, she stepped out back to make her daily call to Katie, surprised to see a message from an unfamiliar number. Praying it was a potential job, she clicked on voicemail.

"Hello, Martha. We haven't talked in a while." Eddy's smooth tone sent waves of nausea over her.

She dropped back against the building, a hand over her mouth.

"I trust you had a restful stay in the hospital. I wanted to make sure you're doing well now, and to remind you we'll have to have another conversation if you discuss our…relationship with anyone. Including the very lovely Katherine." His chuckle dripped evil. "I won't hesitate to finish what we started. I'm sure you understand."

The phone slipped from her numb fingers, and she lurched toward the dumpster, losing her breakfast behind it. Sagging against the cold metal, she wiped her mouth with the back of her hand. A tear burned down her cheek, followed by several more as the temptation to dissolve into hysteria grew. She sucked in a strangled breath, then another until she'd gained control.

"No!" She pushed herself up straight and brushed the tears away. "I won't let him get to me. I have the pictures."

Squaring her shoulders, she strode back toward the coffee shop door, pausing where her phone lay in the gravel. She reached for it, then yanked her hand back. She wanted him out of her life. Now. "We're done. No more!" With the photo card hidden safely away, she could buy a new phone. She'd earned enough to buy a new one. She stomped on the offending item, grinding it into the gravel.

Gathering up the pieces, she tossed them into the dumpster, her pounding pulse making her steps uneven. She'd wipe Eddy out of her life if it was the last thing she did. And it might be.

The young woman hummed softly as she polished the mahogany table to a gleam. Sam had watched her all morning from where he'd settled in to study the GPS class curriculum.

"You're new here," he said. Worst opening line ever.

"I am." She kept polishing, wincing slightly when she reached across the table. "And you're a regular."

"You picked that up quick."

"Jason briefed me on who to watch out for." A yellow tinge, not completely hidden by makeup, framed the mischief in her dark brown eyes. Long eyelashes gave her a doe-like expression.

"I'm Sam."

"Gus."

"Short for?"

"Gus." She moved on to clear another table, continuing around the shop cleaning, greeting people, chatting with co-workers. Tall and pretty with an abundance of dark wavy hair pulled back in a ponytail. An Ace bandage peeked out from under the sleeve of her white shirt. Between that, her thin frame, and the bruises, it seemed life hadn't been kind to her lately.

He'd done enough counseling to recognize a potential domestic issue. Yet she seemed at ease, not looking over her shoulder or flinching at loud noises. It wasn't his business to pry into a complete stranger's life, but something about her made him want to know more.

She started sweeping at the far end of the shop, working her way toward him. As she neared, he lifted his feet.

"Thanks." She did a quick swipe under his table.

"You handle that broom like a pro." *Shut up, Evans.*

"It's a job for experts only. Don't try it at home."

He laughed. "I wouldn't dream of it. Are you for hire? My place is a mess."

"Schedule's full, sorry." A dimple appeared as she continued sweeping.

"I can see why. You're obviously one of the experts."

She offered a bittersweet smile and shrugged. "I guess we all want to be an expert at something. This is it for me."

"Oh, I doubt that. I'll bet you're good at a lot of things." *Well, didn't that sound suggestive.* He braced for a slap.

She leaned on the broom. "I'm good at getting things done, but not so much with my brain. So…I sweep. Not that I mind," she added quickly. "I'm grateful for the job."

"Are you working your way through college?"

She flinched. "A high school diploma seems to be a requirement."

"Gus!" Jason motioned at her from behind the register, frowning darkly.

She flashed an apologetic smile, then scurried to her boss where they exchanged words. Sam strained to hear, muscles tensed as he watched. The barrel-chested owner, a gregarious, demonstrative man, seemed a bit short-tempered.

The man paced in front of her. She said something and he threw his hands in the air. Sam lifted partially out of his chair but, when she responded calmly, settled back down. Jason swept his hand toward the register and said something to her before disappearing into the back.

Seemingly unruffled by the exchange, Gus stepped to the counter and greeted the next customer with an engaging smile lighting her face. There'd been such defeat in her words. What had kept her from finishing high school?

His cell phone chirped and he checked the message. *Everything set 4 2morrow. Enjoy day off. Don't get used to it.*

Chuckling, he responded to Jimmy's text, then glanced at the clock. Due at GPS in twenty minutes for a class run-through with Richard, the brief exchange with Gus made him eager to start. He gathered his papers and headed out of the coffee shop. He'd return tomorrow. There was a lot more to the pretty barista than he'd glimpsed today.

– 10 –

"Good morning, Gus."

Marti set the coffee pot in position, pressed the "On" button and turned around, her chest suddenly too small for her lungs. "Good morning. Sam, right?"

He nodded with a grin that revealed creases at the corners of his mouth. She searched her memory for yesterday's order. She'd been so busy trying not to look at him, she hadn't paid attention the way she usually did. "Large house dark roast with a shot of almond, right?"

Dark blond eyebrows shot up. "Wow, you're good. And I didn't even order it from you."

"Anything else? Maybe a streusel? Hot out of the oven."

"They smell great. Sure, why not?"

As he pulled out his wallet, she pretended not to notice he was several inches taller than her, or that raindrops glistened on hair curling up at the collar of his jacket. She rang his order and then put the streusel on a plate. "Here you go. Ibrahim will have your drink ready in a second."

"Thanks, Gus. It's a pleasure seeing your bright smile so early this morning."

Her cheeks warmed. "Thanks. Yours too." *Lame.*

He moved away to wait for his coffee, and she focused on straightening the counter, promptly knocking over the gift card holder. Setting it upright, her elbow brushed the tiered rack of treats and she grabbed it before it teetered off the counter.

"You okay over there?" Ibrahim teased.

She shot him a glare, encountered Sam's smile, and nodded, face flaming. Spinning away from their chuckles, she checked the brewing pots, forcing her pulse to slow. She could handle looking stupid in front of Ibrahim, but not in front of their customers. Especially the handsome ones.

The few times a man had paid her attention hadn't ended well. But Sam had a different vibe. She glanced over her shoulder. It wasn't just his looks. His friendliness seemed genuine, without the leering and disgusting remarks she'd gotten from the men who'd visited her mother. *Get a grip. Eddy seemed genuine too, at first.*

"Gus!"

She flinched at Jason's voice booming from the storeroom. He might be hard of hearing, but that didn't mean everyone else was. "Be right there." She raised an eyebrow at Ibrahim. "Cover me for a minute?"

"No prob."

She hurried through the swinging doors and turned into the storeroom, pulling up short when she saw Jason holding her backpack and unrolled sleeping bag. *Busted.* How had she forgotten to roll it up?

"Are you actually *living* back here?"

Grateful he'd lowered his voice, she moved into the room. The customers didn't need to know her issues. "I haven't touched the food or anything," she blurted. "I don't even eat when I'm on break." She dropped her gaze, watching her toe wiggle against the burgeoning hole in her shoe. "I needed a place to sleep out of the rain."

After Ibrahim suggested she stay here the last few rainy nights, she'd found it difficult to sleep under a cloud of guilt. She should have asked Jason first.

"Gus, Gus, Gus." Dropping her things at his feet, he rubbed his whiskered face, releasing an exasperated sigh. "I thought you told me everything."

"I did. Well...except the shelter's full because of the weather."

"And you didn't think you needed to clear it with me?"

Her gaze darted up. "I should have. I just thought it would, you know, be one or two nights."

"Either someone has let you in or you made a copy of the key." When she remained silent, he dropped onto a stool and shook his head. "I should boot you out on your skinny rear, you know that?"

Jaw clenched against the burn of tears, she nodded.

"I told you to eat something on your breaks. Why aren't you?"

"It didn't feel right to eat food I didn't buy."

Jason snorted. "For crying out loud, Gus. You're going to shrink into nothing and Lorna will blame *me*. When I say it's okay to eat, I expect you to eat. Got it?"

"Got it." Hope flared. Maybe she wasn't being fired.

"As for staying back here, it's wrong on so many levels. You want me to get fined?"

Because she slept in the storeroom at night? "If you did, I'd pay it."

His bark of laughter made her jump. "That's rich. With what money?"

"I've saved everything you've paid me." After paying for the make-up and buying a cheap phone. She'd slipped the rest into his desk drawer with a note promising to pay it all back.

"You obviously don't buy groceries. You're going to blow away in a stiff wind."

Warmth crawled up her neck and she crossed her arms. She'd always been thin, but now the thrift store clothes hung on her. Another reminder that she wasn't pretty like Katie.

"Well, you can't sleep here anymore." Thick eyebrows lowered. "I'll change the locks if I have to."

The spark of hope fizzled. She nodded and reached for her backpack but he scooped it up first.

"I said you can't sleep here. I didn't say you have to leave." He held the pack out to her but kept hold when she took it. "Lorna and I have a room over the garage where you can stay until you get back on your feet."

She stared at him blankly. "What?"

He released the backpack, and she stumbled back a step. "We talked about it the other day and decided that if you were still staying in the shelter, we'd have you take the garage apartment, now that our renter has moved out. However," his voice deepened in warning, "we will *not* tell Lorna you've been sleeping here. Right?"

She closed her mouth, shaking her head quickly. The buffeting in her chest threatened to throw her off-balance. "No. Yes. Right." A real place to stay?

"After your shift is done," he said, writing on a scrap of paper, "you can head over there. Here's the address." He held the paper out. "Lorna's expecting you so don't make me look bad by not showing up."

She clutched it to her backpack, frowning. "Why are you doing this? You hardly know me."

He shrugged. "When Lorna likes someone, she takes care of 'em. She took a liking to you the first time you stopped in for coffee." He headed out of the room, then added without a backward glance, "You've grown on me too, kid."

She replaced him on the stool, gaping at the doorway. What just happened?

Sam checked the clock. Gus and her burly boss had been gone nearly fifteen minutes. Tapping his pen on the papers, he debated going to find her. Maybe there was something between her and Jason. No. He couldn't imagine that. Jason reappeared long enough to speak with the young man Gus had called Ibrahim. Still no Gus. Maybe he fired her. Maybe he'd lost his temper and—

There she is. The tapping stopped.

She emerged slowly from the back of the shop, a lopsided frown on her face. Standing at the register, she stared unblinking out the window. She seemed dazed but unharmed.

He approached the counter. "Gus? You okay?"

Her attention drifted to him and then snapped into focus. "Oh! I'm sorry. Can I get you something?"

"Sure. I'd like a cookie." *Sheesh. At least pick something manly.*

"Which one?"

"Oh. Uh, chocolate chip?"

Both dimples appeared. "Is that a question or a request?"

He forced a chuckle to hide the warmth creeping up his neck. "A request. And could I get a refill?"

"Sure. I'll top that off for you." She took his nearly-full cup and added a bit more, then set a mammoth cookie on a plate. "It's $1.50 for the cookie.

Baked fresh this morning. You'll love it."

He paid her and slipped another dollar into the tip jar. "So how's your morning going?"

An eyebrow lifted, as if the question startled her. "Fine. Great, actually. Have you ever..." She waved a hand in dismissal. "Never mind."

"Have I ever what?"

Pink washed across her cheekbones and she fidgeted with the gift card holder. "It's silly."

"I'm up for silly." *Because you are, Evans.*

"Have you ever had a need answered in a way you could have never, ever imagined?"

He'd had a list of needs that were never answered at all. Jillian hadn't changed her mind. Andrew was still dead. Shareen's family still grieved. He had no clue what his future held. "Not that I can think of. Have you?"

Her brows pinched upward in a sweetly confused way. "This morning. I still can't believe the way it happened. And right when I figured God didn't care what happened to me." Her face filled with color and she fiddled with a pen on the counter. "Sorry. I'm blabbering away and you have work to do."

"Nothing that can't wait." He'd figured the same thing about God, but no great response had dropped from the sky to change his mind.

"Gus!" Jason bellowing again.

"Excuse me. The boss is calling." A shy smile flashed. "Thanks for chatting."

"My pleasure. Anytime, Gus."

She disappeared through the swinging doors, and he returned to his booth. He wanted to know more about the wary young woman with bruises under doe eyes who'd heard from God.

– 11 –

Marti stood on the sidewalk, scrap of paper in hand, and stared in wonder at the beautiful two-story house. Tan stucco with dark green shutters. Wicker rockers on the wide front porch waiting for an occupant. Window boxes overflowing with a riot of colors. And a woman waving a welcome.

"Marti!" Lorna held the front door open, beckoning her. "I'm letting the bugs in instead of you. Hurry up, girl."

She shifted the backpack, picked up Grandy's bag, and coaxed her feet to move. This couldn't be real. Any minute now she'd wake up in her little alley niche. But Lorna's gesturing seemed real enough, as did the delicious aroma wafting out the door. Her stomach growled.

The front steps creaked under her feet as she crossed the porch. Lorna greeted her with a hug before propelling her into an alternate universe. A real home, not a dingy apartment. In the living room, bookshelves held actual books. Beautiful paintings and artsy things hung on the walls. Framed photos of smiling, happy people filled tables.

"I'm so glad this has worked out for both of us," Lorna said. "When our renter left, we weren't sure whether we wanted to find a new tenant, leave the apartment empty, or wait to see what came up. And look who's the answer to prayer."

Her round cheeks lifted, squeezing her face into a happy squint. Her brown hair, lightly brushed with gray, bounced in a crazy wave of curls. "This is our home, and we want you to feel it's yours as well. You're welcome here in the house anytime, so don't think you have to stay in your apartment for fear of bothering us. With the kids all married off, it's gotten too quiet."

Marti nodded, speechless. Had she ever been welcome anywhere? Even in her family's dingy apartment with its smoke-darkened walls, she'd felt like an outsider. And *she* was an answer to prayer? More like the other way around.

"Through here is the kitchen," Lorna motioned her to follow, "which is our favorite room in the house. Jason is always trying new recipes for the shop." She patted her wide hips. "Unfortunately, he's very good, and I love being the guinea pig."

A granite-topped island filled the center of the room. Strange-looking machinery lined the counters—mixers of some kind, alongside bottles of little wrinkled vegetables. She couldn't remember her mother ever making a meal, but Grandy's kitchen had always smelled like fresh-baked cookies. She breathed deeply and smiled. Like this.

"Your apartment is out this door, right over the garage." Lorna led her out the back door and along a short sidewalk to what looked like another house with three garage doors.

They park their cars in there? It's nicer than the apartment I grew up in. Marti swept her gaze up the outside stairs and across the expanse of windows above the doors.

"Jason rebuilt these steps last year so they're nice and sturdy. And there are motion sensor lights so you're never out here in the dark."

Marti followed her up the stairs and through the doorway, where her breath caught. Instead of a room filled with old car parts, and odds and ends, it was an actual apartment.

"Wow," she breathed.

"It's not much, but it's safer than you living in that shelter."

"It's…amazing." The main living area glowed with sunlight streaming through the front windows. Walls a soothing pale green, the room had *two* couches and a comfy chair. She'd had a camp chair and a battered loveseat in the apartment. On the antique chest-turned-coffee table sat a vase overflowing with a riot of summer flowers.

"Go explore," Lorna encouraged. "This is your home now."

The open floor plan included a kitchen at one end, set apart by an island with a breakfast bar and two stools. Marti slid out of her shoes, eliciting a chuckle from her hostess, and wandered to the kitchen. She ran her fingers over the quartz-topped island where a plate sat heaped with chocolate chip cookies. This was a place to make her own meal and enjoy it without strangers bumping into her, or getting into arguments over a slice of bread. Or Eddy showing up and ruining her appetite.

Past the living area, she discovered a bathroom. An actual tub! The bedroom to the left was filled with light, windows stretching across the two outside walls. Her beloved bedroom at the farm had had only one window. She'd slept on the couch in her family's apartment. Her fingers itched to throw every window open wide.

A dresser sat along one wall, ivory candles of various sizes tied together with a sweet pink ribbon gathered on a crocheted doily. On the bedside table were a lamp with a ruffled shade, a clock, and magazines.

On the other side of the bathroom, a second bedroom. With windows lining one wall, the room was bright and airy. It would be perfect for— She cut the thought short. One day at a time.

Jason had mentioned a room over the garage, and she'd hoped she wouldn't have to sleep near a car. She'd never expected an actual apartment. Lorna continued chatting, her voice barely audible over Marti's pounding heart. Something about closet space. Extra bedding and pillows. Towels in the bathroom. This wasn't real. It couldn't be.

"Marti?"

Her focus swung back to the older woman who frowned at her. "What?"

"Are you okay?"

"Yes." Although she might hyperventilate soon. "Fine. I'm fine."

"But you're crying. Is there something wrong with the place? Do you need anything?"

Marti touched two fingers to her cheeks, surprised at the wetness, and managed a wobbly smile. "I'm so grateful."

Lorna's frown relaxed into an understanding smile. "You are so welcome, dear. When Jason mentioned you needed a place to stay, I knew you were supposed to be right here with us."

"But you don't know me." She seemed to be saying that a lot lately.

"We know enough. Now, you have time to put your things away and rest for a bit. Dinner will be at 6:30. I hope that's not too late for you."

Marti blinked. "Dinner?"

"Men! Jason should have told you that dinner is part of the package." Her perusal swept over Marti in a blink. "We want you to be healthy and happy while you're here. You can let yourself into the kitchen anytime, but we'll eat at 6:30." She paused at the door and wagged a finger. "No reminders. This isn't a hotel. It's your home."

Marti stared at the closed door, listening to Lorna's footsteps on the stairs. *Home.* Complete with flowers and fresh baked cookies. She sank onto the couch, dropped her face into her hands, and cried.

Sam quietly filled his lungs as he took his place at the front of the crowded room. "It's great to see you all here on this beautiful evening. I'm Sam Evans and I'll be facilitating this GED prep course." He took a swig of water. The last time he'd been in front of a group was in a courtroom. A lifetime ago. He sounded as stiff now as he had then.

Twenty-two people had crammed into a room designed for eighteen. "Each of you is here because you want to be. You can quit at any time, but I hope you won't. I believe anyone who wants to succeed, can. One small step can change your future, and that's what we're here to do—take that small step together, one day at a time."

They looked back at him silently, a few nearly asleep, some with hopeful faces. The fidgety guy in the corner, knee bouncing, apparently needed a cigarette, or something stronger. He squinted at Sam, scruffy face screwed up as if he were thinking hard. And they hadn't even started the first lesson.

What am I doing here? Somehow he had to keep them awake and actually teach them something, for the next two months. He stepped to the side of the room and opened a window, welcoming the fresh air that mingled with stale cigarette smoke, body odor, and fruity perfume. "It's a little warm in here so let's get some air circulating."

He returned to the front and put his attention on the outline. *Focus, man.* "Okay. First, let's get to know each other. Tell us your name and what made you decide to take this prep class. We'll start here." He gestured toward a young woman with diamond studs rimming her ear, and piercings in her nose and eyebrow.

"I'm Petula, an' I'm here 'cause my PO told me to get my act together."

A few chuckled at her blunt response. Sam smiled. "Glad you're here, Petula. And I'm glad you listened to your parole officer."

She shrugged. "Beats goin' to jail. An' I figure it can't hurt. Might help me get a job someday."

"It will definitely help you with that. Okay, how about you, sir?"

A young man with dirty blond dreadlocks. "James. I wanna get it right this time. I got a little boy now to take care of so I need a job."

"Great plan, James," Sam said, then added, "But I have to ask. How long did it take to get that done?" He gestured toward the hairstyle.

"Mmm, about six hours. I had to take a break in the middle. Sitting in the chair made me nuts. I'm pretty ADHD. Hey, I gotta get a new lawyer. Do you know any?"

"Let's talk after class."

Introductions continued around the room. Ronnie and Marcel, twins planning to start a business. Robert, the oldest at thirty-five, wanted a better job so he could buy a house. Muriel, Poncho, Elliot the antsy guy, Mary. Stories colored with regret and longing, and a desire for something better. He'd heard the same in Gus' voice.

"Thanks, everybody," Sam said when the last person, tiny Louise in the back corner, had finished. His shoulders had lowered from their earlier position near his ears. "That will help me as I organize our class time."

"What about you?" Poncho asked. His sweater was a riot of bright colors.

"Fair enough." He perched on the edge of the front table. "As I said, I'm Sam. I got my GED a year after getting booted out of high school. I was a counselor over at the Teen Center before it closed, and—"

"*That's* where I seen you before!" Elliot exclaimed. "I knew you looked familiar."

Had they met at the center? Sam started to reply, but the young man continued. "You were the guy who got fired for hittin' on a couple of the girls!"

Sam's heart leaped into overtime as comments rippled through the group. "Wait a minute. Everybody, listen up." Being cleared didn't mean people forgot. Was it going to follow him forever?

It took a lifetime before he'd regained their full attention. Sweat beaded at his hairline. "I never hit on any girl there, or anywhere else. The girl wasn't even a client. The court ruled that she made it up, which she had, so those charges were dropped and I was cleared."

That sounded a bit desperate. He cleared his throat and forced his hands to steady as he picked up his notebook. "Now, let's go over some housekeeping info, and then jump into our first lesson. As we go along, let me know if I'm going too fast, or too slow, or if the lesson doesn't make sense. I don't want to waste your time here." Although it might be too late for that.

– 12 –

Sunlight tickled Marti awake, enticing her from happy dreams. A picnic with Katie, working beside Gramps in the barn, tasting Grandy's raspberry muffins, butter melting across the top. She stretched and opened her eyes, then frowned at the ceiling. *Where—?*

Yesterday's events crystallized and she smiled. Clutching the covers to her chin, she pulled in a breath of fresh linen. A tiny giggle slipped out, followed by a heartier one. She actually lived here! She wiggled her feet and laughed aloud. Tonight she would sleep here again. Not in the alley or at the shelter, not on the cement floor of the Depot, but right here where it was soft, and comfortable, and safe. An actual home for her, and maybe Katie as well!

Refreshed from her best night's sleep in nearly a year, she jumped out of bed, made a quick stop in the bathroom, then headed to the kitchen for a glass of water. Once she got an actual paycheck, she'd buy a few groceries. Imagining an overflowing bag on the counter, she opened a cupboard to see how much room she had to fill.

The shelves were stocked. Soup, crackers, cookies. She opened another. Baking supplies. Cereal, both cold and hot. A whole new jar of peanut butter, unopened! Bread. Pasta and sauce. On the counter stood glass canisters filled with sugar and flour. She opened a third and inhaled deeply. Her own coffee! A folded piece of paper sat propped against the toaster. How had she missed all this yesterday?

Note in hand, she sank onto a stool at the counter. She'd been so tired after a delicious meatloaf dinner last night, she'd gone right to bed.

We're glad you're here, Marti. Make yourself at home. Please let us know if you need anything. Lorna and Jason

A tear dripped onto the note. What had she done to deserve such kindness from strangers? A job, then a home, and now cupboards stuffed with food, all for her. No rats or cockroaches skittering along the wall, no stale smoke. No mass-produced food in the long line at the shelter. And no Eddy.

This was her home! At least until they decided to have a paying renter. She straightened. They hadn't asked for a penny, but she'd pay what she could for now. Once she had a better paying job, she'd pay more. And she'd be the perfect guest. There'd be no mess, no screw-ups. No visitors ever, except Katie. They'd hardly know she was here.

She figured out the coffee-maker, then poked through the rest of the cupboards and drawers as the heavenly aroma filled the apartment. Enjoying her first cup in her new home, she treated herself to two slices of toast slathered with peanut butter, savoring every bite.

Life looked very different with a full stomach and a rested mind.

Settled at his favorite corner table in the Java Depot, Sam studied the information sheets his students had completed. Marcel wanted help with math so he could be the finance guy for their new business. Petula wanted mentoring on how to turn her life around. Poncho needed time—for his family, for studying, for work. The information on each page was unique, but their dreams were similar. A microcosm of the neighborhood. No matter their race, religion, financial status, or background, everyone desired change, a better life.

Poncho's comment about building a future for his children made Sam's stomach clench. The moment Jillian had revealed her pregnancy, he'd started planning his future as a dad, and what he'd do with his son or daughter. How to climb a tree, ride a bike—

"Good morning, Sam."

Slow to pull away from the memories, he encountered Gus's bashful smile. He shoved the pain aside. "Good morning to you, Gus. You're looking very cheerful today."

"We have a new treat I thought you'd like to try." She set a napkin in front of him with a small chocolate cookie. "It's Jason's newest venture—chocolate macadamia nut. Let us know what you think."

She moved around the shop offering samples as Sam took a bite and sighed. Rich chocolate, the crunch of nut, and...a hint of cinnamon? Amazing. He caught Gus's eye where she now stood at the register, and gave two thumbs up. Her smile widened, and she nodded with a knowing lift to her brow. She looked healthier this morning, her eyes bright, a flush to her face that almost completely hid the bruises.

Whatever answer God had given her yesterday was exactly what she needed. He wanted to know more. When the last of the line of customers had ordered, he approached the counter, cup in hand.

"So you liked it," she said.

"Yup. He's definitely onto something." He held out his cup. "Could you top it off?"

"Happy to."

As she handed it back, he blurted, "Gus, I'd like to hear more about what you mentioned yesterday, how God answered your prayer."

Her mouth opened and closed as her cheeks turned a pretty rose color. "Oh, that." She waved his request away. "It was nothing. Sorry if I came off like a crazy person."

"You didn't at all. And something like that is never nothing. If you want to talk about it when you have a break, you know where to find me." He returned to his table before she could protest. The real question was would she want to? She probably thought *he* was crazy for nosing into her life.

Marti watched Sam resettle at his table before snapping her mouth shut and scurrying to the storeroom, hands on her burning cheeks. What had she been thinking yesterday, blurting out her thoughts like that? And why did he care? Who was he, anyway?

Ibrahim appeared in the doorway. "We need more cups up front when you're done hiding out."

She straightened. "Just taking a breather."

"Whatever. Bring the cups."

Before he could step away, she said, "Hey, you've been here forever, right?"

"Five years. I guess that's forever in the coffee world. Why?"

"Do you know anything about Sam? The guy I was talking to?"

"A little." He folded his arms and leaned against the doorframe, wiggling black eyebrows. "You interested?"

"No! It's not that. He seems nice and all." She turned away and grabbed a stack of cups. In the silence, she closed her eyes. *Why did I even ask?*

"Well, I don't know much."

She looked over her shoulder, hoping her ears hadn't doubled in size.

"He used to work at that teen center over on 33rd, as a counselor-type guy, I think. People seem to like him."

"He doesn't work there now?"

"It closed a year or so ago. There was something about him being fired for…" He frowned. "Something about a girl and a trial. I can't remember. I'm fuzzy on details."

Her heart stuttered. "A trial?"

"I don't think it lasted long. I've never heard anything bad about him, but it's not like I know the guy. Sorry I can't remember more. Don't forget the cups."

Marti stood still, her thoughts spinning. Sam on trial? He seemed genuine, nothing like Eddy. It hadn't taken long to pick up bad vibes about Eddy once he started hanging around, but there were no warning bells about Sam.

With an armful of cups, she returned to the front. Waiting on customers over the next hour, glancing toward the handsome man at the corner table, she wrestled with whether to take him up on his offer. Why did he care what happened in her life? Did she look like an easy mark?

When Jason sent her on break, she filled a cup with ice water and started toward the corner. She wasn't the gullible girl Eddy had preyed on. She'd play along for now, and pay attention to her radar.

When she neared, a smile brightened his face. "Oh, good. I'm glad you want to talk."

Taking a sip to moisten her dry mouth, she took the opposite chair. "I don't know why I told you that yesterday. It's not like God spoke to me in some big voice or anything."

He laughed. "Well, that's disappointing."

"He'd have scared me half to death if He had."

"I think He'd scare a whole lot of us, which is maybe why He skips the big voice routine. Or," he raised his brow, "maybe He actually has an annoying high-pitched voice."

"Or He's a She and nobody would expect to hear a booming woman's voice."

"There's that option," he said. "However He did it, I'd like to hear how He answered your prayer. And how you knew it was Him."

"Well, the answer wouldn't make the news or anything."

"That doesn't make it any less important."

Marti considered that. While the amazing answer wouldn't be a big deal to anyone else, it had totally rocked her world. "I guess that's true. Well, I needed a job and a place to live. First I got the job, this one, and then yesterday I was offered a place to live. Out of the blue." It didn't sound all that miraculous when she said it aloud. People found jobs and housing all the time. "See? It's not that big a deal."

"You're right," he said. "That's not a big deal."

She flinched, mortified. That's what Eddy would have said.

"It's a *huge* deal," he corrected, a twinkle in his green eyes. "And it's amazing."

The flush of embarrassment cooled. "I think so," she said softly.

After a brief silence, he leaned back in his chair. "Thanks for sharing that with me. I've needed some answers, and it's always good to hear how that's happening with other people."

He needed answers? "Have you gotten any yet?"

He rubbed his jaw, frowning out the window. "I'm not sure. Maybe. I'm in wait-and-see mode. So, tell me how you like working here."

The conversation shifted and Marti shared a few of her blunders as she'd learned to use the register and make drinks. Sam laughed easily and often, listening with apparent interest. During a lull in their laughter, she sipped her water and tried to study him nonchalantly. He had an adorable smile with creases at either side of his mouth. His eyes crinkled at the corners. And he had a great laugh. She couldn't remember hearing Eddy laugh ever.

"So, what's it like working for Jason the foghorn?"

"Shh." She tried to look firm as she leaned forward, her mouth twitching. "He's a really nice guy, but he's a little hard of hearing so he doesn't realize how loud he is sometimes."

Sam leaned closer. "Then why are we whispering?"

"Oh." She straightened. "Good point."

A few minutes later, her break over far too quickly, she strolled back to the counter. For that brief time, she'd felt like someone worthy of attention. It was ridiculous, of course. From what she'd seen, he treated everyone the same way.

The rest of the morning passed in a rosy hue.

– 13 –

Up with the sun on Saturday, Marti's heart sang as she took a long, steamy shower. Finally—her day with Katie. Never again would they go this long without seeing each other. She banished any thought of Eddy. He would *not* darken this special day.

Her stomach too crazy for breakfast, she settled on the couch with a fashion magazine. A few pages in, the photo of a blond model sent her focus to the man she'd fallen asleep thinking about. Sam—obviously educated, and so handsome her insides went wonky when he smiled at her. Her—tall, skinny, and according to most people, stupid. Even Jason had made it abundantly clear she wasn't pretty. Not that he meant to be hurtful.

She slapped the magazine closed and went to stand at the window overlooking Jason and Lorna's house, forehead against the glass. Sam's attention was baffling. What did he want? A man like him wouldn't be interested in a nameless girl working in a coffee shop making minimum wage. No, he'd want a beautiful girl with blameless character. Someone who hadn't messed up every area of her life, who would never get tangled up with the likes of Eddy. Classy, funny and way smart, dressed in the nicest clothes—

"Oh, for Pete's sake!" She whirled from the window, leaving the silly daydream behind as she scooped up her bag. "Get over yourself. Sam probably isn't what he seems either."

Maybe she'd never get that kind of attention from someone like Sam, but she did have Katie's attention, and she planned to be the best big sister, the best family Kat could ever have. That was a thousand times better than the fleeting attention of a guy she barely knew.

She yanked the door shut behind her and flinched when it rattled. Though her legs itched with the desire to run the eight blocks to Gloria's, she maintained a dignified stroll, with a few race-walk steps thrown in. Halfway up the front walk, the screen door of Gloria's tired-looking rambler burst open and Katie flew down the steps, launching herself into Marti's waiting arms.

"Marti! I've missed you!"

Marti tightened her embrace, eyes stinging. "I've missed you too, sweetheart." She clung to the moment before leaning back to admire Katie's side ponytail. "Your hair is adorable. And I think you've grown again."

The answering giggle warmed her straight through. "I'm taller than Gloria now, but Tim is still taller." She twirled her fingers in the ponytail, a wistful smile teasing her lips. "He likes my hair down but it gets in my face. So when he's not around, I like to pull it out of the way."

The warmth faded. He told her how to wear her hair? "I want to hear all about this new friend of yours," Marti said with forced lightness. "Let's get your stuff and get moving. I want to hear about *everything*, so I'm glad we have all day."

Arm in arm, they started toward the front step to gather Katie's purse and ever-present flowered backpack. "We have the whole day," Katie agreed, "until four o'clock."

Marti stopped. "What happens at four?"

"Tim is coming over for dinner, so Gloria is teaching me how to make meatloaf." She grasped Marti's hand. "You can stay, right? For dinner? I've told Tim all about you, and he's dying to meet you. Please?"

Katie had always begged to spend *more* time together; she'd never cut their time short. Marti swallowed hard and managed a toothy grin. "Of course I'll stay. I'd love to help with dinner, and I definitely want to meet Tim."

Color bloomed on Katie's face as she did a happy dance, still clutching Marti's hand. "It will be perfect. And he might be more than a friend someday." The pink deepened as she dropped her gaze with a tiny laugh.

What? She wasn't ready for that kind of relationship. She might never be. What did this guy think he was doing, raising her hopes like that? Marti pinched her lips tight against a rush of angry words. They'd get to know each other all right, maybe more than he cared to. No way would he break Katie's sweet heart and walk away. She'd make that clear before the day ended.

The morning passed far too quickly for Marti, while Katie seemed to check her watch every half hour. She'd always been the center of Katie's world. Kat was certainly the center of *hers*, every decision made with her baby sister in mind. Maybe they'd been apart too long. Well, today marked a fresh start.

Katie counted every one of the 108 steps on their way down to view Minnehaha Falls. They took selfies in front of the thundering waterfall, then hiked the meandering trail toward the Mississippi River. Settled on the river bank, eating the lunch Marti had packed, they told jokes, asked questions, and shared memories.

"Oh, remember when we used to go to the farm?" Katie asked, resting back on her elbows. "Remember how fun it was?"

Marti smiled. "I loved it. What did you like best?"

"Being in the kitchen with Grandy. She baked the best cookies! And she'd let me help." She frowned. "Did you ever help making cookies?"

"Nope. That was your job. You and Grandy were the chefs, and Gramps and I worked in the barn."

Katie wrinkled her nose as she popped a grape into her mouth. "You were always dirty."

"Hey, that wasn't dirt!" Marti sat up straight and pretended offense. "That was sawdust from all the stuff we made. Do you still have the jewelry box?"

"It's my very favorite thing from Gramps. What do you have from him?"

A sigh weighed on her heart. "Only the little box he showed me how to make."

"I miss them a lot. Don't you?"

"Very, very much, sweetheart." Marti blinked back tears, and watched birds flit from branch to branch overhead. She missed everything about those happy times.

"Marti? Is it bad that I miss Grandy more than Mom?"

The admission echoed her own feelings, and she reached for Katie's hand. "No, it's not bad. I miss them more too."

"Mom slept a lot. She didn't like to do things with me. I had way more fun with you, and Grandy and Gramps."

"Me too." She squeezed her sister's slender fingers. "Mom had a tough life. She wasn't a happy person." Her death from alcoholism sent Katie into foster care five years ago. Marti hadn't mourned her passing, but she'd harbored bitter anger at the lack of love and protection in Katie's young life.

She'd use the lingering anger to be ready for Katie's impending freedom from foster care. "Let's go take more pictures, okay?"

They climbed the stairs and took photos at the top of the falls, in the covered surrey they pedaled along the pathways, and, of course, eating ice cream. Twice. By the time they returned to Gloria's, she couldn't keep up with Katie's excited pace.

"I can't wait for you to meet Tim." Katie bounced up the front steps. "He might even be here by now. He doesn't like to be late. And he's super excited to meet you."

She stopped and spun around, frowning. "Marti, you'll be nice to him, right? I know you want me to have good friends, and Tim is."

The plea stung. Hadn't she always been nice to Katie's friends? "Of course I will, Kat." She tugged her sister's ponytail. "Sweetie, I want you to be happy. If hanging out with Tim makes you happy, I'm sure I'll like him. I just want to make sure he treats you like he should."

"He treats me like I'm a princess!" Katie flung her arms around Marti. "I know he'll like you too."

Marti leaned back to brush the hair from her sister's flawless cheeks. She was so pretty, eyes sparkling, face flushed from the sun. And so grown up. "I'll be on my best behavior, I promise."

Inside, Katie greeted Gloria with a hug. Marti clenched her jaw. Katie treated everyone with the same infectious joy, but the conversation at the theater still grated. Marti greeted Gloria politely.

They'd barely settled in the living room when the doorbell rang. Katie shot out of her chair and dashed toward the front door, and Marti steeled herself to meet the interloper. *Be nice. Katie likes him. Be nice.*

Katie returned, dragging the lanky young man by the hand. "Here he is! This is my friend, Tim."

Marti stood and held out a hand, shaking his firmly. His tentative smile contrasted with the iridescence of Katie's. Up close, he was younger than he'd seemed at the theater, a point in his favor. If he were older, she'd have sent him packing this minute. "Hi, Tim. I'm Marti, Katie's sister."

Reddish tufts of facial hair gave the semblance of a beard, but a light case of acne made the tufts more boyish than manly. "She's told me a lot about you. I think I'd know you in a crowd of strangers."

Katie clung to his arm. "But we aren't strangers. Isn't that cool?"

"Very cool," Marti said. *Or not.*

"Katie, let's get that meatloaf started." Gloria had stayed in the background. "Tim and Marti can get to know each other while we work."

"Ohhh." Katie's shining smile drooped. "I thought Tim could help."

"I'd like to spend some time getting to know him, Kat," Marti said. "How about once you get the meatloaf in the oven, you come join us?"

Katie looked between them before reluctantly releasing his arm. "Okay. We'll be done in a bit. Don't go anywhere."

Tim's wink brought Katie's smile back out. "We won't go far." His promise made her giggle.

Marti's heart squeezed. As Katie and Gloria went into the kitchen, Marti motioned for Tim to head toward the back door. She settled silently across the picnic table from him, pleased to see him squirm under her attention.

"So. Tim. Tell me about yourself."

His shoulders lowered as he chatted about playing lacrosse, and finishing high school in the spring, his favorite subject being math. He was a counselor at a local day camp for the summer. He liked working with kids. Maybe he'd be a math teacher someday.

"How did you and Katie meet?"

A smile hovered at his mouth. "I was hanging at the park with my step-brother and some other guys, and she and Gloria were there. We talked a little, but then they left. I saw her a couple more times, and I thought…" His ears reddened and he picked at a fingernail. "I thought she was the prettiest girl I'd ever seen so I introduced myself."

"Katie's beautiful," Marti agreed. "She's also vulnerable."

His eyebrows pinched together. "How do you mean?"

She waited for a twitch or a smirk. His confusion seemed genuine. "She's not like other girls."

His face relaxed as he nodded. "She sure isn't."

Now they understood each other.

"That's what I liked about her right away. She doesn't act like other girls I know."

So much for understanding each other. Her mouth opened, but he continued.

"She's not all girly and pretend-dumb." His words picked up speed. "She's just herself. She's smart and really funny. That's what made us friends at first. We make each other laugh."

Wait. What? "You think she's smart?" The words shot out before she could stop them.

He frowned. "Don't you?"

"Of course." He had to be kidding. She was definitely pretty, and very silly. But smart? Her delay had always made school difficult. "Why do you think she's smart?"

"Well, lots of reasons. She understands people and what they're feeling. Like, she picks up on emotions super easy. And she knows stuff. She likes to watch National Geographic and nature shows, and she knows all kinds of details about plants and animals. Even space. But you know all that."

"Mmhm." Her heart tumbled to her feet. Tim knew her sister better than she did. And he seemed honestly infatuated with her. She cleared her throat. "So tell me about your family, where you grew up, what you want to do with your life."

He laughed. "Boy, she wasn't kidding when she said I'd get the third degree! Well, I grew up here in Uptown." He'd only recently reconnected with his brother, who was twelve years older, so they didn't know each other very well. He loved playing basketball at the park, hanging out with friends. His short list of careers included teaching, but also maybe being a counselor or somebody who worked with troubled kids.

The back door swung open, and Katie announced, "The meatloaf's in the oven." She pushed the door wider with her hip while holding a tray with three tall glasses of lemonade. Tim jumped up and took the tray from her, color filling his face when she blessed him with an adoring smile.

"Here's one for you, Marti. I squeezed the lemons myself. Gloria showed me how to make real lemonade."

Marti forced a sip past the lump in her throat. *She* should be the one teaching Katie things like that. Instead, it seemed she was peeking through a window on what should be her life with Katie, and discovering she wasn't even in the scene.

Katie and Tim talked about movies they'd seen lately and trying to inline skate, the conversation punctuated with laughter. Marti nodded and smiled, asked a question or two, and tried to sort through the chaos in her heart.

Maybe Katie didn't need her as much as she used to. She shook the thought away. *Don't be ridiculous. She's not even 18 yet. She'll need you for years to come.* Tim would move on and she'd have to pick up the pieces of her sister's heart.

She studied the young man who seemed to smile nonstop at Katie. He listened to her intently, acting like the girlish chatter was the most important thing he'd heard all day. She gave an inner snort. She might look grown-up, but Katie was only seventeen.

Tim glanced her way, his smile vanishing under her perusal. Uncertainty flashed across his face as he turned back to Katie and nodded at her question. *Good. He needs to know I'm watching.*

"Oh, Marti, guess what?" Katie's voice cut through her focus.

"What, sweetie?"

"I got to meet Tim's brother last week. He wears these cool suits, and he was really nice. He took us out for hamburgers, and shopping. He told us we could pick out anything we wanted." Her face glowed. "He actually bought Tim a computer, can you believe it?"

"And Katie got a new purse."

Of course. Kat loved purses. Anything with pockets, actually.

"And matching shoes," Katie added with a giggle. "Red!"

"Wow. How generous of him." Yet another thing she couldn't do for her sister. "He must have a well-paying job."

"I'm not sure what he does," Tim admitted. "He has his own business but we haven't talked about it."

"He's so nice," Katie added with a dreamy smile. "Even his name is cool. Eduardo."

Marti's glass shattered on the patio, lemonade splattering her feet. Tim leaped up, hand outstretched. "Don't move. I'll get a broom."

Images spun as she tried to slap her heart back into a normal rhythm. *Get a grip. There must be a thousand Eddys in Minneapolis alone.*

"What—" She cleared her throat. "What does he look like?"

Katie moved her feet out of the way as Tim swept up the glass. "He's tall. Super short hair. He has a big diamond in one ear."

The terror faded. Eddy's black hair was his pride and joy; he'd never cut it off. And she couldn't imagine him wearing an earring, although he'd loved his gold chains. He certainly wasn't tall.

"Does he ever go by Ed? Or maybe...Eddy?" Her breath stuck as she waited for an answer.

Tim emptied the dustpan into the bag he'd brought out. "Never. He hates that name. He's always been Eduardo. I think it's sorta weird but he likes it."

"Oh." The air left Marti's lungs in a silent whoosh. Every person she'd dealt with had called him Eddy. And Tim looked nothing like him. Tall, lanky, with wavy brown hair, pale complexion. Eddy was dark and solid as a tree trunk. Relief shivered through her. No way were they related.

"Dinner's ready," Gloria called out the back window.

Marti pushed out of the chair onto shaky legs. Not everyone named Eddy was a psychopathic, abusive drug dealer. Still, she'd ask Gloria to keep Katie close to home. She trailed the kids toward the back door. If she went to the police, maybe— Not unless she wanted to go to jail. No, she'd protect her sister herself.

Katie paused at the back door, reaching for Marti's hand as she neared. "Thank you for being so nice to Tim," she whispered. "I knew you would be."

"He seems like a great guy, Kat." The words, and the truth behind them, choked her.

"He is. I'd be sad if you didn't like him. I don't think I could like someone you didn't like." She rested her head against Marti's shoulder for a moment. "You're my family. I love you."

Tears rushed up her throat as she wrapped her arms around Katie. "I love you too, sweetheart," she managed. "You're all the family I have."

Katie gave her a quick squeeze. "Let's eat!"

Marti laughed and followed her into the house. They were family. That would never change.

– 14 –

Settled on her favorite bench on the south end of Lake Calhoun, Marti lifted her face to the sun. The early morning light wrapped her in warmth, relaxing her shoulders, releasing the clench to her jaw. She'd tossed and turned most of the night, visions of Katie and Tim laughing over private jokes overlapping Gloria's sharp words at the theater.

She'd felt like an outsider, not unwelcome but not essential either. What if Katie didn't *want* to live with her? It was no secret Gloria wanted to keep Katie living with her. Probably to keep the money coming in as the caregiver of a vulnerable adult. What if the courts decided it would be better for Katie to stay in Gloria's care?

The scenic view blurred. If she didn't have Katie, what did she have? What was the point of trying so hard if it all got taken away from her in the end? Crossing her arms tightly, she shook her head. *Don't go there. It's not an option to be kept out of Katie's future.* She had to stay focused on the goal, be ready when the big day arrived. Maybe she needed a lawyer to make sure she became Katie's guardian. Right. Like she could afford that.

"Gus?"

She blinked. "Sam?"

He stood a few feet away, hands on his hips. Dressed in a T-shirt, shorts, and a baseball cap, he'd obviously been running. "Nice to see you on this beautiful Sunday morning."

"You too. Good run?"

"Yup. I usually run with my brothers in the afternoon, but since they couldn't make it today, I decided to beat the heat." He gestured to the end of the bench. "Mind if I join you?"

"No." The rhythm of her heart was a sort-of dance step, so different from the pounding when Eddy was around. Part of her wanted to run away. The other part kept her in her seat.

He angled to face her, a smile tipping his mouth. "Do you usually come out here on Sunday mornings?"

"When it's nice like this. I'm so used to being up early for the Depot, I can't seem to sleep in on the weekend." Questions about the future made sleep an elusive dream.

"Me neither. But as a teen, I couldn't sleep long enough. My dad never understood that."

"Isn't that what teens are known for? Staying up late and sleeping half the day?"

"As a cop, he didn't get it. And since I was the oldest, I was supposed to set a better example for the kids." A shadow skimmed his face. "So, what does your dad do?"

Stints in prison. "He's not in my life. Never really has been."

"Mine died three years ago. I'm sure he's been busy monitoring everyone's behavior in heaven. If they hand out tickets, he'll be the winner. Following rules was his life, along with making sure other people did too. Not that there's anything wrong with that, of course. Some of us aren't quite as zealous about it."

It didn't surprise her that he came from such an upstanding father. His dad had probably been the one to throw hers in jail. It was almost funny—the son of a police officer chatting with the daughter of a convict. Who would become one herself if Eddy ever got arrested.

Sam leaned back against the bench, propping his elbows on the backrest, and stretched his legs out. His smile brightened as he released a contented breath. "Man, what a great morning. Perfect temps. Blue sky. No humidity. Gotta love it."

"Sure do." Especially now. *Stop it.*

Gentle waves lapped the shoreline. Occasional dog barks in the distance, and the quiet conversation of people walking past filled the silence between them. It felt oddly comfortable sitting with him, as if she'd known him a long time. She gave herself a mental slap. *Didn't you learn anything from being around Eddy? People are not what they seem.*

"How about a cup of coffee at the concession stand?" he suggested. "I'll even buy."

She hesitated before nodding. "I never pass up free coffee."

"So I've found your Achilles heel," he said. "That might come in handy someday."

"Probably not," she countered. He chuckled. Chatting with Eddy like this at her restaurant job had been a bad move, but it felt completely different with Sam. Still, she would keep her antenna up. She'd never be manipulated again.

As they strolled the asphalt path, cups in hand, Sam glanced sideways at the silent young woman beside him. Shy and quiet most of the time, she could shoot back a smart response to his teasing in a blink. Those dark eyes, that made his insides goofy, held surprise, intelligence, and laughter, all tinged with wariness.

"So what's all that stuff you're always studying at the Depot?" she asked.

"Secret plans to take over the coffee shop," he said, relieved when she laughed. "Actually, I'm teaching GED prep classes and I'm trying to stay ahead of everyone. It's been a while since high school."

"What do you teach?"

"All the basics. Comprehension, science, math. We're covering each topic separately, then we'll review and take the practice tests together."

"I suppose everyone is around high school age?"

"A few, but most are ten or more years out. The reasons they didn't graduate are varied, but you know what? They all want the same thing."

"A diploma?"

"There's that," he chuckled. "They also want the chance to better their lives. Some have kids, some are stuck in a low-paying job, others just want to get a job." He motioned toward an empty fishing dock and they strolled out to the end. "It's cool to hear their dreams and see their passion to succeed."

Standing side-by-side in the morning sunshine, he wrestled with wanting to ask about her own story. Her pensive profile made him hesitate. "Gus—"

"Marti."

"What?"

She leaned on the railing. "My name is Martha but people call me Marti."

Elation swelled at her admission. "So where did Gus come from?"

"It's a nickname. I use it with strangers."

"Like me."

"They don't come any stranger." Mischief sparkled on her face.

He threw back his head with a laugh. "You got that right."

They settled on the edge of the dock and she pulled off her sandals to swirl her toes in the water, kicking droplets out into the lake. Sam sat quietly beside her while noise filled his head. *She could join the next class. But she might be offended if I suggested it. But it could change everything. Is this about her or you, Evans?*

"I don't know if you remember," she said, "but I didn't...I couldn't finish high school."

"I remember." He bit his tongue to keep from blurting out twenty questions.

She leaned forward, resting her elbows on her knees, and her thick hair became a curtain. Another pause before she continued. "Things were sort of a mess at home. I needed to get a job."

"A lot of people in the class said the same thing." He crammed his hands under his thighs to keep from sweeping her hair aside to see her face. Ducks skimmed to a landing in the water, quacking their own quiet conversation. "I didn't finish high school either."

Doubt colored the dark gaze that jumped to his. "You?"

"Yeah, me. The one and only in my family to get kicked out of high school." This was the first time he was actually glad he hadn't graduated. "Eventually I got my GED and got a job."

She lifted her face to the sun, dark curls tumbling over her back. "I have a sister. She went into foster care about five years ago, when our mother died. Before that, Mom stayed home with her, so I had to quit school and get a job. I didn't earn much but at least we could eat."

And he'd thought he had it bad. "That's pretty amazing for someone so young."

She shrugged and kicked more droplets into the air. "You do what you have to do. I've always wished I'd finished, so I'm glad you're helping people change their lives. Everyone deserves a second chance." Regret colored her words.

"Including you, Martina." Martina fit her better than Marti, and definitely better than Martha.

When she started to correct him, he winked. Her cheeks turned a pretty pink, a shy smile touching her mouth. His heart did a goofy backflip. "Hey. Why don't you come to the class?"

"Me? Oh, I…" She waved a hand. "I need to focus on work. My sister gets out of foster care soon, so I need to be settled and ready for her. We're finally going to be back together."

"You're taking her in? Wow, you really are amazing." And on a barista's salary, no less. So his dad had been a little rough on him. At least they'd had food on the table.

A gentle melody played from her pocket, and she pulled her phone out. "Speaking of my sister. Excuse me."

Sam got to his feet and moved across the dock. Though she spoke quietly, her voice carried across the still air. He leaned on the railing and tried not to listen.

"Yes, I know, Kat. That's what Gloria and I talked about…No, I'd rather you didn't…Because it's too soon, sweetheart. You barely know him…I *do* like him but…I know it's hard. Here's an idea. I'll come too but I won't sit with you…Of course I know how old you are, but…Okay, how about I come over tomorrow and we'll talk about it over ice cream…I know, sweetie. Hang in there and we'll get it figured out…I love you too…I'll see you about 7:00. Bye, Kat."

Silence enveloped the dock, then she blew out a long breath. "Sorry about that."

He turned to find her standing, sandals on, an apologetic smile on her pale face. "Not a problem. Ready to head back?"

"I should. I have stuff to do before I work at noon."

They retraced their steps, chatting about the newest coffee on the Depot menu, and Jason's latest cookie creation. At the concession stand, she faced him and gestured over her shoulder. "Well, I'm heading that way, so—"

"Me too. Let's go." He headed in the direction she'd pointed, the opposite of his place. After hesitating, she joined him. "Marti, I hope you'll consider coming to the GED class. I think you'd be surprised at how much you still know, and how quickly you'll pick up the rest."

She focused on the sidewalk ahead of them, a mix of desire and regret coloring her profile. "I'll think about it."

"For more than three minutes?" *Lay off, Evans. You can't save the world.*

The corner of her mouth lifted. "At least five."

"Days? Great."

Her answering laugh was light and relaxed. He hid a grin of triumph.

Two blocks later she stopped and faced him. "Okay, well. Thanks for walking with me."

"My pleasure."

She cocked her head, studying him. "You don't really live this direction, do you?"

"Sort of." When she raised an eyebrow, he shrugged. "No, but my mom taught me a gentleman always sees a lady home, so that's what I'm doing. I need the practice."

"Hardly," she said, so softly he nearly missed it. A rosy hue brushed her cheeks again.

Without thinking, he reached up to brush her hair to the side.

Her hand shot up in defense, then dropped as quickly. "Sorry. That was— I'm a little jumpy sometimes."

"I didn't mean to startle you." *Stupid move, Evans.* It confirmed his idea about her bruises. "My bad."

She took several steps back. "Well, thanks for the coffee and the walk."

"You're welcome. I'm glad I got to spend some time with my favorite barista."

With an awkward wave, she hurried down the street and turned into an alley. He retraced their path toward the lake, kicking himself every step. What a bonehead move. She probably thought he was some kind of stalker guy now.

He'd gotten a peek under the first layer of a complex young woman. *You've always been a sucker for the underdog, Evans. Especially those with big brown eyes and a sweet smile.*

– 15 –

Monday morning and no early shift. Absolute heaven! After sleeping in until eight, Marti snuggled on the couch cradling a cup of coffee and pondering her walk with Sam yesterday. She'd never been comfortable around men. Aside from Gramps, she'd never known one she could trust, starting with her dad. Sam seemed nice. Respectful. Conversation flowed easily, and he made her laugh. But even Eddy had appeared genuine when they first met.

When Sam reached toward her, the movement had triggered a memory far too fresh to forget. She frowned. What had he been about to do, anyway? He had no reason to touch her. A shiver pushed her deeper into the couch, and she pulled the afghan up to her chin. Maybe it hadn't been a coincidence they'd run into each other by the lake. And by trying to walk her home, he'd figured out generally where she lived. Good thing she'd left him blocks away from Jason and Lorna's.

She breathed slowly, deeply. *Calm down. You're smarter now.* Memories of the beating still shook her to the core, but new ones were crowding in. There were people in her life now who didn't have an agenda other than helping a stranger. Hard to comprehend but still true.

From the kindness of the nurses in the hospital, to Jason taking her in like a stray kitten, and Lorna teaching her to bake. Even the visit from the blonde girl who came bearing the plant. She frowned. *What was her name? Something with a V. Vicky? Valerie?* A vague memory of a business card sent her to retrieve her backpack from the closet. *Here it is. Vanessa, that's it.*

89

Fingering the card, she struggled to remember details of their conversation. The girl had offered help, but for what? A job, maybe. Had she offered legal help? With Katie coming out of foster care, Marti needed to be ready in case Gloria put up a fight. She had nothing to lose by asking.

Dressed and out the door in ten minutes, she found the house ten blocks away. A piece of paper taped over the doorbell invited her in. She pulled the screen door open and stepped inside.

A young woman seated at a desk at the far end of the room offered a bright smile. "Hi. Welcome to GPS. Can I help you?"

Business card in hand, Marti approached. "I think so. I met Vanessa recently, and she told me to stop by." She lifted her shoulders. "Maybe I should have an appointment?"

The girl shook her head as she stood. "No appointment needed. We're a drop-in, get-to-know-ya kind of place." She extended a hand. "I'm Tiffani, with an i."

"Marti," she said, "also with an i."

Tiffani laughed and motioned toward the couches. "Nice to meet you. Have a seat and I'll see if I can track Van down. She might have gone back to River House."

"I don't want to bother—"

"You won't. Help yourself to a soda. I'll be right back."

Choosing a root beer from the mini-fridge, Marti wandered toward bookshelves filled with photos. Young men and women mugging for the camera, arms slung around each other's necks. Some wild Frisbee leaps. Heads bowed in prayer. A touchdown dance. Faces lit by firelight.

Longing swept through her. How amazing to be part of a group like that, to not face life alone day after day. To actually have friends.

"Marti!"

She turned at the happy greeting.

Vanessa approached, hands extended. "I'm so glad to see you. I've thought of you every day."

Marti accepted her hug, careful not to spill soda on the girl she towered over. She hadn't seemed quite so tiny from the hospital bed perspective. "Am I interrupting anything?"

"Not at all." She kept hold of Marti's hand and led her to a couch. "Come sit. I want to hear how you're doing. You look wonderful—color in your cheeks, no more bruises."

The unexpected welcome clogged her throat. "I'm doing well. I wanted to thank you for coming by the hospital. And for the plant."

Vanessa squeezed her hand. "Totally my pleasure, hon. I'm thrilled to see you looking so much better. Tell me what you've been up to."

Marti shared bits and pieces of the past few weeks. So much change in such a short time. Vanessa listened intently, asking questions, laughing occasionally.

"I'm curious about what GPS is. And...," Marti glanced at the card, "River House?"

Vanessa's smile deepened, a sparkle lighting her blue eyes. "I'll try to give you the short version, but once I get started, it's hard to stop. See that house across the street with the white porch?"

Marti turned. Vanessa pointed at an older two-story; the wide front porch hosted a handful of kids. Laughter and conversation filtered across the distance.

"That's River House. Kurt, my husband, started the ministry as a place for high school kids to come for tutoring and counseling, to hang out after school, but especially as a place to experience God. It took off in ways only God could design."

Two boys tossed a football back and forth on the front lawn while a girl sat on the porch steps chatting with them. The earlier longing burned into her heart. What if she'd found River House when she got kicked out? Everything might be different now. She moved her attention back to Vanessa.

"Eventually we realized we needed a place for the kids as they graduated from high school, where they could find their passion and get the skills needed to find the right job. When the owners of this house died, we were stunned to learn they'd left it to us." An affectionate smile filled her distant expression. "Such a God-thing. So we launched GPS, which stands for Gathering Place Services, and here we are."

She pressed a warm hand briefly on Marti's arm. "And here *you* are. I can't wait to find out how we can work together. How is your sister? Katie, right?"

Startled, Marti nodded. "She's doing great." *As long as Eddy keeps his distance.*

"How can we help the two of you?"

As in the hospital, her offer seemed genuine. "Well, I've been on my own for a long time, since I was fifteen. Always paid my own way. But in the hospital, I lost my job." How much could she say without revealing her connection to Eddy? The less, the better.

"Do you need help finding a job?" Vanessa asked.

"I found something part-time, which has been great, but I'm still looking for full-time. I'm not picky about what I do, and I learn fast, but I..." She focused on the large photo over the fireplace. "I don't have a lot of skills. I'm grateful for the job I have now. I take as many hours as I can get, but I need to make more money."

She swallowed the little pride she had left. "How much does it cost to get help here?"

"Nothing. Our funding comes from a private party, so we're able to offer classes and services free to whoever needs them."

Marti pressed her lips together. In the real world, "private party" meant drug money, loan sharks, or some other source. No such thing as free.

"We won't ask for your first paycheck," came a male voice from behind her.

She looked over her shoulder in surprise.

A tall, slender man wearing wire rims and a pleasant expression approached. "I know the idea of free makes people roll their eyes, but because a family wanted to honor their daughter's memory in a concrete way, we're able to offer our services at no cost to our clients."

No smirk, no glimmer in his eye suggested more to the story. He held out a tri-fold brochure. "Here's our info."

"We've all experienced tough times in our lives," Vanessa said, "so we do what we can to help others when they need it. And we have amazing volunteers."

Marti looked from one to the other, then down at the paper. "I'll check this out."

"Great." He extended his hand. "I'm Richard, by the way."

"Marti." Why hadn't she told Vanessa to call her Gus?

"I hope we'll see you here again soon, Marti." He winked, then joined Tiffani to retrieve papers she held out.

"Helping people find a job is one of our specialties," Vanessa said, drawing Marti's attention back to their conversation.

"I have another question, about getting legal help? Katie will age out of foster care in a few months, and I want to be sure I'm named as her legal guardian. She's considered a vulnerable adult because..." *Because of me.* "Well, she's vulnerable."

Vanessa nodded. "We're partners with several local lawyers who provide legal services for free, so we'll make sure you've got everything in order."

Marti blinked against the burn of relief. "Thank you."

A smile lit Vanessa's face. "Marti, I'm so glad you came by. I've been praying we'd get to work together. I'll talk to our lawyer friends to see what needs to be done for you and Katie, and let you know. Do you want me to call, text, or email?"

"Call or text." She recited the number, adding Vanessa to the very short list of people who knew the closely guarded secret. "Thanks for the soda. And the help."

"You're welcome." Vanessa walked with her outside. "Now that Richard is running GPS, I'm at River House more than I'm here, but holler and I'll zip over, or we can meet for coffee." She pulled a business card from her back pocket. "Here's another of my cards. I can't wait to get together again."

She gave Marti a warm hug, then crossed the street toward the larger house where she received a raucous greeting. Marti turned away from the laughter. She could work with Vanessa, but that Richard guy had appeared out of nowhere. He seemed too nice, too much like Sam, actually.

Who were these guys that kept dropping into her life? First Jason, then Sam. Now Richard. Was she naïve to trust them? Maybe she should run like crazy the other direction. She didn't have much of a choice. When had life gotten so complicated?

– 16 –

After Tuesday's lunch rush, Marti left Jason at the front counter and ducked into the storeroom for more napkins, pausing to open the boxes delivered that morning. She'd unpack them after her break. She wasn't letting anyone mess up the order she'd brought to the chaos back here. Heading back, a deep voice slammed her flat against the wall.

"Yes, I'd like a large black coffee."

Eddy?! The smooth baritone set her legs wobbling, her heart crashing against her ribs. She clutched the bag of napkins to her chest, knees knocking. *Hold it together. C'mon. If you faint, he'll see you.*

"Any bakery item with that, sir?" Jason's voice.

"No, thanks. You're the owner, am I correct?"

Marti inched back toward the storeroom, a hand pressed over her mouth as nausea churned. Thank goodness the swinging doors kept her hidden.

"Yes, I am. That will be $2.25 for the beverage. Ibrahim will get that going for you."

"Thank you. Say, I'm wondering about a friend of mine who I haven't seen in a while. She used to come in here regularly, so I'm wondering if you've seen her lately. Martha Gustafson? I believe she also goes by Marti."

In the brief silence that followed, Marti's throat squeezed shut. If Jason said yes, she'd make a run for it out back. "Here's the change for your fifty. Hmm. Tall brunette, right? Slender girl, looked like she could blow away in a stiff wind?"

Eddy chuckled. Marti shivered. "That's her. I've been worried about her."

"Over the past year, she stopped by occasionally, but I haven't seen her in a few weeks, maybe a month. Ibrahim, have you seen her?"

"Now that you mention it," came Ibrahim's casual response, "it *has* been a while. I enjoyed seeing her. Sir, would you like a shot of almond in your drink?"

"No, thank you. That's too bad. I'm disappointed she hasn't been here recently. I'm getting more concerned as time goes by."

"When you do catch up with her, tell her to come by the Depot for her free cup of coffee," Jason said.

Marti slipped into the storeroom and tiptoed to the back corner where she huddled on the floor, arms wrapped tightly over bubbling panic. Did he believe them? Was he checking every inch of Uptown?

Her head snapped up. Katie! Eddy would assume Katie knew how to find her. She had to warn Gloria. She yanked her phone from her back pocket. After three trembling tries, she punched the correct number. *Come on, Gloria, please!* It went to voicemail.

She cupped her hand around the mouthpiece and whispered, "Gloria. It's Marti. I need to talk to you. Katie might be in danger. You all might be. Please don't let her out of your sight. Not even with Tim. *Please* keep her with you until we can talk. Call me as soon as you can."

Drawing a calming breath, she dialed Katie's number. When her sister answered, she put a smile on her face and whispered, "Hi sweetie. It's Marti."

"Hi, Marti! I tried to call you earlier but you didn't answer."

"I must have turned my phone off."

"Why are you whispering? Can you come over today? It's been like forever since our last time. I miss you."

Seeing Katie would mean Eddy would find *her.* She clutched the phone. *What do I do?* "I can't today, hon. I'm at work. But soon. Katie, I want you to listen to me for a minute."

"Sure, Marti. But first, can I tell you what Tim and I did yesterday? We went to the zoo with Gloria. There's a baby giraffe now. He's got really big brown eyes with long lashes like yours." She giggled. "Not that you look like a giraffe, of course. And—"

"Katie, listen to me!" She flinched at the edge to her words. Kat hated it when people were abrupt with her.

After a pause, Katie answered in a tiny voice. "Okay."

"I'm sorry, hon, but I have to get back to work so I need to tell you something quick. When we talk later, I want to hear all about the zoo. Okay?"

A sniffle in response.

"I promise I'll hear every detail."

"Okay."

She steadied her tone, hand still cupped over the phone. "Now this is really important. You can't leave the house without Gloria. Not for any reason. Not even with Tim. I don't want you to even go out into the yard without Gloria with you. Okay?"

"I'm old enough to go outside alone, Marti." The words were surprisingly sharp.

"I know that, honey. It's not about that. I need you to be really careful right now about being alone. If anything happened to you, Kat, I—" Terror wrapped tentacles around her throat. "I don't know what I'd do."

"Don't cry, Marti! I won't go out alone, I promise. Don't cry. It makes me sad."

Marti bit hard on her lip and pushed the tears down. "I'm sorry. It's just so important that you stay in the house for a few days. I'll see you soon, and then we'll be super happy and silly, right?"

"Okay."

"I love you, Kat."

"Love you too, Marti."

As she hung up, the click of the closing door made her spin toward it, still crouched low. Jason held a finger to his lips and joined her in the back corner. She pushed to her feet, leaning against the cool cement.

"He's been gone for a few minutes. Did you know he's looking for you?"

She shook her head stiffly.

"I'm pretty sure he believed us, but if he comes back, I don't want you in sight."

"I shouldn't be here."

"This is the safest place for you. You can't leave now, not when we know he's looking for you."

She lowered her head. "I'm sorry," she whispered. What a mess she'd made of so many lives.

His arms came around her and held her tight against his barrel chest. "It's not your fault. There are rotten people in the world that we have to steer clear of."

The unexpected hug calmed her. "But I'm too stupid to recognize them." Her words were muffled against his shirt.

"You are anything but stupid. Trusting, and a little gullible, maybe. Not stupid."

Tears continued to push up her throat. Crying wouldn't help. She stood straight. "I need to find another place to stay."

"Like sleeping in an alley would be safer?" The retort was harsh. "I think we've seen you're no match for him."

"The shelter has security."

"Only while you're inside. Don't you think he's been watching it?"

"I don't know. Why would he?" Nausea threw a cold chill across her skin. "He'll go after Katie to get to me."

"I have a friend on the police force. I'll ask him to keep an eye on her."

"He can't watch her 24/7. That's what *I* need to be doing." She paced. *Think. Think!* "Maybe I should take her away from here. We could move to Chicago, start over."

"She's a minor in foster care. It would be kidnapping."

She whirled on him, fists clenched. "She's my *sister*! I have to do something. This is my fault so I have to fix it. If Eddy ever—"

"Gus, stop." He grasped her shoulders and gave a gentle shake. "Think about it. This is where your support system is. This is where people can protect you. If you take her and run, we can't help you."

He was right. They had no place to go, no money. No guarantee that Eddy wouldn't find them anyway. She agreed reluctantly. "You're right. It wouldn't be safe to take her away. But if I left town, he'd leave her alone. I'd do that if it would keep her safe." *It might kill me but I'd do it.*

He released his grip "You can't be sure he'd leave her alone. And if you disappear out of her life, she'll be devastated, right? Let's play it by ear, kid. Lay low for a bit and we'll see how things shake out. Lorna needs some stuff done around the house. You can stay home for a few days to help her, and we'll go from there."

"But don't you need me here?"

He chuckled. "We'll manage. I'm betting he'll move on and that will be the end of it. He's pretty hard to miss, so we'll know if he's hanging around. I think you'd better stick with "Gus" for the time being. Unless he knows you by that name?"

"No. At least, I don't think so." She didn't know what to think anymore. "I want this to be over."

He returned to the front of the shop, and she dropped back against the wall, trembling violently. This wasn't over by a long shot.

– 17 –

Resting on her side, Marti watched growing light slide between the blinds, pushing against the blackness of a night that seemed to never end. She had tossed and turned, weighing their options, considering every angle. Now, in the silence of dawn, she still had no answer. No way to ensure Eddy left them alone, and in one piece.

Maybe her only choice was to go to the police. The information on the memory card might get her a shorter sentence, maybe more visiting privileges with Katie. She sat up, dropped her aching head into her hands, and massaged her temples. If only they could go back to the farm, away from city life and all its dangers, the only place she'd ever felt safe and truly loved. Grandy would know what to do.

Long-forgotten images formed—a gray head bowed in prayer, hands clasped around the dinner table for a blessing, Gramps reading Bible stories at bedtime. Grandy soothing her back to sleep after one of her frequent nightmares, singing quietly about how Jesus loved her.

Marti lifted her head from her hands, desperate to hold onto the memories. If Grandy were here, she'd tell Marti to pray. He'd answered her prayer for a job and a place to live, but this seemed different. Worse, somehow. She hadn't led a life like Grandy. She'd stolen the make-up, and a few pieces of fruit when she'd been really hungry. She'd lied and had horrible thoughts, especially about Eddy. She'd ignored the drug deals to keep Katie safe. And she'd never read the Bible.

"God?" She cleared her throat. "It's me. Martha Joy. First, I'm really thankful for my job at the Depot, and for a place to stay. I probably shouldn't ask for more since you've already provided so much, but I don't have anyone else to talk to.

"You know I was just trying to be nice to Eddy at the restaurant, but that turned out to be the worst mistake ever." She swallowed hard and clenched her hands in her lap. "I'm afraid for Katie, that he'll do something awful to her. Would you protect her? Please?"

Eyes squeezed shut, she breathed deeply against the quaking fear. "And could you figure out a way to get Eddy out of our lives? So he can't hurt Katie, or me, or anyone anymore?"

She sat in the silence like Grandy so often had, waiting. No lightning bolts or raging wind. Only silence. But— She blinked several times. The fear no longer choked her, the pounding in her head eased.

Sunlight filled every corner of the room, making the endless night a distant memory. A smile quivered at the corners of her mouth. She had no more answers than before she prayed, but she wasn't nearly as frightened. She smiled up at the ceiling. "Thank you."

She scrambled off the bed. There was a ton of work to do around the house, and Lorna had promised to start teaching her how to cook. She'd stay busy and keep praying.

~∞~

"That phone call scared me half to death." Gloria glared at her, tapping the ashes off her cigarette. "And why did you call Katie? Now she won't leave the house."

Marti released a heavy sigh where they stood on the corner near Gloria's the next evening. She probably shouldn't have called Kat, but panic had clouded her judgment. "I didn't mean to scare her. I needed to warn you both."

"About?"

She pressed her lips together. Every detail she shared with Gloria could be ammunition for a prosecutor to use against her, either to keep Katie from moving out or to link her to Eddy. But Katie's safety was the focus here. "So, you know I had a run-in with someone."

"Obviously. At least you don't look like death warmed over anymore."

Thanks. "A coworker at the restaurant turned out to have a shady side business. He thinks I'll go to the police with what I know."

Gloria's pale blue eyes narrowed. "Will you?"

"Not so long as he leaves me and Katie alone."

The woman cursed as she tossed the smoldering cigarette into the street. "Which puts my family in danger too. Nice work, Martha."

She masked an inner cringe with a neutral expression, chin lifted. Her poor choices continued to affect more and more people. "Had I known what he did, I'd never have even spoken to him, but I can't unring that bell. He's not going to hurt you or Katie as long as I stay quiet, but he's holding it over my head to make sure."

She reached into her pocket and pulled out two cans of Mace that she'd bought on the way over. "I think you and Katie should keep these handy. For peace of mind."

Gloria accepted them. "I wouldn't know how to use it."

"Point and spray. I'm sure you won't ever need it, but I'd feel better knowing you both have them. I'll talk to Katie, assure her she can leave the house. I'd just rather she not go out alone."

"She never does." The woman slowly shook her head. "It's amazing you've survived this long on your own."

Marti bit back a response. Her survival instincts made up for her lack of brains. Most of the time. "I'll go back to the house with you and talk to her now."

Gloria stalked away, muttering. Marti followed at a distance, berating herself for the impulsive call to Katie. She'd need to say something believable so Kat could go back to normal life.

When she passed through the front door, Katie flew off the couch and knocked her back a step as she threw her arms around her. Marti hugged her tightly, praying for wisdom, for forgiveness. For a way out of the mess she'd made.

"Hi, sweetie." She leaned back and smiled. The tears on her sister's face seared her heart. *God, I'm sorry I've made such a mess of things.* "You give the best hugs."

"Why can't I leave the house, Marti? Did I do something wrong? Are you mad at me?"

Ignoring the heat from Gloria's glare, she led Katie back to the couch. "You didn't do anything wrong, Kat, and I'm not mad at you at all. I'm sorry. I didn't mean to scare you like that. You *can* leave the house with Tim or Gloria, or even your friends."

"You sounded really scared on the phone."

More like terrified. "I'd had a bad dream and I wanted to make sure you were safe." Eddy was a nightmare that consumed her days and nights. "I feel much better now."

"I have bad dreams sometimes." Katie sniffed, clutching Marti's hand. "When I wake up, I always wish you were with me."

"I'm only a phone call away, sweetie. And I can be over in two shakes of a lamb's tail."

Grandy's silly saying made Katie smile. "I'm still going to live with you after my birthday, right?"

Yes! Marti swept strands of hair from her sister's flushed face. "Definitely. And that's not very long from now, is it? Now, tell me all about your trip to the zoo."

– 18 –

Returning to the Java Depot Friday morning, Marti happily reunited with the people who had become her family. Ibrahim, an irritating yet endearing older brother, teased her for skipping work. Jason, the dad she never had, beamed at her when she took her place behind the counter. And Sam. She had to rein in her widening smile when he arrived mid-morning.

Keeping one eye on the front windows for Eddy, Marti threw herself back into work. She welcomed customers, rang orders, and cleaned every inch of the front of the shop. But each time the bells jangled, her heart skipped a beat.

At noon, Sam approached the register. "So, I hear you're about to go on break."

She glanced sideways at Ibrahim. "Are you talking about my personal business?"

"No way. I'm smarter than that."

"I thought so."

Sam chuckled. "I overheard Jason tell you to take a lunch break. Actually, I think everyone on the block heard him."

She laughed.

"So I'd like to show you something, if you don't already have plans."

"Oh. Um, no. Nothing planned." Except eating alone, as usual.

"Great. Lose the apron and let's go."

She tossed the black Java Depot apron aside and joined him at the door, feigning nonchalance over the tickling in her chest. "Where are we going?"

"I've seen where you work, so now you get to see where I work. At least, when I'm not teaching. Or hanging out at the local coffee shop. It's not far from here."

"That's good because I only have an hour."

Sam lengthened his stride. "Well, hurry up."

Five blocks later, Marti pressed a hand to the stitch in her side, breathless. "Not to sound like a four-year-old but are we there yet?"

He laughed and pointed across the street. "Right there."

As they approached the building, she read the sign. "North Country Woodworking and Design. *You* do woodworking?"

He pulled open the front door and gestured her in, a twinkle in his eyes. "You don't have to sound so surprised."

Her cheeks flushed. "Sorry. I'm just...surprised."

"Come on back and meet my cousin Jimmy. He owns the place."

The showroom, filled with handcrafted items, drew Marti from one side to the other. Beautiful tables with intricate inlaid designs. Chairs, stools, bedroom sets. Picture frames and jewelry boxes. Oak, mahogany, cherry, redwood. She was in heaven.

"Wow." She stopped beside a game table and ran her fingers lightly over the wood. "The detail is amazing. He does all this himself?"

"A lot of it." Sam paused next to her, surveying the room. "He's the main designer. A few flunkies help him out."

"You being the main flunky?"

He threw back his head with a laugh that tickled the edges of her heart. She hid a smile.

"Hey, Evans. Why aren't you working?" A man with shaggy blonde hair and a light beard emerged from the back of the showroom, safety glasses hanging at his neck. "Ah. Entertaining a young lady, I see."

"She's entertaining me," Sam corrected him, throwing a wink at Marti. "Jimmy Bergstrom is my cousin and owner of this amazing array of art. Jimmy, this is M—Gus."

Jimmy extended a hand, eyebrows raised. "You don't look like any Gus I've ever known. Nice to meet you."

She shook his hand. "There aren't many girl Gus's, I guess."

"The name suits her," Sam said with a nod. "She's on a lunch break so I thought I'd show her one of my hideouts."

"Great! Come on back and I'll give you a tour."

Leaving the showroom, he described how he'd started the business in his garage ten years earlier, moved it to a large shed in his backyard, and finally to this location two years ago. She listened closely as he explained his design process and how the various tools worked.

Since the early days of working with Gramps, she'd loved the aroma of fresh cut wood, the feel of shavings between her fingers, and the whine of a saw.

"This is a scroll saw," Jimmy explained. "It's used for the more intricate designs. Want to see how it works?"

"Sure!" It had been too long since she'd been near equipment like this. She felt like she'd come home.

He retrieved safety goggles and handed them to her and Sam. "Safety first around here, even when you're observing."

Sam drew her back a few steps as they pulled their glasses into place. She clasped her hands behind her and leaned forward to study Jimmy's technique. She loved watching a block of wood transform into something beautiful under a woodcrafter's expertise. She'd stood for hours as Gramps created amazing items with practiced ease, impatient for her turn.

Jimmy's design came into focus as he deftly moved the wood this way and that. The buzz of the saw faded and he handed the piece to her, the word Dream in cursive. "To remember us by."

"It's beautiful." Did she even know how to dream anymore? She ran her fingers over it. "Thanks."

"Want to try?"

"Yes!" She thrust her gift at Sam and stepped forward. She hadn't touched a scroll saw in years.

Jimmy gave her basic instructions, and took a small step to the side. She adjusted her safety glasses and set the cedar board in place, then paused, focusing on the wood. Something simple. A heart for Katie.

After an initial jitter, the wood grew compliant under her hands and the shape took form. Over the noise, she heard Gramps's voice, felt his gnarled hands guiding hers. She finished the heart with an extra curl, and carved Katie's name in the center.

She stopped the machine and blew the shavings away. Long-forgotten joy sparked to life deep inside. Pulling the glasses down, she turned to the men. Sam stared at her, mouth open. Jimmy nodded, arms folded and eyes narrowed, his smile growing.

Her cheeks flushed under their attention. "Thanks," she said to Jimmy, handing him her glasses.

"You're welcome. And that, my friend," he told Sam, slapping him on the shoulder, "is some massive natural talent."

Warmth sparkled through her. She'd put aside the dream of creating art out of wood to focus on survival. To know she could still handle a saw thrilled her to her toes.

"Wow," Sam said, brow raised. "I didn't know you could do that."

"You don't have to be so surprised," she teased. "You never asked."

"What else should I be asking about?"

She shrugged, clutching the heart to her chest as if she could ward off questions that might lead to things she didn't want to share.

Jimmy pulled bottles of water from a nearby mini fridge and nodded toward his office. Once they'd settled around his desk, he turned his attention to her. "So where did you learn woodworking?"

"My Gramps. When we were young, my sister and I went to their farm every summer. Katie would help Grandy in the house, and Gramps let me hang out in the barn with him. He designed really beautiful things." She could see sunlight streaming through the high barn windows, highlighting pieces in various stages of completion. A dresser, a bench. A swing for her and Katie.

"I wonder where it all went," she mused, then pulled away from the memory. "Anyway, as I got older, he let me try things. Turned out I'm better with my hands than my head."

"Ever consider doing it for a living?"

"Right." She waved off the ridiculous question. "Since I stink at school, there's no point."

"How about an apprenticeship?" he asked.

She gnawed her lip, unwilling to voice her ignorance.

Sam leaned forward in his chair beside her. "An apprenticeship is a way to learn on the job, with hands-on experience."

"*After* going to college," she added dully. Jimmy would laugh if she told him she never finished high school.

"Instead of going to college." He glanced at Jimmy. "There might be some certification classes but not official coursework."

Something stirred in her heart. She flattened it. They'd find out real quick that she couldn't do a job like that. She forced a sip of water down her tight throat. "Right now I need to get a full-time job so I can support Katie."

"An apprenticeship *is* an actual job, Gus," Jimmy said. "You get paid because you're a contributing member of the team. And your employer pays for any certifications you need."

That sensation flared again, rattling her resolve. She couldn't afford to get caught up in dreams. "That sounds great, but I can't go looking for that type of job. I need to focus on my sister."

"This would be a great way to do that," Sam said.

She held back a snort and got to her feet. "Chasing dreams isn't gonna put food on the table or pay rent. Speaking of which, I need to get back to work." She smiled at Jimmy as he stood to face her. "Thanks for the tour, and letting me use your equipment. And for my gift."

He held out a hand. "Anytime, Gus. Pleasure meeting you." His grasp held her in place. "I'd like you to consider what we talked about. I'll take you on as an apprentice whenever you're ready."

She froze. "What?"

The corners of his eyes crinkled. "I'd love to have you work here. Take some time to think about it. The offer's open."

As she and Sam left the shop, the conversation rolled around in her head like an errant gumball. Had Jimmy just offered her a job? Doing something as cool as woodworking? But he didn't know the truth about her. Her mother had always said she had a smart mouth but no brains in her head. As soon as she had to read something for a project, he'd fire her on the spot. And if he didn't, he would if he ever learned about Eddy.

Sam bought two hot dogs and sodas at a sidewalk vendor. As they continued walking, he said, "I'd sure love to know what you're thinking."

"Me? Why?"

"Because one minute you've got a huge smile on your face and a bounce in your step, the next you're frowning and dragging your feet."

She blushed, swallowing a bite of her ketchup-soaked hot dog. "Things get a little crazy in my head sometimes."

"It's like watching a movie," he said as they crossed the street, laughter in his voice.

She shoved him. "Maybe I'll start charging you." His full laugh danced across her skin. "Keep that up," she warned, "and I'll charge you double."

He put an arm around her shoulders in a brief hug. "Marti, you're priceless. I think you should consider Jimmy's offer."

"He was being nice." She kicked a rock, sending it tumbling ahead of them. She'd cherish the memory forever.

"Huh-uh. Jimmy wouldn't make an offer like that unless he meant it. We both know you'd be an asset to his shop."

"Sam, it's nice of you, both of you, to say that, but I can't… I'm not good at…" The truth choked her.

"Reading?"

Humiliation ripped through her. *It's that obvious?*

"You mentioned you hadn't graduated. When I worked at the Teen Center, a lot of kids struggled with reading." His words held no hint of judgment.

Cheeks flaming, she focused straight ahead. "Well, lump me in with the 'kids.' I like numbers," she added quickly, "not words so much."

"We all have things we struggle with, *kid*." He bumped her with his shoulder. "It's numbers for me."

His kindness soothed the embarrassment. Stopping in front of the Java Depot, she cocked her head. "Am I like your community project or something?"

"Meaning?"

"You're being so nice when you don't know anything about me. Neither does Jimmy."

"We know enough."

"Maybe it's be-nice-to-a-stranger month," she mused.

"I guess I thought we'd become friends. A stranger wouldn't know that you're smart and funny, and you have a huge heart."

She stared at him, lips parted in silent protest.

"You have a great laugh," he continued, pink dusting his cheeks. "You're brave, and pretty, and extremely resourceful. And you're—"

"Hey, Gus. You coming back to work?" Ibrahim's voice broke between them from where he'd poked his head out the door. "I want to have lunch before my shift's over, you know."

She blinked several times to focus on her coworker. "Oh. Yeah, sorry. I'll be right in." She turned back to Sam, a smile wobbling onto her face. He'd called her pretty!

"So." He tapped her nose. "Think about Jimmy's offer. That's all I ask. Okay?"

She managed a nod, staring after him as he sauntered away. Why would a man like him be so nice to her? When he turned the corner, she went inside and slipped into her apron. She tucked her priceless souvenirs in a cupboard, took her position behind the register, and greeted the next woman in line. "What can I get for you?"

When Sam stepped back into the shop, Jimmy greeted him with a slap on the back. "Okay, spill it. Where'd you find her? And how do we get her working here?"

Sam laughed. "Slow down, pal. Why all the excitement?"

"Are you kidding? It's not very often you see raw talent like that, especially in a gorgeous female. We have to snap her up."

"Well, you can find her at the Java Depot usually first thing in the morning." He grinned as they walked through the showroom. "Not your favorite time of the day, I realize, but she's there early. With a smile that might wake even you up."

"Funny. I'm serious about getting her here as an apprentice. I have a hunch she'd be a real asset."

"Of course she would." Sam stopped at his workbench and faced his cousin. "But convincing her of that is going to be a bigger challenge than that carved headboard you're working on."

Jimmy nodded, arms folded. "I could see she wasn't taking me seriously. So that's where you come in. Convince her I'm an amazing boss. That this is a huge opportunity for her. And for us."

"The convincing has to come from you, *Boss*. She thinks she's my community project or something. I encouraged her to consider your offer but that's about all I can do without weirding her out."

Once Jimmy returned to his office, Sam absently studied the half-finished cradle. His gut told him the same thing—she'd be an asset to the shop. But she'd have to believe in herself before she took either of them seriously.

Sanding block in hand, he touched up the cradle base. There had to be a way to help her do that. He saw her potential; he doubted she did. He'd have to watch for a chance to build her up. Something that would open her heart to the truth. *I could use some help with that, God. Any ideas?*

– 19 –

Sam's mouth fell open as he stared at his twin across the table. "You what?!"

Lizzy smiled sweetly. "I RSVP'd for you and said you'd be bringing a guest."

"Great. That's really great, Lizzy." He dropped back in his chair and ran a hand through his hair. "And where am I going to come up with 'a guest' for a wedding that's only weeks from now?"

She picked through her salad and shrugged. "You'll figure it out."

Before he could reply, their siblings swarmed the small restaurant. Lauren slipped into the seat beside him and bumped his shoulder. "Howdy, big brother. What's up?"

He shot a glare across the table. "Your sister is at it again." Lizzy might be happily married, but that didn't give her the right to butt into his life.

"I guess she gave you the news."

"*You* know?" He looked around the table. "Who else is in on this lousy idea?"

Joey, next to Lizzy, raised his hand and grinned. "I'm all for it." No surprise there. He'd been dating the same girl since tenth grade. Lauren raised her hand as well. Between their mischievous smiles and dark hair like Dad's, they looked more like twins than he and Lizzy.

Jessie, the baby of the family, rested her blonde head on Sam's shoulder. "I think it's romantic."

"Right." He wasn't buying her innocent sigh. Most often, she was the instigating prankster. "Scrounging for a date is the definition of romance." Her tattooed, man-bunned boyfriend wasn't his definition either.

Ben cocked an eyebrow at him from across the table. "We must use different dictionaries. But hey, it'll be good for you to have a date."

"And what would you know about it? It's not like you're an expert in romance."

"True," he nodded, then raised his glass of soda and winked. "But I have a date."

"*You* have a date." That didn't help. "Since you're married to the department, you must owe someone a major favor."

Ben chuckled. "Every once in a while, bro, you've got to break out of the norm and try something new. Like going on a date."

Their siblings hooted at his remark, then the pizzas arrived at the table, saving Sam from a response. He took a bite of pepperoni and chewed irritably. He'd be willing to try it, if he had someone to ask a favor of. After the trial, he'd fallen off everyone's radar, and he'd been happy about that. Too bad there wasn't at least one person from the old crowd he could call. If he were still married, this conversation wouldn't be happening. *Thanks again, Jillian.*

Conversation bounced around the table, punctuated with laughter and teasing. From Lauren's new job and cute boss, to Joey's concert schedule, and the antics of Lizzy's two young children. He watched Joey and Jessie try to out-joke each other. Ben joined in while regularly checking his phone.

Sam released a quiet sigh and drained his glass. They deserved better from him. He'd screwed up in high school but got his act together, showing them how to make better choices. And he'd been on a decent path until his marriage, job, and life imploded. Instead of showing them how to bounce back, he'd demonstrated how to hide from life.

As the group broke up, he hugged each of them. Jessie hugged him back fiercely, her adoration turning him into embarrassed mush as it always did. Lauren kissed his cheek and promised to keep an eye out for a fun date for him. Ben and Joey reminded him of Sunday's run, Ben on his phone before he left the restaurant. Then Sam stood alone with Lizzy in the parking lot, keys in hand.

"Sam, I know you're mad about the invite—"

He waved a hand in dismissal. "I'm not mad, Lizzy. Just embarrassed to be the family loser."

Her green eyes widened. "That's not true. There aren't losers in the Evans family."

"According to Dad, which is why he tried so hard to mold me into his image."

"But he never succeeded," she replied, "which set the example for the rest of us to stand up for ourselves and be who we wanted to be."

Sam blinked. *What?* "I thought I had set an example of how to fail at life."

"Oh, hardly." She set a hand on his arm. "Sammy, you have to quit beating yourself up. We all look up to you."

"I am the tallest," he conceded.

She laughed. "Aside from that, you goon. For the boys, you're their example of being authentic. And the girls adore you, as you well know."

"And you're stuck with me," he added.

"No one's luckier." Her brow pinched upward. "Sam, I know how hurt you've been, but don't let Jillian be the last word for your heart. You deserve so much more."

He didn't want his failed marriage to be the last word either.

"If you don't have a date for the wedding, it's not the end of the world." She hugged him tightly. "I just thought I'd give you a little kick in the pants."

"I know. And in a weird way, I appreciate it." He offered a crooked smile. "But don't get your hopes up."

"We'll see. God might be at work in this whole wedding event."

He climbed into his car and sat in silence. He'd been blessed with an amazing family. They'd stood by him during the divorce, the firing, even the assault charge. Rallied around him, encouraging and supporting him. Yup, he was blessed.

He started the car. Now to surprise them by bringing a date to the wedding.

Marti waved at Ibrahim and left the Java Depot, pulling in a deep breath of fresh early evening air. She'd take the long way home and go by the—

"Hey, Marti."

She whirled, a hand to her chest, then collapsed against the brick wall. "Oh, my gosh, Sam. You scared me!"

Grinning, he straightened from where he'd been leaning against a sign. "Sorry. Didn't realize you'd be so jumpy after work."

"Only when someone sneaks up on me." The pounding beneath her ribs eased into a soft-shoe routine. "What are you doing here?"

"I have a job offer for you. Want to grab a hamburger from Millie's?"

A job offer? And dinner with him? "Oh. Well…sure. I guess I could do that."

"Great. Let's go."

On a bench near the lake, burgers in hand, Sam talked about the students in his classes, the people he worked with, and asked about her day, her coworkers. His easy conversation released the nerves that had made it hard to swallow, letting her enjoy their light supper as they chatted.

The sun lowered to the horizon, spreading a golden tint across the water. A gentle breeze rippled over tall grasses lining the shore, filling the air with the musky aroma of lake water. A plane crossed over them, heading for the airport.

Sam deposited the remnants of their simple dinner in a nearby trash can. "How about we walk off that meal? Unless you need to get right home?"

She shook her head, finishing the last of her chocolate shake. "Not right away." As long as she got home in time to call Katie before she went to bed.

They strolled the path in comfortable silence, laughing over the duck family that paddled along with them. Being with Sam created an unfamiliar sense of safety. She didn't understand his attention, but she'd enjoy it while it lasted. No doubt this would end all too soon.

"I mentioned a job offer," Sam said. "It's temporary, but it could become somewhat permanent, if you wanted."

Whatever that meant. She waited for him to continue.

"Remember our conversation about you having trouble with reading and me having trouble with numbers? I meant it."

She raised a skeptical eyebrow, and he chuckled. "Numbers aren't my thing. A student in my class needs math help, but I am not math tutor material. However, I think *you* are."

"Oh, right. You want *me* to tutor him."

"Yup."

"You do remember I never finished high school."

"I do."

His request didn't make sense. A high school dropout tutoring someone in math. There had to be a bazillion other choices. "Why don't you ask someone at the high school? Or at one of those tutoring places?"

"Because I'm asking you."

She rubbed the back of her neck. Maybe he meant the offer as a compliment, but she didn't need yet another setup for failure. "Well, thanks, but ask someone who could actually help him."

"I think that's you."

Stopping abruptly, she faced him. "Look, Sam. It's nice of you to make the suggestion, but we both know it's not realistic. I haven't been in school for years, and I was barely hanging on when I was there. So if you're trying to make me feel better, it's not working. I don't need to prove myself to you or anyone else. I know who I am, and who I'm not."

His unwavering gaze sent a burning wish through her, to be that person who could step into a request like this and make a difference. Someone he could admire. When he remained silent, she resumed walking, forcing her shoulders back. He fell into step beside her, hands in his pockets.

"Now, if you'd offered me a maintenance job," she said eventually, "we'd be having a different discussion. I can fix things, build, repair. I can get a whole room painted in no time flat," she added with forced cheerfulness, "so keep me in mind for something like that."

"I will."

"Good. Thanks." She picked up her pace. Now to get home and forget this whole humiliating conversation.

115

As they rounded the end of the lake in deepening dusk, Sam watched her proud stance crumble. She obviously believed what she said, but he saw so much more. The prompting to ask her to tutor Marcel had been a constant nudge. "My student still needs help with math and my offer still stands."

She whirled on him, fists clenched at her side. "Okay, I'll spell it out for you, Sam. I'm too stupid! I'm not the person to tutor him or anyone else." Deep pink blazed across her cheekbones, highlighting the tears she tried to blink away. "Don't waste your time trying to make me one of your success stories. It's not going to happen."

She stalked across the beach toward the lake, jaw clenched. When she reached the water's edge, she folded her arms and lifted her face toward the star-speckled sky. His heart ached over the lies that controlled her life. Stupid. Worthless. Waste of time. It made sense now, how she reached out and then snapped back into her shell.

Leaving her shoes on the beach, she waded into the water. He did the same and stood silently beside her, the water tickling his calves. Moonlight shimmering across the still lake highlighted her pensive profile.

Her heavy sigh filled the space between them. "I'm okay, Sam," she said quietly, the fight gone. "You don't have to worry I'll do something drastic."

"I'm not. I'm hanging with a friend."

Lips pressed together, she turned her face away. A fish splashed nearby. A bird call echoed across the water. He wiggled his toes against the sandy bottom.

"What do you see when you read?" he asked.

She shrugged. "Most of the time the words make sense. Then sometimes they float up and down. I have trouble with some of the small letters."

"When you're tired?"

She thought for a moment. "I guess. Numbers never do that. But word problems are…a problem," she added with a wry twist to her lips.

"For you and me both." They stood quietly again. "Marti, I know a little about dyslexia. Several kids in my youth group struggled with reading but it wasn't because they were stupid. Sometimes the signals in the brain get mixed up which has *nothing* to do with intelligence."

Arms folded tight, she glanced sideways at him.

"I'm no expert by any means, but I know it has to do with how the brain processes language. Dyslexia makes reading more difficult. But everybody has areas of strength and weakness."

"Yeah, well, some of us excel in the weakness category."

Give me the right words, God. He faced her. "You can't make dyslexia go away, but there are ways to work around it, things you can do to cope with it. I could help you. I'd like to."

Silence. She frowned across the lake.

"You aren't stupid, Martina. Far from it actually."

"How would you know?"

He waded closer. "Would you look at me, please?"

Her arms tightened across her chest. "I can hear you fine this way."

"I'm sure you can, but I'd rather talk to your face than your ear."

She rolled her eyes and turned slightly, jaw set.

He smiled. "Thank you. As I was saying, you are far from stupid. I've watched you at work, how you handle different situations. You're great at problem solving."

"When you have to figure out where your next meal is coming from, it gives you lots of practice. Desperation isn't the same as smart."

"You picked up the register training in a couple hours."

"How would you know?"

"Ibrahim told me."

Her brow dropped. "Why were you talking to him about me?"

He held up his hands to ward off the flash of anger in her eyes. "We weren't. Not directly, anyway. We were talking about how long he's worked there, the staff he's seen come and go. And he mentioned that you picked up the training faster than anyone he's worked with." He lowered his hands. "And that's all he said about you. Honest."

"Fine. Keep it that way."

"Martina, the world isn't out to get you."

"That's easy to say when you get life handed to you. For the rest of us, it's every man for himself. They might not be out to get me, but they aren't looking out for me either." A tiny sigh escaped. "It's easier flying under the radar."

He knew a thing or two about that. "You know, you could help Marcel with math and he could help you with reading. And you and I could work together over your lunch breaks."

She flung her arms out. "We can study until you grow old and die, and I still won't be any smarter. Even you said there's something wrong with the way my brain works. You can't *will* me to be smart."

He gritted his teeth. She refused to see herself in any other light. "Why not? You've willed yourself to be stupid." As the words left his mouth, he flinched.

The world froze for a long moment before she splashed toward the shore.

"Marti." He followed. *Who's stupid now, Evans?* "That's not what I meant."

"Whatever. Go away."

He took her arm to stop her, and she spun around and slapped him. Hard. He kept his grip on her as he rubbed his cheek. "I deserved that."

"And a whole lot more. Leave me alone." She tried to pull away. "I don't want your help or your pity."

"Marti, I'm sorry. Really." He took her shoulders in a gentle grasp. She kept her head down. "I didn't mean it the way it sounded. It came out all wrong."

Stillness blanketed them. Finally she lifted her gaze, the corners of her mouth tugging downward. His heart squeezed.

"No," she said, "it came out right. Whether I will it or not, it's the truth. My mother told me. My teachers told me. People I've interviewed with have told me. As I've said before, I know who I am, and who I'm not. Let's leave it at that."

His careless words had burned that untruth deep into her heart. As she stepped back, he dropped his arms. There'd be no damage control done tonight.

She stood for a moment looking up at him, her expression softening. "Thank you for wanting it to be different. You're the first person who's ever cared."

He reached a hand toward her, but she swept up her shoes and walked away. Chin still up, she seemed neither angry nor dejected. She thought she knew who she was, had convinced herself she was fine with it. But he would prove her wrong on all counts. She needed to know the real truth—she was smart, worthy. And beautiful.

He grabbed his shoes and followed at a discreet distance until she went up the front steps of a white two-story and around to the back. Turning for home, he rubbed his still smarting cheek. He needed a plan going forward. She couldn't afford to win this battle, and he wasn't about to lose.

Keeping her mind carefully blank, Marti made it into the apartment before letting Sam's words sweep over her. "Why not? You've willed yourself to be stupid."

She pressed her fist to her chest, the keys in her grasp stabbing into her. She focused on that outer pain rather than the inner throbbing his words caused. He thought she *wanted* to be stupid? That she chose this?

Dropping onto the couch, she leaned her head back against the cushion. How many times had she prayed before a test at school that *this* time she'd pass? She'd begged God over and over to make her different, capable. If not smart, at least not dumb. She didn't want to be this way, to be someone kids mocked. People had always been quick to point out her mistakes. Why did it even bother her after all these years? She should be used to stunned expressions followed by pity.

Sam had seemed as surprised as everyone else when she revealed she hadn't finished high school. Pressing her fists against her eyes, she tried to rub the image away. She wasn't right for someone like him. She should never have been friendly in the first place.

She pushed off the couch. It didn't matter. Life was fine with just her and Katie. She didn't need to be good enough for him or anyone else. She didn't need any of them. Puttering around the apartment, she rearranged items on shelves, folded laundry, and cleaned the already-clean kitchen. Sam's words were never far from her thoughts. *You've willed yourself…willed yourself.*

Disjointed dreams and memories disrupted her sleep that night. Grotesque faces laughing at her, long fingers pointing. Jason offering her a job—and handing her a golden broom. Standing before a blackboard trying to spell cat. Childish snickers erupting behind her.

Sam smiled at her over a cup of coffee at the Depot, then left her at the lake saying she wanted to be stupid. Ibrahim told her how fast she caught on, then shook his head while she tried over and over to ring an order for a sneering Eddy.

A customer wrinkled his nose at the cup of pink coffee she gave him. Jason poked her awake where she slept inside the dumpster. The same words echoed over and over—too stupid. Too stupid.

"No! I'm not!"

The shouted words woke her where she sat in the middle of the bed, hands pressed against her ears. Her heart slowed its frantic pounding as hot tears trickled down her cheeks.

"Maybe I am," she whispered to the darkness, then curled on her side.

– 20 –

When the phone rang Saturday afternoon, Marti debated ignoring the unfamiliar number. But if she missed a call from Katie calling from a different phone…

"Marti? Hi, it's Vanessa. Am I interrupting anything?"

She sat up straight on the couch. Vanessa? "Not at all."

"I have a couple things. First, Kurt and I talked with one of our lawyer contacts. She'll be happy to work with you regarding Katie's guardianship."

"Really?" Air vanished from her lungs. Someone was willing to help?

Vanessa laughed. "Yes, really. I'll text you her info, so you can contact her when you're ready."

"Wow. This is amazing. Thank you so much." The thought of help filled her with tingling relief.

"You're very welcome. Also, I'm wondering if you're free tonight, and if you'd consider coming to church with me."

Go to church? The last time she'd been in one was Grandy's funeral ten years ago. "I haven't been for a long time."

"We can sit in the back, if you'd prefer. Kurt is out of town and I'd rather not go alone."

"Sure. I'd like to." The words flew out before she could slap a hand over her mouth. What if she embarrassed her new friend somehow?

"Great!" Vanessa sounded genuinely happy. "I go to Faith Community on Hennepin. There are also Sunday services, but the Saturday evening service is the most fun. Want to meet there or should I stop by your place?"

"There's fine. It's over by the library, right?"

"Yes. The church that looks like a warehouse. How about we meet at five?"

Marti glanced at the clock. That gave her plenty of time to change her mind. "Okay. Five o'clock."

"Wonderful!"

Two hours later, Marti sat on a bus bench across the street, watching people stream into the gray stone building that looked nothing like a church. Lots of young people, and older people too. Families, singles. People dressed in jeans, shorts, skirts. So why was her heart trying to escape her ribs? No one would notice whether she went in or not.

Sunlight glinted off Vanessa's white-blonde hair as she approached the front door, then paused to search the crowd of people. Marti stood, tempted to slip away. It had been so long, she'd no doubt embarrass Vanessa somehow. From across the street, Vanessa's face lit up and she waved. So much for an escape.

After a cheerful hug, Vanessa tucked her arm through Marti's as they entered the building. "I'm so glad you were free tonight. It's always more fun to have someone to sit with, don't you think?"

Marti nodded. She'd never had anyone to sit with, unlike girls like Vanessa. It was like walking beside royalty. People greeted and hugged Vanessa, and smiled at Marti. A few stopped to introduce themselves.

When they slipped into a pew near the back of the large room, Marti discreetly wiped her brow and drew a shaky breath, turning her attention to the band onstage. A mix of men and women playing guitars, a violin, drums, keyboard. Dressed like everyone else in jeans, skirts, leggings. At Grandy's church, no one would have dared wear jeans or a bandana. She smiled. Or dreamed of having dreadlocks like the drummer.

The large room vibrated with energy, rows filled with swaying, clapping people. Marti rubbed her arms, wrapped in a strange sense of welcome, as if she were right where she belonged.

The song ended, and a dark-haired man strode to the front of the stage, a smile on his bearded face. "That was some amazing worship! God is good."

"All the time," the crowd shouted back. Laughter and applause erupted. Vanessa nodded and clapped too.

"All the time…" he said.

"God is good!" came the response.

"Do you believe it?" he demanded with a broad smile.

"Absolutely!"

Marti smiled at the exchange. Obviously something repeated often.

"Glad to hear it," the man continued. "Have a seat. I'm Joel Barton, one of the pastors here at Faith, and I have the privilege of spending the next hour or so with all of you. I'd like the ushers to come forward for the offering. If you're visiting, please sit back and let the plate go by. For those of us who call Faith our home, this is our chance to give back to the God who has blessed us abundantly. Pray with me, will you?"

Marti relaxed into the cushioned pew, absorbing the prayer, tapping her foot to the music playing as the offering plates circulated. The pastor returned to the front and opened his Bible, directing them to verses toward the back of the book. Vanessa leaned close to share her Bible. Marti smiled and whispered, "I'll listen, thanks."

Eyes closed, she let Joel's voice flow over her as he shared words she hadn't heard since Grandy died. Promises of life and love. Assurance of forgiveness and mercy, safety and protection. His passion reached deep inside her weary body, igniting a need for…something. Change. Direction. A way to bring Katie home.

She lowered her head, hands clutched in her lap. *God? It's me again. I know I'm not like all these people but…I feel close to you here. The way I did with Grandy and Gramps. I don't think I ever thanked you for them. They always reminded me of how much you loved me and Katie. I hope that's still true. I don't deserve it, but Katie does.*

Words poured from her heart, swirling up to the rafters, lifting her as well. The shame and guilt that dogged her every day quieted under a reassuring peace. Tasting the freedom of forgiveness, she longed for more, begged for more.

"Marti? Are you okay, hon?" Vanessa's voice broke into the moment.

"Yes. Sorry. I was…praying." Wiping her wet cheeks, she offered a sheepish smile. "I guess it made me a little teary."

Vanessa smiled. "Praying does that to me sometimes too."

"It does?"

"Lots of time, actually. It's amazing to be right in the moment with God, don't you think?"

The worship leader returned to the stage and encouraged them to stand. "C'mon, everyone. Let's worship God with some singing, dancing, clapping, or whatever moves you."

Marti frowned. "I missed the rest of the sermon?"

"I don't think Joel minds if we get swept away in prayer." She smiled and squeezed Marti's arm. "I think he likes it, actually. I'm sure God does."

People around them lifted their hands as they sang. Marti did the same, feeling ridiculous with her hands in the air, smiling like an idiot, happier than she'd been in a long, long time. Swaying gently as she joined her voice to Vanessa's, she hoped the evening would never end.

In the lobby area a short time later, Vanessa introduced her to several people, then Marti heard a squeal behind her.

Tiffani bounded through the crowd and hugged her. "Yay, you came! Vanessa said she was going to invite you, so I prayed that you'd want to come."

Tiffani prayed for her?

"Richard's over there," she pointed and waved, "and I think Parker's here somewhere. Oh, there he is. Hey, Park! You've gotta meet him, Marti. He's a hoot."

Surrounded by GPS staff, Marti chatted like she'd known them forever. Here, amidst new friends in what Grandy had always called God's House, she reveled again in the sense of being exactly where she was supposed to be.

"So who do we have here?" came a man's voice.

"Hey, Joel," Vanessa greeted him. "This is my new friend, Marti Gustafson. Marti, this is Joel Barton, the senior pastor here."

Warm fingers enveloped hers in a welcoming grasp. "Glad to meet you, Marti. And glad you came to Faith tonight."

In more ways than one. "Me too. I enjoyed your message."

"It made her cry," Vanessa added with a teasing wink.

Marti blushed. "In a good way."

"Well, if they were sad tears, I'll take the blame. But happy tears are definitely from the Holy Spirit."

Richard claimed the pastor's attention, and Marti turned back to Vanessa and Tiffani. They chatted about the upcoming barbeque that *of course* Marti would come to. She smiled and nodded. Maybe someday, when her past was finally past.

Stomach growling, Marti reluctantly said goodbye to her new friends and started for the door.

"Marti! Hold up." Pastor Joel hurried toward her. "Glad I caught you. I wanted you to have this."

She accepted the book he held out—a Bible. Tears smarted as she ran a hand gently over the leather cover. She managed a wobbling smile. "Wow. Thank you. This…means a lot."

"We can never have too many Bibles."

"This is my first one," she admitted. Would he be disappointed in that revelation?

His smile widened. "Well, that makes this even more special. Be sure you come see me when you have questions. I don't have all the answers, but I'll bet we can figure it out together."

A busy man like him had time for her? "Okay. Sure. Thanks." Clutching the Bible to her chest, she hurried out the door. She might not be able to read much of it, but looking at it, holding it, would be enough. For now.

She glanced upward and again whispered, "Thanks."

– 21 –

Sam stayed away from the Java Depot for a few days, afraid Marti would throw coffee on him if he showed his face. The days seemed empty without their daily conversation, her laughter over his inane attempts at humor, her brown eyes lit with fun as she teased him back.

After long hours in the woodshop, he graded papers, rewrote lesson plans, and went on long, exhausting runs. His careless words dogged him around the lake, her stricken expression still seared into his heart. *You've willed yourself to be stupid.* Man! Sometimes he fit so many feet in his mouth, he could be a circus act.

Ending another ten-mile run, he put his hands on his knees, breathing hard. He couldn't outrun the nudging to fix things, repair the damage. Pressuring her to tutor Marcel, at least right now, would push her farther away. He'd line up someone from the high school to help instead.

He stretched his burning muscles, then walked slowly back to the concession stand. The morning he'd come across her sitting on that bench, when they'd had coffee and she'd told him her real name, had been a breakthrough. She'd let down her guard enough to trust him, at least for a few minutes. And when she'd been so focused on designing the heart, she forgot he and Jimmy stood nearby.

He smiled, remembering the shock on her face when Jimmy offered her an apprenticeship. She'd nearly danced her way back to the Depot, only dragging her feet when she'd let the doubts in. He stopped abruptly and slapped his forehead. Woodworking! Of course! She'd glowed with excitement when Jimmy gave her a turn. She never looked like that serving coffee or sweeping floors.

His eyes narrowed. During the tour of GPS, he and Richard had talked briefly about basic woodworking classes, to go along with computer and music classes. An idea took root, and he headed for home at a jog. He had phone calls to make, a plan to set in motion.

Late the next morning, he finished prepping the wood for his next project at the shop, then set out for the Depot. Marti had asked if she were his project. Maybe. He was determined to help her see herself in a new light. The truth she lived by wasn't true at all. He'd taken a step or two back into real life over the past month or so, rediscovering his own truth. It was time for them both to move forward. They could do it together.

He'd hardly slept as his brain worked out the details, but he'd woken more energized than he had in months, itching to get started. If his proposal went as he hoped, it would change more than how she saw herself. If not, she might be done listening to his ideas.

The Depot buzzed with pre-lunch activity, and he snatched a corner table to start Operation Truth. He rolled his eyes, setting his backpack on the table. A little dramatic but appropriate. He took his place at the end of the line, fidgeting as he inched toward Marti at the register.

She blinked in surprise when he stepped forward, then nodded politely. "Sam."

"Hello, Gus. I'd like a—"

"Double Frappuccino with two shots of mango spice."

Probably the largest drink she could throw at him. "And how did you know that's what I wanted today?"

The tiny smile wavering at the corners of her mouth seemed like a peace offering. "A professional guess. Okay, what would you really like?"

"Whatever you said. I'm in the mood to try something new. And I'll have one of Jason's cookies too. Your choice."

"Being adventurous today," she observed as she entered the order.

"I am, and…I hope you are too." He glanced behind him. No one was waiting. "When you get your lunch break, could we take a walk? I'd like to talk. And I have an idea I want to share with you."

"That's $4.42." Her brow knotted. "I'm not tutoring anyone."

"I know. Got the message loud and clear." He handed her a ten, then rubbed his cheek and grinned.

Color infused her face but he held up a hand when she started to speak. "Let's talk when you're on break."

"Should I be worried?"

"Nah. I'm harmless." *Unless I open my mouth.*

"That's what they all say." She held out his change, the sparkle in her eyes snuffing the rebuttal on his tongue.

His shoulders relaxed. She'd either forgiven him or was putting on a great act. "So, a walk at lunch?"

She stepped away, returning with a cookie on a plate, and dipped her head. "Okay."

"Great." He walked away before she could change her mind, and quietly asked Ibrahim to make two lunches for later. Collecting his beverage, he returned to his table.

After reviewing class notes, he propped his chin on his hands and watched people pass by the window, trying to tame the doubts that dodged in and out of his thoughts. *God? I know I've been AWOL the past few months. Or year. I don't have an excuse other than sulking since everything blew up. But I want to help Marti learn to believe in herself. And get to know you so she can find out who she really is. And…I need to do the same. I'm ready to get back in the game.*

"Sam?" Marti stood beside his table.

He started. "Wow. Time for your break already?"

Doubt clouded her face. "Well, if you're not ready, or you don't want—"

"I'm ready." He crammed papers into his backpack, and grabbed the bag Ibrahim had waiting at the counter. "Let's go!"

He held the door open for her, which she acknowledged with a shy smile, and turned their path toward the lake.

"So," he said after two silent blocks, "how did your morning go? It seemed pretty busy the whole time."

"From the moment we opened the doors," she agreed. "Some days are like that."

"Are you working full-time?"

"As many hours as Jason can give me. We've been short-staffed so that means more hours for now, but he's planning to hire someone soon. It's not great having him at the register," she confided. "He's a really nice guy, but I think he scares people with his big voice."

He chuckled. "I'm pretty sure you're right."

He steered her toward a shaded bench, and pulled two sandwiches from the Depot bag, along with bags of chips, bottles of water, and cookies. "Lunch is served."

"Thank you."

"I heard you like roast beef, so I hope that's okay."

"Talking to Ibrahim again?"

"Guilty."

Swallowing the first bite of sandwich, she sighed. "Fine. This time only."

Sitting in comfortable silence, they watched runners, walkers, and bikers parade by on the path that followed the winding shoreline. Marti was so easy to be with. He hadn't realized how high maintenance Jillian had been until she'd walked out and he crashed in exhaustion.

Marti took their lunch wrappings to a nearby garbage can, and Sam drew a steadying breath. *I could use that help right about now, God.* When she resettled on the bench, he faced her.

"Thanks for having lunch with me. I hate eating alone." He cleared his throat. "So. I've been pretty disgusted with myself since the other night. Sometimes I'm amazed at the stupidity that comes out of my mouth." He shifted on the bench and met her gaze. "I hope you'll accept my apology. I'm really sorry I said that. Unfortunately, I can't guarantee I won't say something stupid again, but I'm working on it. I never meant to hurt you, Martina."

Her chin trembled. "I'll accept your apology if you'll accept mine. I can't believe I slapped you. I am so sorry."

He offered a crooked smile. "I deserved it. What I said was totally untrue. Let's call it even. Deal?"

"Deal." Her brow relaxed as color filled her pretty face.

He released an exaggerated sigh and wiped his brow. "Phew. Thanks. The next time I make you mad, I'll try to be out of reach."

Her laughter filled him with teenage goofiness.

"Okay, there's one other thing I want to talk about, but I need to give you some background so you know where I'm coming from."

She waited, her unwavering attention a little unnerving.

"Okay. Well, here goes nothing."

Touched by his apology, Marti waited for him to continue.

"You know those monster roller coasters that lift you way up and then send you hurtling down to the ground? That's been my life over the past year or so."

"Sounds scary." A lot like hers, actually.

"Yeah. Things have settled down. I really enjoy working at the shop with Jimmy. It's not the direction I thought my life would go, but it's been way more rewarding than I expected. I just feel like there's more I could be doing to help people. Teaching the GED class is a start, and it's actually been fun."

"You didn't think it would be?"

He shrugged. "I didn't know what to expect. I really like the people, and it's been cool to help them set goals and move forward in their lives."

She smiled. He seemed made for that kind of work—kind, encouraging, smart. Not to mention cute.

"But something's still been bugging me, and the other day I had a lightbulb moment. This is where I need your help. One of the things we want to offer is a program on trade skills. Carpentry, electrical, plumbing—that sort of thing. To help people understand what that entails, how to get the right skills. Options that are out there."

"Like when Jimmy mentioned the apprenticeship." Someday she'd take him up on that offer.

A smile lit his handsome face and her heart bumped against her ribs.

"Exactly. Not enough people are going into the trades nowadays, but the work still needs to be done." *Get on with it, Evans.* "So, this is where you come in. The first class I want to start is basic woodworking."

"I like that idea."

"Glad you approve because I want you to help teach it."

"What?!" First he wanted her to be a math tutor, now a shop teacher? "I can't do that!"

"We'd do it together—design the class, figure out what parts each of us wants to teach and how, and then teach it together." He leaned forward. "Marti, Jimmy is still talking about you. He's serious about wanting you to work with him. This would be a great way to see if you want to work with us."

"Sam." He seemed determined to make a fool of her. "I don't know how to teach someone. I barely know how to do stuff myself."

"You know far more than you realize. And we're talking basics here, nothing fancy."

She pinched the bridge of her nose. "I appreciate you trying to help me. Really. But I can't teach woodworking, and I can't tutor someone in math or anything else. Working at the Java Depot is fine. I'm not trying to be anything other than who I am."

"And who do you think that is?"

"Well, I..." Good question. "I'm a big sister who will soon be a guardian. I'm a reliable barista at the Depot." Loser came to mind.

"Okay. Those are fine, but what do you like to do? Really, really like to do?"

She frowned. "The world needs coffee, and that's fine with me. I like being a barista."

"I doubt you grew up dreaming about serving coffee."

She folded her arms, lips pursed. Why was he trying to run her life?

"I'm not saying you shouldn't work there, Martina. But there's more to you, to what you can do. More than what you give yourself credit for. I think you'd have fun teaching other people about woodworking. And yes, I think you'd be really good at it.

"And...I'd like to do it with you." His shoulders lifted shyly. "I think we'd make a great team. We have fun together. Or at least, I have fun when I'm with you. A guy-girl team would interest people, especially young women."

She opened her mouth to argue but no words emerged. He seemed truly excited about the idea. Wrapping her fingers around the edge of the bench, she ignored the excitement that pulsed deep inside.

"That's the other reason I want you to do it with me," he said, filling her silence. "Women need to see this as a career option. Too many people think it's a guy's profession, but there are some amazing female woodworking professionals. If girls saw what you can do, they'd consider it as a viable option for themselves."

Her feet itched to run away from his persuasion. Her heart said stay. She so wanted to make amends to the community she'd harmed by allowing Eddy to do his evil from her apartment, to offer something positive to people. But what if she screwed up his idea?

She chewed her lip. If she could encourage even one woman to follow her dream, it would be worth trying. She knew her way around power tools, and how to take the hard knocks life handed out. If they were successful, it would be an example for everyone, including Katie.

Don't be silly. When have you ever been successful at anything? The biting words hit hard. "Sam, I don't see—"

"We could do a small class first. Maybe three or four women."

She blew out a short breath. He had an answer for everything. But…she could maybe handle a small class. *What could you possibly teach them aside from how to make a heart?*

"At least consider it, Martina. Please?"

The hope in his "please" pulled a wavering smile out of her. And when he called her Martina, her heart melted. For whatever reason, he believed in her. There was something sweet about that.

"Fine. I'll think about it." She'd do far more than that. His idea would keep her mind occupied for quiet nights ahead.

His smile deepened as his shoulders relaxed. "Thanks."

Hours after he'd walked her home, she mulled over their conversation. Teaching a class would mean less hours at the Depot, which wouldn't matter if they paid the same. If she even got paid. Working with Sam and having access to power tools could be fun, but she couldn't do it without pay. She needed every penny for Katie.

She had to admit, the crazy idea was growing on her, but his answer about pay would make the final decision.

– 22 –

Marti settled on the couch and pulled her new Bible onto her lap for the first time. Trailing her fingers across the cover, she smiled. Simply holding it filled her with a strange urgency, as if she teetered on the edge of an amazing discovery. The sensation had stayed with her the last few days, since she'd attended church with Vanessa, and especially after the talk with Sam.

She'd been afraid to open it. What if it held all the answers she needed but she couldn't read it? She hugged it to her chest, eyes scrunched shut. "God?" she whispered. "I'm so glad I didn't chicken out of going to church with Vanessa. I think maybe you pushed me into it? If you did, thanks. Now I have my own Bible but…what if I can't read it? I don't want to miss what you have to say in here. Could you help me?"

Sitting in the silence, she waited for the prodding she'd gotten before. Nothing. Only the sound of Jason with his hedge trimmer outside. She drew a breath and set her shoulders. "Okay, then. I'll do my best, which isn't all that great, as you know. But it's all I've got."

She flipped open the cover and gently turned the fragile pages until she found the Table of Contents. Her heart sank at the long list. She'd be old and gray before she got through even half of it. She turned a few more pages and discovered a folded piece of paper. The handwritten words were few and easy to read: "To Marti. This Bible is God's Word, a love letter written for you. Listen to it. Peace, Pastor Joel."

Listen to it? How could she do that? Maybe you were supposed to read it aloud, but that would be painful, not to mention taking forever. He'd called it a love letter. Written for *her*?

Below the words, it said John 3:16. His signature made her smile. At least she had someone to go to when she needed help. Turning back to the Table of Contents, she found "John," and flipped through the pages toward the back.

She put a triumphant finger on the page. "Yay me." She frowned at the small print, blinked several times, then read aloud, "For God so loved the world, He gave His only degot—degotten? What's that mean? He gave His only degotten—oh! *Be*gotten, you goose. His only *be*gotten Son that whoever believes in Him should not perish but have eternal life."

Grandy had spoken those words to her, but she hadn't known they came straight from the Bible. They brought the same comfort now as they had then.

"I can do it." A triumphant smile stretched her cheeks. "I can read the Bible! Not very fast, but I can." She dropped her head back against the couch and sighed. "But God? This will take forever." She heard Joel's voice during church. Passionate, encouraging, challenging.

"Okay. Let's read the next verse." She'd figure it out if it took all night. Whatever else she might be, she was no quitter.

Whistling, Sam pulled open the door at Java Depot and paused to let his eyes adjust from the morning sunshine. Ibrahim stood in his usual spot creating amazing drinks, Alicia at the register. And Marti? Expecting her to be wielding a broom, he found her at his usual table, bent over a book, dark hair hiding her face.

"I see someone is sitting at *my* table."

She jumped, looking up wide-eyed, then grinned. "First come, first served."

He chuckled and dropped into the opposite chair. "On break?"

"Yup." She checked the time on her phone. "Unfortunately, it's almost over."

"What are you reading so intently?"

"My new Bible." She held it up like a prized possession. "I went to church on Saturday and the pastor gave it to me." Her cheeks glowed pink. "Isn't that cool? Do you have one?"

"I do," he said. *Collecting dust.* "It's very cool that he gave you one."

Her smile faded. "I wish I could understand it better. Some of the words are a little hard to figure out."

"How about we read it together during your lunch break?"

"Really?" she squeaked. "That'd be great, except my break doesn't happen until after the lunch rush, as usual."

"No problem. I'll be here going over classwork. Let me know when you're ready."

Clutching the book to her chest, she scurried away with a bounce in her step. He settled in to review the new curriculum, but his mind followed Marti. Her usual reserve had slipped enough for him to get a glimpse beneath the wariness. He grinned like an idiot. Her joy was contagious. And beautiful.

Three hours later, settled side-by-side at Millie's Restaurant down the block, they read words that reminded him how far he'd drifted from his faith. *More like stomped away from it.* Marti peppered him with questions, and mused aloud over words that fascinated her. Face lit with interest, her observations challenged him to think, prodding him to dig deeper.

Before life imploded, he'd never have believed he could turn his back on his faith. It had been a lonely time without God. Seated beside Marti now, he whispered his thanks for a second chance.

"It's a disaster." Sam slumped into a chair in Richard's office two days later and pinched the bridge of his nose.

"How bad?"

"Five passed. Ten crashed and burned." He snorted. "But since I obviously can't do or teach math, don't take my word for it."

"Ahh. Taking full responsibility, I see."

"Wouldn't you?" Humiliation burned up his throat. "And yes, you would so don't try to deny it."

"I probably would," Richard agreed, "for a day. Then I'd get back in the swing of helping people work toward their goals."

"Yeah, right." Sam pushed to his feet and went to the window. "I guess this answers the question of whether I should stay on here."

"I suspect my answer differs from yours right now."

Sam turned. "You can't possibly think I'm a good fit after such an epic fail."

Richard met his frown calmly. "Well, first of all I don't see this as *your* failure. Second, I'd hardly call it epic. And third, my opinion hasn't changed one iota." He held up a hand when Sam started to argue. "How about you take a seat and we figure out what went wrong for your students?"

Great. What could be better than dissecting my failure in minute detail? "I think right now I need a run to clear my head. Canada oughta do it."

Richard laughed. "Fine. Go run, but make sure you have a return route."

"While I'm gone, you'd better start thinking of hiring someone more effective and capable than me. That shouldn't be hard."

Kicking himself back to the townhouse, Sam changed into running gear and set out around Lake Calhoun. If he wanted to make it to Canada and back, he had to pace himself despite the urge to run hard and fast. The third lap had him sweating, the fourth out of breath.

He slowed halfway through the fifth to cool down, and walked back to the townhouse. Couldn't he do anything right? A monkey could teach from that curriculum. The cold shower did little to lighten his mood. Maybe coffee would do the trick. And a chat with the lovely Martina, who deserved someone far better than him. He should do her a favor and stay away from her. He would, if he had her best interests in mind.

The Java Depot was unusually quiet when he entered. Marti swept at the far end. When she looked up, a delighted smile lit her face. Okay, that was way better than coffee. Or running to Canada.

As he approached, her smile faded. "What's wrong?"

"Nothing. Why?"

"You look upset." Her eyebrows pinched together. "Did something happen?"

Was he that much of an open book? He managed a half-smile. "I wanted to see my favorite barista."

"Oh." Color filled her face. "That's nice."

He wasn't sure what he was aiming for, but nice wasn't it. "You due for a break anytime soon?"

"Actually, I get off in," she glanced over her shoulder, "ten minutes."

"Great. Do you have anything planned?"

She shook her head.

"How about we walk over to see Katie?"

A smile bloomed, lighting her eyes. "I'd love that. She's been asking to meet you."

"Hopefully you've only told her good things."

"That's all I know about you," she admitted softly. "Let me finish here and we can go. Maybe she'll be up for ice cream."

He settled by the window, her revelation sweetly mocking. Apparently he'd done a great job only showing part of himself. Their daily Bible readings had revealed the many facets that were Marti Gustafson. Despite her struggle to read smoothly, she was a quick study, intuitive, and thrilled to be reading a Bible. She'd shared a bit about the grandmother she'd adored, and the part faith had played during the summers she spent at the farm with her grandparents.

The more she shared, the more he wanted to know—about her, Katie, life before the Java Depot. What made her so strong and yet vulnerable, sweet and opinionated? And especially what made her reach out only to pull away. She had a wicked sense of humor, and made spot-on observations of life and people. Life shone brighter now; he felt more hopeful because of a certain dark-haired beauty.

Man, he was falling hard.

− 23 −

Katie squealed with excitement when Marti called. *Of course* she wanted to meet Sam, and duh on the ice cream idea. When Marti introduced her to Sam thirty minutes later, Katie was on her best behavior. She carried on such a polite conversation with him, Marti had to force her mouth closed.

Tim joined them at the ice cream parlor and declared the treats were on him. With a wink toward Katie, he said overtime pay was burning a hole in his pocket. Once she'd been assured there was no actual fire or hole in his pants, Katie ordered a triple cone. He laughed. Marti had to smile at what a cute couple they were, even if she didn't want to think about Katie dating. At least Tim seemed reliable, and treated her like fragile, priceless glass.

Seated at a high table, Sam entertained the young couple with stories of growing up with a cop father. Suspecting more than a few were embellished, Marti laughed along with Katie and Tim.

"That's so cool that your dad was a real cop." Katie raised her blonde eyebrows at Marti. "Hey, maybe he's the one who put Dad in prison!"

In the awkward silence that followed, Tim cleared his throat and asked Katie what she thought of the movie they watched the other night. Marti excused herself to use the restroom.

The mirror reflected pink spots on pale cheeks, dark eyes filling with tears. Katie's innocent question reminded her who she was and where she came from. She could pretend that she deserved someone like Sam, but the truth would always win out.

She pulled in a deep breath and stood straight. "You can't change where you came from," she told the girl in the mirror, "but you can be proud of what you're doing for Katie. That's what matters."

When Marti returned, Sam offered an encouraging smile as she slid onto her stool, cheeks still flushed. She'd been so quiet about her background, he should have guessed secrets haunted her as they did him.

"Marti, tell Tim I'm a way better skater than him," Katie insisted.

Marti gave a half-hearted smile. "That's hard to do since I've never seen him skate."

"Well, I am," she told Tim with a triumphant smile.

"Maybe Sam's better than both of us," he countered.

Sam lifted his hands. "Don't put me in the middle of that discussion. Besides, I don't skate."

"What?" Katie squeaked. "Everyone skates in Minnesota."

"Except me. And don't get any ideas about dragging me out on the ice."

She giggled. He edged closer to Marti and stage whispered, "But I play a mean game of broomball."

"Hey, me too," Tim said. He checked his watch. "I've gotta get home. Can I walk back with you guys?"

Katie bounced off her stool and claimed his hand. "Of course! Those two walk too slow."

Sam winked at Marti as they trailed the energetic twosome out of the shop. "I guess we've been relegated to being the old people who totter along behind."

"Old before our time," she said with an exaggerated sigh. "I didn't realize it would come so fast."

He chuckled. "Me either."

They followed at a leisurely pace in comfortable silence. Everything he learned about her made her more amazing. Coming from a family with a dad in prison, she displayed a fierce loyalty to her sister, and a determination to make a life for them together.

He bumped her lightly with his shoulder. "You're a pretty amazing big sister."

Her cheeks bloomed. "Thank you," came the faint reply.

At Gloria's, Katie hugged him tightly and wagged a finger at him. "You be good to my big sister."

"I intend to," he said with a nod. "She deserves the best."

Her smile brightened. "I think so too. I'm glad you two are dating."

Eyes wide, Marti opened her mouth but Sam took her hand, stopping the response. She sucked in a quick breath but didn't pull away.

"I am too," he said. He shook hands with Tim. "And you take care of this little beauty, or you'll answer to both of us."

"Yes, sir."

The girls shared a long hug, Marti said goodbye to Tim, and Sam led her away. They were halfway to Jason's, her hand still tucked in his, before she spoke. "Thank you for making that such a fun visit."

"I think we all did our part. Katie is full of dynamite, isn't she? Like her *old* sister."

"I may be old," she said quickly, "but I've got plenty of dynamite left, so keep that in mind."

He chuckled and knew a moment of sheer joy, followed by panic. What if he messed things up with her, like he had with Jillian? The idea of hurting her punched the air from his lungs.

Stopped at the stairs to her apartment, he took both of her hands, watching color infuse her face again. "I'm glad you were free this afternoon. That was fun."

Her shy smile deepened. "Thanks for suggesting we see Katie. I'm sure you made her day. I know you made mine. You were very patient with her. She can be a bit—"

"Energetic," he supplied.

She nodded, then bit her lip. "I'm sorry about her dating comment."

"I'm not. It's what I've been thinking."

Her mouth formed a silent "O." She pulled her hands from his and folded her arms. "My dad's in jail, Sam, for the rest of his life. And my mother was a drunk. A mean drunk."

Ah. Another piece to the puzzle that was Martina. "So?"

"So?" She tossed her hands up. "The daughter of a convicted felon is hardly dating material for the son of a decorated cop."

"Whoa. I don't want to go through life being defined by who my dad was."

"I would if my dad were a cop instead of a career criminal."

"Well, be glad he wasn't." The bitterness still surprised him. He gently grasped her shoulders. "We aren't defined by our parents, Martina, so how about we focus on who we are, not who they were?"

She dropped her gaze, silent. He lifted her chin. "I'd like to spend more time with you, Marti. We don't have to call it dating. Just friends hanging out together. Unless you don't want to. I'm cool with that." *No, I'm not.*

She relaxed into a smile that sent his hopes soaring. "I'd like that too," she said softly.

"Well, how about a couple of friends have dinner Friday night?"

Delight beamed. "Sure."

"Okay. Great." He slid his hands down her arms and took her hands. "Thanks for this afternoon."

Her fingers trembled within his grasp. "You're welcome."

He whistled all the way back to the townhouse. Whatever had formed between them had transformed him into a complete idiot. A babbling, bumbling, deliriously happy idiot. He was finally getting his life back on track, a track that included the spunky and beautiful Martina.

He needed to think up date ideas. Amazing ideas. Knock her off her feet. He rolled his eyes. *That's sweep her off her feet, Evans.* Roses. No, too formal. Wildflowers? Definitely more her. Maybe he could make dinner. She didn't have to know he could only cook three things.

He started a new tune, hands in his pockets as he strolled. Who'd have thought he'd get so excited thinking of date ideas? He would be a new man this time around. Only the best for Martina. Oh, he'd have to make sure there was lots of chocolate around. *But what if she doesn't like chocolate?* He scoffed. What woman didn't like chocolate?

From his front steps, a figure stood and faced him. His whistling stopped on a sour note.

"Hello, Sam."

Unable to breathe, he managed a stiff nod. "Jillian." That's right. Jillian didn't like chocolate.

− 24 −

"So? Did you like him?" Marti asked, then held the phone away from her ear when Katie squealed.

"I love him! He's sooo cute, Marti, and he sure likes you. That was like a double date, wasn't it? How cool is that?"

Marti flopped back on her bed, smiling at her sister's chatter. "I guess so, in a way. How nice of Tim to treat everyone."

Katie sighed noisily. "Isn't he the best? I'm so glad you like him. He's the sweetest guy. And he really liked Sam too. He called him a cool dude. Isn't that funny?"

Sam was definitely a cool dude. "It was his idea to come see you today."

"Really?"

"I guess I talk about you so much, he wanted to meet the real person."

Katie giggled. "Did he like me?"

"Very much, sweetie. How could he not?"

"I hope you marry him someday."

Marti blinked. She was hardly the type of girl Sam would bring home to meet the family. But they did have fun together, and he'd held her hand.

"Marti? Don't you want to marry him?"

"Kat, we're friends. He's a great guy, but I'm not ready to get married. I'm too excited to finally get to live with you again. There's no way I'd pass that up."

"Really? You're excited too? I can't wait."

143

"I can't either." Marti set her forearm over her eyes. *Please don't let anything ruin this, God. We've waited so long.* "It won't be long now."

"Will I get my own room?"

"That's the plan." She prayed that Jason and Lorna would be okay with a second renter.

"Tim and I prayed about that. About finding the right place for you and me. He says if we pray and believe it, God will work everything out. I want to live with you."

The admission brought a burn to her eyes. "Me, too, Kat. Me too."

Sam remained motionless as they studied each other. Jillian was thinner than when they were married, less polished. She'd always had every hair in place.

"You look great," she said.

"Why are you here, Jill?"

"Boy, right to the point." She released a short breath. "I'm doing well, thanks for asking."

"We can skip the formalities. It's not like we parted friends." His clenched jaw barely allowed the words out.

Lips pursed, she nodded. "True." She swept a hand toward the steps behind her. "Mind if I sit?"

"Go right ahead." He widened his stance and folded his arms. Had a shadow crossed her face? Hyper-driven Jillian had never been uncertain about anything in life.

She perched on the top step. "Okay, well, this will make you laugh. Ryan kicked me out."

Due justice, perhaps, but not funny. "What about the baby?"

"Her too. She's at my mom's right now. Nap time, you know."

"No, I wouldn't know." He'd have liked to, but that ship sailed two years ago. "He kicked his own child out?"

"Not exactly. But there's no way I'd leave her with him. He doesn't care about anything but himself."

Had she looked in a mirror recently? He pushed the uncharitable thought away. He was hardly one to throw stones.

A wistful smile relaxed her frown. "Adrienne is so…perfect. I mean, she's a feisty two-year-old, but she's adorable, and smart, and has a big heart for such a tiny person." She pressed a hand to her chest. "You'd love her."

Did she really have no clue she was twisting the knife still in his chest? "Why are you here?"

She bit her lip. "I'm in a tight spot at the moment. I'm looking for a full-time nursing job, but there aren't many out there right now."

"I'm sure something will turn up." His toe tapped in rhythm to a distant car alarm.

"In the meantime, I'm at my mom's. The thing is, she's in a one-bedroom apartment, and she has a big dog. We're all sort of on top of each other."

He waited. So?

"The thing is, she wants her boyfriend to be able to come and go, but having me and Adrienne there makes it a little awkward."

"I see."

The cords of her neck tightened as she frowned. He'd forgotten she did that when she was annoyed. "You aren't going to make this easy for me, are you?"

"I have no idea what you want, Jill." He lifted his hands. "Do you need money? Food? A reference?"

"I need a place to stay."

Seriously? His mouth opened and closed. She wanted to move back in with him? After walking out on their marriage with the baby that was his and then wasn't?

"You still shouldn't play poker," she said. "Your thoughts are written in neon on your face."

Hopefully not all of them. "I'm…surprised. That's the last thing I expected you to say."

"Ironic, hmm? Serves me right, I guess."

Yes, it did, but that's how the old Sam would react. He'd have been ecstatic for this chance to boot her off his property, to watch her wallow in her mess. He drew a slow, silent breath. The Sam deserving of Marti wouldn't go there.

Slapping her hands on her thighs, she pushed to her feet. "I knew this was a bad idea. Forget I mentioned it. We'll manage. Take it easy, Sam."

She was several steps away before he found his voice. "I didn't say I wouldn't help." She turned slowly and he gestured her back. "We'll figure something out."

− 25 −

Marti thanked the woman, then turned to the next customer and froze. Even with his black hair super short and slicked back, dressed in a starched white shirt and jeans, there was no mistaking him. The menacing smile that had haunted her dreams now mocked her across the counter.

"Good morning, Marti. Or shall I call you Gus?"

The silky tone sent a tremor through her. She locked her knees and lifted her chin. "What can I get you?"

He chuckled. "I'll have a large coffee and a cookie." He leaned slightly forward and lowered his voice. "And I'll have you thrown in jail if you breathe one word about me to anyone."

"That's $5.25." She accepted the fifty-dollar bill and added quietly, "I don't speak of you. Ever. I prefer to forget that time in my life."

"Then why are they looking into my private affairs?"

"Here's your change." She slid money across the counter. "I'll get your order for you." Refusing to acknowledge Ibrahim who watched the exchange, she retrieved the cookie, then filled a cup with steaming brew. Remembering he preferred his coffee strong and black, she dumped a scoop of creamer in before snapping a lid in place.

"Here you go," she said with a forced smile. "Perhaps they're looking into your affairs because everything you do is illegal?"

His toothy smile matched hers. "You remember what happened the last time you made me angry, don't you, Martha?"

She blinked at the memory of the knife coming at her.

"I see you do. Keep that in mind if you ever consider speaking of me to anyone. I meant it when I said I'd take you down with me. And I'll see that your beautiful sister goes too."

Fire shot up her spine and she leaned toward him. "If I find out you've so much as looked at her from a distance, I'll make sure it's the last thing you see," she hissed.

His brow lifted as he nodded with appreciation. "Well, haven't we grown a backbone since we last met."

"I have no intention of ever saying your name again," she narrowed her eyes, "unless you force me to. If *ever* speak to me or Katie again, I'll take my photos right to the police station."

"You don't have any photos. But I do, as I'm sure you remember."

"I have photos of your precious paperwork. Names, addresses, transactions." She kept her chin lifted, teeth clenched to hold back the rising hysteria. "You have yourself to thank for that idea."

His smirk faded, the muscles in his jaw flexing as his black eyes glittered. She stiffened her spine to keep her defiance in place. Eddy wasn't someone to mess with. She prayed her threat hadn't made things worse.

"So I'm sure we understand each other," she said. "You go your way and I'll go mine." She looked past him. "May I help the next person, please?"

His smile returned. "Until we meet again, Gus."

Marti kept her expression pleasant as she waited on the woman, forcing her voice and hands to stay steady. Then she looked at Ibrahim and pointed toward the storeroom. He nodded and she fled, crouching in the far corner where she covered her face and sobbed.

"Rich? Got a minute?" Sam stood in Richard's doorway.

"Always. Grab a seat. I'll finish this up quick."

Sam settled in a chair and looked around Richard's sparsely furnished GPS office. Oversized closet would be more accurate. Family photos were the focus of the décor—the kids playing in leaves, Amy smiling over blazing candles on a cake, a family shot at Disney with even the baby wearing Mickey Mouse ears. Happiness radiated from the photos, belonging, fam—

"So what can I do for you?"

He swung his attention back. "I've talked to Jimmy about the woodworking class, and he's onboard."

"Excellent. I'm stoked you're putting this idea in motion. I keep hearing that we're losing our skilled trade workers, so I think introducing these options to people looking for jobs and skills could open a lot of doors for them."

"Jimmy would agree with that."

In the silence that followed, Richard asked, "So what else is on your mind?"

Sam frowned. "What?"

"Evans, I can read you like a book, and your pages seem a little crumpled today. I don't think it's about getting this project up and running."

Sam drummed his fingers on his thighs. "When I got home yesterday, Jillian was waiting for me."

"Oh. Wow."

"Yeah. Things haven't gone great for her. She needed a place to stay."

Richard's eyebrows shot upward. "She's staying with you?"

"No!" He suppressed a shudder. "I'm moving to Lizzy's."

"For how long?"

He shrugged. "Dunno. Jill said she's trying to get a job so she can be out on her own. With the baby, it was too crowded at her mom's place."

"Bizarre. Do you think she wants to get back with you?"

What? He stared at his friend. "No way. She sure didn't act like it."

"Would you consider it, if she brought it up?"

Two years ago, he might have. Now there was Martina. "Not for a second."

Richard studied him with a slow growing smile. "There's someone else now, isn't there?"

Sam shifted in the chair. He wasn't ready to talk about Marti. "Right now I'm trying to figure out what to do about Jill."

"Is she moved in yet?"

"Sometime today."

"Did she sign something saying she'd only stay for a certain length of time?"

Sign something? "It happened too fast for me to come up with paperwork." He frowned. "Do you think I should?"

"Dude, I wouldn't trust her in *my* house, let alone in her former house. Who knows what she's up to."

Great. He probably should have told her he'd think about it, and talked to Richard before letting her move in. Lizzy had gone bonkers when he called. He got up and paced the closet office, two steps one way, two back. Pacing without going anywhere added to his frustration.

"Sam, despite everything you've gone through, you still trust people way too easily. Jillian may need a place to stay, or she's playing you because the bloom is off the rose with her boyfriend."

"There's no way she wants to get back with me," he protested. Right? He dropped back into the chair. He should have thought to pray about it first. He'd been more concerned about how to tell Marti. "I don't think I can boot her out now. Not with the baby."

"I can." Richard shook his head. "Trusting people isn't a bad thing, Sam, but after what she did to you, I'd think you'd be more cautious. Unless you still have feelings for her?"

"No!" The word exploded. What he felt for Marti overshadowed anything he'd felt for Jillian.

"She ripped your heart out and stomped on it, my friend. You can be a good guy, which you are, and let her stay there, or she can face the consequences of her actions."

"Richard?" Tiffani stood in the doorway. "You've got a call."

"Thanks, Tiff." Reaching for the phone, he paused. "She's not homeless, Sam."

Sam nodded his thanks and left the stuffy office, massaging his temples as Richard's words tumble around in his head. His advice made sense but didn't feel right.

He needed a run to clear his head, and listen for God's advice.

– 26 –

After an amazing dinner with nonstop conversation, Marti stared at the dessert tray. From banana cream pie to creme brulee, each choice looked delicious.

"Anything calling your name?" Sam asked.

"All of it, unfortunately. I can't make up my mind."

"We'll have the triple chocolate cake," Sam told the waiter. "Two forks. Oh, and coffee. Thanks."

As the waiter stepped away, Sam grinned. "How does that sound?"

"Perfect." Like the whole evening, starting with him showing up at the Depot to whisk her off to dinner. Even the corner table was perfect; it allowed a clear view of people coming and going. Eddy continued to hover at the corner of her thoughts.

"Hopefully it won't be chocolate overload." Sam's words pulled her back to the table.

She waved a hand in dismissal, smiling. "That's an old wives' tale."

"Sam!" A middle-aged couple stopped beside the table, the man holding out his hand.

Sam stood and greeted them warmly, then gestured toward Marti. "This is my friend, Marti Gustafson. Marti, you've heard me mention Andrew. These are his parents, Bob and Darlene."

She shook their hands, and sat back to let them chat with Sam. They talked with the ease of people who knew each other well, yet there was a tenderness in Sam's manner she hadn't seen before.

Andrew. A familiar name. What was his story? Sam had mentioned a girl as well.

They chatted a few minutes more, then hugged Sam warmly before saying goodbye to her and moving on.

Sam took a long moment getting resettled, lips pressed tightly. He lifted a melancholy smile to her. "I'm happy to see them doing so well. It's been a rough road."

Before she could respond, the waiter delivered dessert with a flourish, setting forks before each of them, then promised to return with coffee. Their first bites elicited groans of pleasure. From the start of the evening to now— a delicious meal she'd never be able to afford, a handsome dinner partner whose smile set her heart spinning, and the most delectable chocolate she'd ever tasted, every minute had felt like a dream. The happiest dream she'd ever had.

Another bite poised, Marti said, "Tell me about Andrew. His parents seem like lovely people."

"They are. Andrew was the oldest of three kids. A younger brother and sister. Drew was a special kid. Funny, smart. Reminded me of me at that age." Sadness filled his eyes. "When he died, the family was devastated. We all were. Can't imagine you ever get over something like that." He sighed and took another bite of dessert.

She couldn't imagine that pain. Losing Katie was unthinkable.

The waiter appeared with two cups of coffee. She waited until he stepped away. "I'm sorry I don't remember—how did he die?"

"Drug overdose. A little over two years ago." He shook his head, regret shadowing his face. "He'd done so well in treatment, I really thought he'd kicked it. My life was sort of a mess then, and I didn't see the changes."

His fork clanked onto the plate and she jumped. The intensity in the green eyes that met hers pinned her in the chair, choking her breath. The raw pain on his face made her heart ache. To keep from reaching for his hand, she tightened her grip on her fork.

"He had so much potential, so much to offer the world. He had college plans, tons of friends. Everybody liked him." His chuckle was strained.

"Especially the girls. Then drugs messed everything up, and eventually killed him." He leaned forward, brow lowered. "Which is why we can't *ever* give up the fight against the drug dealers. We've got to keep fighting to get them off the streets."

Marti shrank back from his fierce expression. She set her fork aside and reached trembling fingers toward her glass of water. Beads of moisture formed along her hairline. She was "them."

"When Shareen died the day before Andrew's funeral," he continued, "I promised God, myself, and anyone who'd listen that I'd find the guy responsible and take him down, no matter what. I hounded Ben night and day, canvassed the neighborhood begging people to share what they knew about this guy named Eddy. Nobody would."

Conversations around them faded. Marti sat frozen in her chair. She didn't want to hear any more, see the angry pain glittering in his eyes.

"Andrew was an honors student. Shareen was a cheerleader. They were making something of their lives, despite bad choices." His deep sigh seeped inside her. "I wish you could have known them."

The heartbreak in his quiet words made it impossible to breathe. She was as responsible as Eddy for the destruction of these kids' lives. She'd looked the other way. It didn't matter that she'd thought it was for Katie's safety. She'd let others die instead.

"Hey." His hand covered hers. "Sorry. I'm being a downer when we should be enjoying this amazing dessert." He squeezed her fingers. "And the great company."

You're a fraud, Marti Gustafson! A murderer! The words screamed through her head, the truth burning into her marrow. She tossed her napkin on the table and stood, a hand at her mouth. "I don't feel well. Thanks for dinner."

Ignoring the startled expressions of other diners, she zigzagged through the restaurant and stumbled out the door, dragging in deep breaths of fresh air to keep from losing her dinner right on the sidewalk.

I'm no better than Eddy. She ran, tears blurring the way. She ran from the memories. From Sam. From herself.

"Marti!" Sam's voice faded as she turned the corner.

How had she forgotten her real identity? Sam deserved the best of everything, and that wasn't her. The daughter of a drug-dealing inmate. A petty thief. Responsible for Katie's issues. Now a drug dealer and murderer who would no doubt join her father in prison.

She reached the lake and ran along the path until her feet stung and her lungs burned. Sam would be waiting at Jason and Lorna's. After his third call, she turned off her phone and sat by the water until moonlight danced over the ripples.

When the mosquitoes forced her to move, she retraced her steps. Past the restaurant and the Java Depot, she paused at the front door of Faith Community Church. Would they let her in again if they knew who she really was? She'd be forever grateful that she'd returned to God in this place, but she didn't belong here, not among these people.

Unwilling to walk away from the church quite yet, she followed the sidewalk around the building. A garden area nestled in back, overhead lights spreading a glow that illuminated a path. Peaceful stillness beckoned.

Just be.

She breathed deeply as she followed the path, the sweet aroma of roses a balm to her soul. She could "just be" when she was alone in the dark, but not with Sam's gaze reflecting the pain in his wounded heart. His guilt pounded at her.

"Marti?"

She spun with a squeak then released a short breath. "Oh. Pastor Joel." Her shoulders dropped. "What are you doing here?"

He approached with a chuckle. "I work here. Sometimes pretty late, as you can see. What about you?"

She slipped her hands into her pockets. "I've been walking. And thinking."

"Maybe praying?" he asked gently.

"If I had the right words."

"How about we sit for a minute? I'd like to catch up with you." He settled on a curved cement bench, patting the space beside him.

The kindness in his face pulled her forward.

"So, what's got you wandering the neighborhood so late?"

Head down, she searched for the right words. "I've made a mess of my life."

"I see."

His tone was sympathetic, not at all surprised. She picked at her jeans with shaking fingers. "How does God feel about sin?"

"He hates it."

She flinched. "Even when it's unintentional?"

"Even then. And you know why?" He waited for her to look up. "Because sin of any kind pulls us away from Him. It puts the focus on us instead, which was never how we were designed to live. The thing is, Marti, we all sin, intentionally and not. Unfortunately, it's human nature."

They sat quietly, cars humming in the distance.

"You know that old saying that confession is good for the soul? It's true. God created us to live in community, to share our burdens, and help and encourage those around us." After a pause, he added, "And did you know that conversations between a pastor and a parishioner are confidential? Whatever we talk about goes no further than this bench."

The assurance was the pin that punctured her balloon of secrets. She lowered her head. "I'm a drug dealer." He'd be reaching for his phone now to call 9-1-1. Any minute.

"I've met quite a few drug dealers, but you sure don't fit the mold."

The story of Eddy and her downward spiral spilled out. Even details of her childhood slipped into the telling, and her new friendship with Sam. Unable to stop the barrage, she stayed focused on a distant light and let the words flow.

"The worst part is knowing I had something to do with the death of kids Sam cared so much about. And who knows how many others." She lowered her head. "I'm sure there's a special place in hell for people like me and Eddy."

The thought of eternity with that monster sent icy terror coursing through her. As her words floated beyond the glow of the overhead lights, silence blanketed them. No doubt he couldn't figure out what to say after such a revelation.

"Marti, I'm sorry to hear about all the lousy stuff that's happened in your life. You didn't deserve any of it. You're amazingly resilient."

Elbows resting on her knees, shame colored her sigh. "More like stupid and gullible."

"Hmm. I heard the compassion of a young person trying to do the right thing. Persevering despite the roadblocks. You asked about sin earlier. Do you think God won't forgive the choices you've made?"

"Why would He?"

"Because He doesn't see our sin. Jesus has stepped in front of us and taken the blame."

She frowned. Grandy had reminded her often that Jesus loved her, and she'd believed it then. She wasn't that child anymore. "Maybe for people like you, and Grandy and Gramps."

"For everyone. It's not something we'll ever understand this side of heaven. Did you get a chance to read John 3:16?"

The words were engraved on her heart. "Yes. My grandma said that verse a lot."

"Remember what that verse declares?"

"God gave His Son so whoever believes in Him won't die."

"Ah, but it's more than that. God loves you so much, Marti, He was willing to let Jesus die in your place, for your sins, so you can live with Him forever. Amazing, don't you think?"

His words stirred the longing she'd lived with her whole life. She pushed it away. "He didn't mean people like me and Eddy."

"He meant everyone, Marti. Everyone."

"But you and Sam are good. Eddy and I aren't. It's not fair that we'd get to live with Him along with you."

He chuckled. "Our idea of fair and God's aren't the same. Our thoughts and His aren't the same. Salvation isn't based on our level of goodness but on the depth of His love. While we can't understand how or why, we can choose to believe God's promise, try to soak it into our bones."

"Killing people is unforgivable. Drug dealers are murderers."

"Drugs can and do kill people," Pastor Joel acknowledged, "but your involvement with Eddy has no bearing on what happened to Andrew or Shareen. Those kids died two years ago. You met Eddy only recently. That's not a guilt you need to carry."

"But there are so many others." She dropped her head into her hands. "I can't fix what I've done."

"You're right." His agreement sliced into her. "None of us can change the past, but we can make a positive difference going forward, choose to live in the new life we have in Christ."

She was silent.

"Have you told God you're sorry?"

She dropped her hands to her lap and nodded. Over and over and over.

"Do you want to live differently now?"

"Yes." She ached with the desire.

"Then your job is to accept what God is offering you. Because you've asked for forgiveness, Marti, it's been granted. He knows your heart, that you're sincere, and He'll help you start over."

"But..." There had to be more to it than that. "That's too easy."

"So you can't fix the past, but you don't deserve a future. Is that right?"

"Yes." She'd made too big of a mess. She could sweep the Depot floors for twenty years, make Katie's life a paradise, volunteer every free moment to teach classes with Sam at GPS—it would never erase what she'd done, never repay the debt she owed this community.

"Hmm." He flipped open a notebook and wrote quickly, then tore the paper out and handed it to her. "I'd like you to spend some time on these verses. Read them several times and ask God to show you what they mean. Then let's talk next week, whenever it works for you. Bring some coffee from the Depot and we'll hash it out together. Okay?"

She looked at the verses he'd written, a glimmer of hope struggling against the darkness in her heart. She smiled in response to his raised eyebrows. "Okay."

"Good. Now let me drop you off at home."

"Thank you." The chaos in her mind had quieted, as had the turmoil in her chest, sitting here with the pastor. She wanted the peace he had.

Her fingers curled around the paper. Maybe she'd find it in these words.

– 27 –

Sam dragged up the townhome steps and unlocked the front door. After waiting nearly two hours at Jason's, he'd admitted defeat. He'd gone over and over their conversation, looking for whatever had set her off.

In the kitchen, he turned on the light over the sink and started a pot of coffee. The evening had gone great. Hadn't it? She'd laughed and talked, blushed at his wink, chatted with the goofy waiter. Maybe he got a little forceful about getting drug dealers off the street, but the rest of the conversation had been light and fun.

The overhead light snapped on, and he turned in surprise. Jillian stood in the doorway wearing a baggy T-shirt and shorts, hair tousled. He smacked his forehead. "Sorry. I forgot you were here."

She slid into a chair at the table. "Freaked me out at first, but I figured most burglars don't make coffee before ransacking the place."

He glanced at the microwave clock. Midnight. "Go back to bed and I'll get out of here."

"I think I'll have a cup of tea first."

Sam pulled a mug from the cupboard, filled it with water, and put it in the microwave. "Still use Splenda?"

A smile touched a corner of her mouth as she cocked her head. "I'm surprised you remember."

He retrieved a teabag and Splenda packet from the pantry, and set them before her with a spoon, then went to the microwave for the mug. "We were married a long time, Jill."

"Not long enough," she said softly, dunking the teabag.

He poured a cup of coffee and leaned back against the counter, putting the assortment of toddler cups, plates, and bibs behind him. His focus returned to Marti. How had he messed up so bad? Where had she gone? He should call her again. Maybe something bad happened. He rubbed his cheek, still able to feel her slap from weeks ago. She was plenty capable of taking care of herself, but that didn't mean—

"What has you frowning so deeply this time of night?"

He glanced at her and shrugged.

"A woman, perhaps?"

The only sound was the clink of her spoon against the mug as she stirred. Finally, she sighed. "Sam, thanks for letting us stay here. I didn't expect you to agree so I want you to know how grateful I am. *We* are."

He nodded. She could thank God for changing his attitude. "Any luck with the job search?"

"Not so far. I heard the Teen Center closed. What a shame." She sipped her tea. "What are you doing with yourself these days?"

"Refining my woodworking skills with Jimmy. I'm also teaching GED classes at a new program for young adults."

"That's great. Whatever happened with the trial?"

He flinched. "It didn't last long, but she did plenty of damage."

"Did they throw the case out?"

O'Neil v Evans. The charge that forced Richard to fire him. "Not until all the nitty gritty details of my life were displayed for everyone in the courtroom, and enough character witnesses for me and against her made it clear it was a bogus charge."

Jillian's eyebrows pinched upward. "Anyone who knows you would never believe you'd assault one of the kids you were trying to help."

"Her lawyer tried hard to prove otherwise."

"I'm sorry you had to go through that right after we split. I told the attorney I'd be a character witness, but he didn't think that would help. So, I prayed for you."

He nodded. He'd survived all of it. The divorce, the baseless assault charge, the firing, the trial. What mattered now was finding Marti and setting things right. He rinsed out his cup. "I'll get out of here so you can get some sleep."

"Something mothers never get enough of."

Did she have to keep throwing it in his face? She followed him through the dark living room. As he opened the front door, she set a hand on his arm.

"Sam, wait. This is your home. I can sleep on the couch, or on the floor in Adrienne's room. There's no reason for you to leave."

He studied her upturned face, pale in the moonlight. The face he'd loved for years. "There's no reason for me to stay."

Pulling the front door closed behind him, he breathed deeply. There was one very good reason to leave. He needed to figure out what he'd done wrong so he could make it right.

Early the next morning, hands shoved deep in his pockets, Sam approached the chalky white headstone. He'd give anything to have one more conversation with Andrew. "Hey, buddy. I haven't been by for a while, so I wanted to let you know I haven't forgotten my promise, and…to apologize."

He lowered to the grass and rested his forearms across his raised knees. "Man, I sure miss you. I know you've heard this a hundred times, but you were another little brother to me. We both screwed up the same way at about the same age. But you were supposed to stay clean. You told me you would."

The flash of anger sputtered. "It was my job to help you, and I blew it. I should have had your back." He looked up at the cloudless sky and blinked rapidly. "I wish saying I'm sorry would change things, but it hasn't after two years. I'm still looking for the guy who gave you the drugs. I won't stop until we nail him."

Memories slid past like a slideshow—playing football at the Center. Long talks over coffee. Praying together in the treatment center lounge. Celebratory steaks with the family when Drew "graduated."

A familiar knot formed in his gut. The glare of flashing lights, a bumpy ride to the hospital. Holding a sobbing father. Standing outside the green canopy at the gravesite, letting the pouring rain pound on him. The stranglehold of guilt kept his tears locked inside even now.

"I saw your folks last night. They miss you like crazy, of course, but they're doing okay." He picked a blade of grass and twirled it between his fingers. He chuckled. "You'd love this—I met a girl. She's gorgeous. I act like a complete idiot around her."

He could hear the ribbing he'd have taken from Andrew, who'd never had an awkward moment around girls. "I messed up a great date last night, and I don't even know how. Go ahead and laugh. I'll admit, I could use a little coaching."

In the silence, he heaved a sigh. "If she gives me another chance, I'll try not to mess it up again. We'll see if I even get the chance."

On his way back to the car, he prayed there'd be one.

– 28 –

Marti moved through the motions at work, squinting in the morning sunshine that warmed the Java Depot. Her thoughts jumped from her conversation with the pastor to dinner with Sam. How could she have embarrassed him like that?

She started a fresh thermal pot of dark roast. *What an idiot I am, God. How can you ever make something decent out of me? I make stupid choices, get involved with the wrong people, and hurt people I care about.*

She flinched and started a pot of light roast. She cared about Sam. Too much. He didn't deserve her, and she certainly didn't deserve him. Pastor Joel's reassurance swam through her veins, calming and then confusing her. God knew she was sorry, so He forgave her? Just like that? She shook her head. It didn't feel right. She needed a way to fix things.

Staring blindly at the back wall, water running in the sink, the answer crystallized. She had to tell Sam the truth. He needed to know who she was— no, who she'd been. He'd probably cut off their friendship, but at least he'd know the truth. After she made amends for what she'd done, maybe then she could accept that God would truly forgive her.

Pain seared into her hands and she jumped back from the steaming water. "Ow!"

Jason appeared at her side a second later, looked at her bright pink fingers, and thrust them under cool water. "You didn't notice you were being scalded?"

She shook her head, tears smarting, and he grunted. "Like a frog in a frying pan."

"What?"

"Never mind." He pulled her hands from the water, studied her fingers, and put them back under the stream. "Keep them there for a bit. Don't let the water get too cold. They should be okay."

Nodding, she kept her head down, eyes squeezed shut. The thought of telling Sam the truth scalded her inside and out. She'd rather throw her whole body into boiling water. But she'd tell him the truth if it meant getting God's forgiveness. And maybe Sam's someday.

Once she'd dried her hands and swallowed a couple ibuprofen, she returned to the register. Welcoming the sting in her fingers that kept her thoughts from Sam, she greeted customers, cleared tables, and chatted with Ibrahim.

"Marti," Jason barked from his office, "go take a break."

She exchanged a grin with Ibrahim. "Don't have to tell me twice," she said, removing her apron. "Back in a few."

Stepping outside, she lifted her face for a kiss of sunshine, Sam once again at the forefront of her thoughts. She owed him the truth for all the kindness he'd shown her. And she would let that kindness propel her to being a better person. A strange peace filled her from deep within, bringing a bittersweet smile to her heart. He'd been such an unexpected bright spot in her life.

She wandered the sidewalk, admiring the window displays of neighboring stores. The clothes at Trudy's Trends were amazing. And way expensive. She paused at the next window. Every piece of the table display at Williams Sonoma, from the place mats to the darling glasses, was on her wish list. Or would be if she had one. If she saved every penny, maybe she'd be able to splurge on one piece for her and Katie.

"Someday," she sighed, turning away from the window and bumping into the person standing next to her. "Oh, I'm—" The apology cut short when she looked up.

"I've thought the same thing about us, Martha," Eddy said. "Someday."

She bit her lip against the bile burning up her throat and stepped back. "In your dreams."

His chuckle crawled under her skin. "This new you is much more to my liking than the little mouse of earlier."

"My mistake. I'll switch back."

"Martha, Martha," he said with an exaggerated sigh. "Would it be so bad, you and me?"

"Horrific comes to mind."

His smile widened then slowly faded. "But perhaps necessary if you want to keep Katherine safe."

She lifted her chin, begging silently for courage. "I prefer my own insurance plan."

"I think you're bluffing. I don't believe you had it in you to be so devious."

She lifted her arms wide, pulse racing. "Then take your best shot, if you're sure I won't have all of your private information turned over to the police the next time I get so much as a bruise."

His eyes took on a feral gleam, his mouth flattening as they stared at each other. "Once I find your hidden treasure, and have no doubt I will, we'll have a different kind of chat. More complete than the one we had in your apartment."

"Marti?" Darling, wonderful Sam stood at her side. "Everything okay?"

She swayed toward him, nauseous with relief. "Yes." She forced a smile. "Everything's fine."

"Aren't you going to introduce me to your friend?" Eddy suggested.

"No need. We're leaving." She turned sharply and started away, then stopped when she heard Sam's voice.

"Sam Evans. And you are?"

She whirled back, frantic to stop Eddy from revealing himself. His hand already clasped Sam's. "Nice to meet you, Sam. I'm Victor."

Victor? She blinked. His middle name. Breathing a choppy sigh of relief, she took Sam's arm. "My break's over. I have to get back to work."

He hesitated, then nodded at Victor. "Nice to meet you. Take it easy."

As they walked away, Eddy's chuckled followed them. "That's the plan."

Marti concentrated on putting one foot in front of the other, still clinging to Sam's arm as they headed back to the coffee shop. If Sam had discovered "Victor's" real identity, the encounter would have turned ugly, with Sam no doubt the loser.

He turned to face her outside the shop. "What's going on?"

"Nothing. That was a…a guy I worked with. A while back."

"A boyfriend?"

She pulled back sharply. "No!"

"Looked like an unpleasant conversation."

"I bumped into him. Literally." She shivered. "I'm glad you came along."

"Me too." He folded his arms. "So, what happened last night?"

Heat bloomed across her face. Now that they were safely away from Eddy, she could tell Sam the truth. "I over-reacted about what you'd said about Andrew and his family, and the girl." That much was true. "It made me sad, but I shouldn't have embarrassed you like that. I'm really sorry."

His frown relaxed. "So, I'm not *that* bad to hang out with?"

She smiled. "Not at all. I am."

"Okay, good. Well, not that you're bad to hang out with." He lifted his shoulders and grinned. "How about we try it again tonight, only no conversation about kids, drugs or past history?"

Bad idea. Very bad idea. Looking into his handsome face, she opened her mouth to decline. "Okay." *Well, that would be her opportunity to tell him everything.*

– 29 –

"Good morning, Gus."

She turned from stocking the drinkware and smiled. "Good morning, Jimmy!"

Without the safety goggles and a sprinkle of sawdust in his hair, Jimmy looked very professional, and intimidating.

"How's my favorite woodworker?"

"I'm sure Sam is doing fine this morning." She certainly was after an evening of walking and talking, eating ice cream, and lots of laughter. Although she'd never found the right time to spill her story, she'd take the next opportunity.

He chuckled. "Okay, my favorite *female* woodworker."

"Working," she replied. "Just not with wood."

"Which is what you should be doing." He leaned against the shelving unit, watching her arrange Java Depot water bottles and ceramic mugs. "So how do I convince you to come work with me?"

Her heart skittered, catching her breath. "Offer me a million dollars?"

"You're definitely worth it. Unfortunately, I haven't reached that level of income. Yet. But with you onboard, I know we could."

She glanced sideways to see if he was kidding. "I'd cost you that much in training hours and mistakes."

"You wouldn't, but it'd be worth it if you did." He straightened. "Gus, I know raw talent when I see it, and I'm determined to be the one who helps you develop it."

He certainly was determined. "I'll admit I used to dream about being a woodworker like my Gramps."

"Now we're getting somewhere," he said with a triumphant grin.

"But then I grew up and life got complicated. I need to stay focused on earning money for Katie."

"Totally get that." He nodded. "So, if I offered you a decent starting salary, would you at least consider it? It comes with health insurance, and the start of a 401k."

Her mouth opened and shut. Health insurance? Savings? He named a salary that made her eyes go wide. How could he offer so much without knowing what she could do?

"Keep in mind that that's an apprentice salary," he added. "After the apprenticeship period, it would go up substantially."

"Up?" she squeaked.

He chuckled. "I'll make it worth your while, Marti. The business continues to expand, and I want to be sure I've got the best talent onboard."

The bells jangled over the door and she glanced over her shoulder, then froze. Eddy ignored her as he approached the counter and placed his order with Ibrahim, but she had no doubt he'd seen her. The coffee shop seemed to darken whenever he entered, stifled by his presence.

"Gus?" Jimmy's voice jerked her back. "Would you at least consider it? I don't need an answer right now, but the sooner you can start, the happier I'll be."

She forced a wooden smile, unable to draw a full breath. "Of course I will. It's an amazing offer."

"I'll check back in a few days, or," he held out a business card, "feel free to call me if you make a decision before that."

"Thanks." She slipped it into her apron pocket. "I'd better get back to work."

"We'll talk soon," he said.

As he left the shop, the salary he'd mentioned pulsed through her. It had to be a dream.

"New friend of yours?" Eddy's smooth voice at her shoulder was a living nightmare.

She'd hoped he'd left. "Java Depot customer."

"You were quite friendly with him."

"We treat all of our customers like friends." She turned and looked into soulless snake eyes. Their venom put her nerves on high alert. *God protect me.* "Almost all of them." She picked up the empty merchandise box at her feet and strode past him to the storeroom. Releasing a shuddering breath, she leaned against the wall.

As long as Eddy remained in her life, she couldn't possibly jeopardize Jimmy or his business by working there. Since she couldn't imagine him ever leaving her alone, the woodworking dream faded away. Eddy was the nightmare she'd never wake up from.

Sam stood outside the Java Depot. Waning sunlight accented Marti's sharp, jerky movements as she wiped the counter. She straightened and stood quietly, eyes closed, then her shoulders sagged. Apparently she'd had a rough day.

Pushing open the door, he caught her attention and smiled. The corners of her mouth lifted. He winked and she blushed, glancing at the clock. Taking a seat near the door, he turned his attention to the crowded shop. Jason's business continued to flourish. A steady stream of regulars, plenty of young people, and families shared Jason's latest creations.

"Ready?" Marti waited beside him.

Startled, he leaped to his feet and held the door for her. "How did you sneak up on me?"

"It's all in the footwork." While her words were light, a shadow dimmed her smile.

As they walked in silence toward the lake, she glanced repeatedly over her shoulder, and frowned at each person who passed.

"So, how has work been so far today?"

"Fine. Why?"

"Uh...it seemed like a polite way to start a conversation?"

Her shoulders dropped. "Sorry. I'm a little cranky."

"Well, this will cheer you up. Jimmy told me you two talked about you working at the shop with us. He's thrilled that you're considering his offer."

"That's kind of him."

Sam chuckled. "Nope. He wants the best talent in town under his roof, and that includes you."

"I made one little heart," she said flatly. "That hardly makes me talented."

So much for cheering her up. "I was there," he reminded her. "I saw how easily you created the piece, how comfortable you were with the equipment."

"Well, that's nice and all, but I can't really fit that into my life right now."

"A full-time job?"

"A *new* job. Working long hours learning stuff. I have enough on my mind." Her pace increased. "I can't think about doing that right now. It's too much. I have to focus on Katie."

The edge to her protest wasn't irritation. He put a hand on her arm and stopped her. "Marti, are you okay?"

"I'm fine." She kicked at a rock. "I've got a lot going on."

"Is that Victor guy bothering you? I could talk to him—"

"No!" She bit her lip, adding more gently, "No, that's okay. I'm a little on edge with Katie getting out of foster care soon. There's a lot to think about."

She continued walking, and he fell into step beside her, hands in his pockets. In the middle of the next block, a neon ice-cream cone beckoned. He waited until they'd reached it before steering her into the shop. "We need ice cream," he announced, directing her to the counter.

"I didn't bring any money."

Sam smiled at the man behind the counter. "The sky's the limit. Anything the pretty lady wants."

Pink crept across her cheeks as she ordered a single cone. Sam held up two fingers behind her, and the man chuckled and added a second scoop. Marti blinked in surprise when he handed it to her. "That's a single?"

"It's buy one get one free," Sam said. "I'll have the same."

Continuing their stroll toward the lake, she thanked him. "I didn't realize this is exactly what I needed."

"You're welcome." He got a smile in response, and bumped her with his shoulder. "Ice cream makes everything better."

Settled on "their" bench, they raced to stay ahead of the melting ice cream. Marti laughed as he switched hands again, licking drops off his fingers. "You need more practice," she said. "Classy ice cream consumption is a fine art."

"Yeah, well, I'm practicing now." He nodded toward her hand. "Looks like you should too."

She squealed as hers dripped over her knuckles, and licked furiously to catch up. The ice cream diversion had relaxed her, letting her smile come out. Now she chatted about her day, asked about his, and munched on her cone.

Treats devoured, they continued walking around the lake, sharing sibling stories. Her memories of Katie were sweetly painful. That they adored each other was obvious, as was the lack of any kind of parental guidance or upbringing. She barely mentioned their parents, focusing on the joy she found hanging out with her sister. The more she shared, the tighter his chest became. He wanted to wipe away the years of neglect, replace them with better, happier times.

"So tell me more about your family," she said. "You said you're the oldest of six? It must have been amazing to have so many siblings to play with."

"And fight with, and have to share with," he added.

"You poor thing. That sounds terrible."

He poked her. "You try living with all those little terrors going through your personal stuff, taking your food, snooping in your business."

"I'd like to." Her smile faded. "I'm sure there were times when you all wanted to kill each other, but there must have been good times too."

"Plenty." He nodded. "I have to admit, I wouldn't give any of them up."

"Memories or siblings?"

"Either." They stood at the edge of the water watching a pair of geese glide past. "Both of my parents came from big families, so I have 42 first cousins. One of them is getting married next Saturday. I'm not looking forward to it."

"You don't like weddings? Or your cousin?"

He chuckled. "My cousin's great. I just hate going alone. My siblings are relentless." To put it mildly. "Hey, how about grabbing a light dinner somewhere?"

"The cone didn't fill you up?"

"I think it whet my appetite." Dinner would give them more time together, and that's all he wanted lately. "So, what do you say?"

In the silence that followed, the long-lashed brown eyes meeting his reflected a surprising struggle. Was he that hard to be around?

"I guess I'm hungry too," she said finally.

Before she could change her mind, he steered her back the way they'd come, dousing the smile that threatened to expose him as a complete idiot.

– 30 –

Marti breathed in the spicy aroma of her favorite Indian restaurant, leaning her elbows on the window-side table. She'd never missed their free sample Saturdays. "Mmm, that smells wonderful."

"I haven't been here in years. Glad to know it's still doing well." He studied the chalkboard menu. "It's hard to decide. It all sounds delicious."

"Then please allow me to choose for you," the waiter said as he stopped beside them. "Chef's surprise."

Sam raised an eyebrow at Marti. She grinned and nodded. She'd agree to anything tonight.

"Okay," he said. "We'll share whatever you want to bring out."

"Very good, sir. You won't be disappointed."

As he moved away, Sam chuckled. "I hope not."

"I haven't had a single thing here that wasn't delicious," she assured him.

Conversation moved back to the dreaded wedding. "I guess this is one of the times having all those siblings is a pain," she mused, "when they give you a hard time."

He gave a crooked smile. "Especially when most of them are either married or in serious relationships, and think you should be too. And there's always Mom."

"Does she give you a hard time about it too?" Her mother had given her a hard time about everything, all the time.

"Not intentionally. She thinks she's helping. Bringing someone to a family event like this ramps up the speculation. I'm not sure which is worse—going alone or bringing a friend."

"No girlfriend right now?" *That's none of your business!*

"Nope. I've been divorced a couple of years. I suppose I'm a little gun-shy."

She sat straighter at the revelation. He'd been married? What else didn't she know about him? She winced. There was plenty he didn't know about her. That she'd tell him about soon.

"How long were you married?" The question slipped out before her brain engaged.

"Nine years."

A long time. His fault or hers? She locked the thought away before it could be uttered.

He squinted past her. "We met in college, about as different as two people can be. It seemed to work, though. Well, I thought it did."

Sadness flickered across his face. She chewed the corner of her lip. It seemed he wasn't over it yet. "I'm sorry."

"Don't be. It's turned out for the best. Anyway, I'm thinking I'll probably skip the wedding. Not much in the mood."

"Oh, don't do that. It's your family." If she had family who cared about her, she'd never skip an event, no matter how bad the teasing got. "Will the comments really be that bad?"

"No worse than any other time, I guess, although the whole matrimony theme will probably intensify things. They try to be subtle, but then it feels like everyone's walking on eggshells."

Go with him.

Marti straightened abruptly, the silent words like a poke in the back. Like when she got the idea to leave the change for the makeup. And when she'd run out on their dinner date and ended up at Faith Church. She shook her head to dislodge the unexpected thought.

A light dawned on his face as he looked at her, then pink crept up his neck. He refolded his napkin, and fidgeted in his chair like a child in timeout. He cleared his throat and reached for his water glass, tipping it instead. "Oh, man!"

They leaped to their feet as water sloshed toward her. Trying to stop the it with his napkin, he knocked her glass over. Those nearby handed them more napkins. A waiter scurried over with a towel.

"No problem, sir. Let me take care of you. Thank you." As he sopped up the water, their first waiter swept in.

"Sir and madam, please come this way. We will get you seated at another table. Please, this way."

Marti struggled to contain herself after a peek at Sam's flushed profile. When he finally looked at her, she burst into laughter. He chuckled and put a hand to her back as they followed the waiter.

Once they were settled at a corner table, he shook his head. "Sorry for that little crisis."

"It was only water."

His brows pinched upward. "I was going to ask if you'd consider going to the wedding with me, but I've probably guaranteed an 'Are you kidding?' response."

She blinked. He was asking *her* to the wedding? As a date? With his whole family there? She squashed the rush of excitement. She had no business going, no matter how his invitation touched her. She'd yet to find the courage to tell him her whole story.

"Never mind," he said. "Your expression says it all."

"Says what all?" She'd definitely lost her poker face.

"That it was a stupid idea. So, how about this great weather we're having?"

His nervousness touched her heart. She'd never made anyone nervous. Well, maybe Eddy about the photos she had. The thought slammed into her. What was she thinking? She needed to tell Sam about Eddy, not go on another date with him. But if she said no, he'd think it was because of the water.

Go with him.

The repeated directive calmed the growing chaos. "I'd love to go," she said, surprising them both. *God, am I going to make things worse?*

"You would? Really?"

His incredulous tone made her smile. She couldn't imagine women weren't knocking down his door. "Really. I'm happy to run interference for you with your family, if it'll get you to go celebrate with them."

"They'll give you the third degree, I guarantee it," he warned.

"I can take care of myself. But…" She played with the straw. "I've never been to a wedding. I might embarrass you." *Yup, I'm that kind of loser.*

"Martina, you couldn't embarrass me." He reached across the table and set his hand over hers. "Ever."

She lost herself in the compassion in his eyes and the warmth of his hand. "Oh. Well, thank you."

He leaned back with a chuckle. "You're welcome. The wedding is late Saturday afternoon, followed by dinner and a dance. It's a lot of time with my family."

How bad was this crowd? "I'm tougher than I look."

"I don't doubt it," he said. "I've got three of the nosiest sisters in the world. And my brothers are…guys."

"I can handle it." No one could be worse than Eddy who already used Katie to guarantee her silence. She couldn't bear Sam becoming a target as well.

The last of the lines creasing his forehead relaxed. "If you're sure, then it's a deal. I think I'll actually enjoy it now."

"I'll bet nobody else will have a bodyguard." Nor will anyone have a drug dealer for a date.

"That's for sure. Especially one that looks like you."

Was having an ugly date worse than no date? No one expected much of a tall, skinny girl whose clothes never fit. She sucked in a silent breath. *Clothes! What do people wear to a wedding?*

Vanessa had offered whatever help she needed. Marti prayed that included fashion advice.

He had a date with Martina. Sam stood at his closet perusing his few appropriate choices, his heart doing a goofy rhythm. Dressing up wasn't something he did very often. Like ever. Thanks to Lizzie, he owned two suits—charcoal and black. The black seemed depressing for wedding attire. He'd look like an undertaker for his first real date in years.

Laughter floated from his guest bedroom. The little girl's shrieks of delight were followed by thudding, then more shrieks, Jillian's laughter mixed in. A bittersweet smile touched his mouth as he pulled the suits out. *Will that ever be my life, Lord?*

He laid the black suit on his bed and dusted the shoulders of the charcoal jacket, searching his memory for the last time he'd worn either one. He'd had a rented tux for Lizzy and Rob's wedding. He'd worn the black suit for their father's funeral. Maybe he'd never worn the charcoal?

The shrieking grew closer followed by Jill's voice. "Addy, stop. Don't go—"

Sam turned. The little one stood staring at him from the doorway, thumb in her mouth. Jillian appeared and swooped her up. "Sorry. I didn't think she'd come in here."

"It's okay, Jill. Maybe she can help me make a decision."

Jillian looked from the suit in his hand to the one on the bed. "Big event coming up?"

"Heather's wedding this weekend. My cousin?"

"I remember Heather," she said, nodding. "Nice suits. Either will work."

He held them next to each other. "Black is depressing, I think."

"Formal, not depressing. It's all in how you spin it." She cocked her head, then pointed. "If you have the right shirt and tie, go with the charcoal."

The right shirt? He tossed the suit on the bed and dug through the closet. Pulling out a white shirt, he sorted through his handful of ties. "How's this?"

"Hmm. What other ties do you have?" She shifted her daughter to the other hip and went past him to the closet. He stepped back, the proximity unsettling. Jillian had always helped him dress for big events. He'd appreciated it back then.

"Here. This one is better."

Holding the shirt and tie under his chin, he checked his reflection in the mirror over his dresser. Jill always did have a better eye for style. "This works. Thanks."

She returned to the doorway, eyebrows raised. "Do you have a date?"

"I do, actually." The realization still flipped his insides.

"You'll have more fun with a date." Her smile lacked energy. "Lucky girl."

He was the lucky one. He returned the black suit to the closet, and gathered dress shoes and socks. "I think this is everything. I'll get out of your hair."

She rolled her eyes. "Sam, this is *your* house. I'm the one in the way."

"It's yours for right now." He slid past her and headed for the front door, eager to be free of memories that surfaced when he was around her. Their marriage seemed a lifetime ago.

"She's pretty."

He stopped. "Who?"

Jillian nodded her head toward the photo on his bookshelf. He and Marti studying the Bible together, pausing for a goofy selfie.

He smiled. "Yeah. She is. Okay, well, you two have a good day."

"I hope you have as much fun at Heather's wedding as you did at ours." Her chin trembled. "You cleaned up nice then too, Sam."

How could he respond to that? There was no point in a walk down memory lane. He opened the front door. "Thanks for the fashion help."

He loaded the clothes into the car and pulled away from the curb, and from his past. Marti was the future and he couldn't be happier. Or more nervous.

– 31 –

"River House. Tiffani speaking. How can I help you?"

Marti cleared her throat. "Hi, Tiffani. It's Marti. I'm looking for Vanessa?"

"Hi! Let me see if I can find her. Hold on."

A moment later, Vanessa came on. "Marti? Hi. I'm glad you called."

She managed a nervous chuckle. "Well, you might not be when you hear what I need."

"Lay it on me, sister." Laughter colored her words.

An hour later, Marti wandered through Trudy's Trends, waiting for Vanessa. She adored the clothes in this store, but not the price tags. She'd tried to convince Vanessa to meet at the thrift store a few blocks away, but the response was firm. "You deserve something new, Marti."

A saleswoman approached with a smile. "Can I help you find something?"

"I'm…I need a dress. But I'm waiting for someone." Maybe she'd get escorted out for being the wrong kind of clientele.

"Well, let me show you the dress area, and you can browse while you wait. Come this way. I'm Susan, by the way."

Marti weaved through the shop behind her like a lost puppy.

"Are you looking for casual or dressy?" Susan asked over her shoulder.

"A wedding. We're going to a wedding." The words were surreal. *I have a date to a wedding.*

"How fun. Evening or daytime?"

"Um, late afternoon?"

"Lovely. A wedding that time of day can be formal or simply dressy. Gowns or tea length would be appropriate. Here we go." Bracelets jangled on the arm she swept toward several racks. "I'm sure you'll find something perfect here."

Marti tried not to squirm under Susan's perusal. She hadn't bought anything new in forever. How would she know what to pick?

"Let's see." Susan searched through the far rack, returning with a flowing dress in a shimmering navy blue. "You're so tall and thin, this would be stunning on you."

"Sorry I'm late." Vanessa's breathless apology came from behind. "Oooh. That's pretty. Definitely something to try on, don't you think?"

Marti pulled in her bottom lip. "Depends on the cost."

"Psh." Vanessa waved a hand at her. "It's all about finding the perfect dress."

Marti had never bought anything without looking at the price first. She usually put it back.

"How about this one? No, that's not the right look." Vanessa pulled another off the rack and held it up to Marti. "This is gorgeous. Such a great color for you."

Susan also pulled dresses out. "I'll get a room started. What's your name, hon?"

She had to give her name to enter a dressing room? Did they want ID too? "Marti."

"Okay, Marti. You keep looking and I'll put these in a room. Hello, ladies," she called to two older women who'd entered the store. "I'll be right with you."

"This one is beautiful." Vanessa chattered as she moved through the selection. "I wish I had your height. Any of these will be gorgeous on you."

She picked another one and nodded, shook her head at the next, then held one up to Marti again, who watched in amazement.

"Oooh, look at this. Gorgeous." Vanessa spun toward her. "What do you—oh." Her smile faded and she quickly returned it to the rack. "You hate it. Okay, we'll put it back, no problem."

"No, it's beautiful. It's just…"

Vanessa faced her, eyebrows pinched upward. "I'm overdoing it, aren't I? Kurt says I get carried away sometimes, and he has to rein me in." She blew out a short breath. "I'm sorry. I didn't mean to take over—"

"Vanessa, you haven't at all. If I were here alone, I'd still be looking at the first dress. Or actually, I'd have gone to the thrift store." She spread her arms. "These are amazing dresses, but I can't afford them," she finished in a whisper.

"Marti, this is the whole purpose of GPS."

Marti cocked a doubtful eye at her friend. "To buy wedding clothes for complete strangers?"

"To provide help where and when it's needed. And then, when people can, they pay it forward. I have no doubt you'll do that when the time is right."

The turmoil in Marti's chest eased. She wouldn't accept a handout, but she could pay it forward. Vanessa must have seen her weaken because she grabbed her hand and pulled her toward the dressing room. "Try a couple on, and we'll worry about the cost later."

A rush of excitement bowled over Marti's hesitation. It wouldn't hurt to try a few. Two hours later, she left the store with the most beautiful dress she'd ever seen wrapped gently in tissue and tucked in a bag along with a pair of shoes and a purse. Settled at Millie's Cafe for lunch, Marti pressed a hand to her roiling stomach, not sure she could eat. Her life had changed before her eyes.

"So I want to hear all about this special guy," Vanessa said, popping a chip into her mouth. "You've been pretty mum about him."

Marti set her turkey sandwich aside, struggling to keep her face from turning its usual shade of fuchsia whenever she thought of Sam. No such luck.

Her friend's smile deepened, and she leaned forward. "He must be pretty amazing. Come on, I want details."

"Well, he's tall and blond." How could she describe the kindness in his eyes? What his laugh did to her stomach? His patience with her?

"Cute?"

Her toes curled. "Very."

THE COLOR OF TRUTH

"What's his name? What does he do? I want to make sure he's worthy of you."

Now *that* was funny. Sad but funny. "It's me that's not worthy. He's such a nice guy. He has an amazing heart, you know?" She set her chin in her hand. "I've never known a man like him. He's funny, and smart, and he even likes his siblings."

"That's huge. Kurt has a brother that he's super close to. It makes me love him even more when I see the two of them together." A shadow crossed her face. "My sister and brother would have adored him," she added softly.

Marti's heart ached for her. "My sister thinks Sam is the best."

Vanessa straightened, eyebrows lifted. "I know a Sam. He's tall and blond, and super cute."

"Sam Evans?"

They stared at each other for a moment, then burst into laughter.

"He's everything you said, for sure," Vanessa said finally. "He's great."

"How do you know him?"

"He's helping us with GED classes. And he's working on starting some intro trade skills classes. How did you guys meet?"

Sam's classes were at GPS? "We met at the Java Depot where I work. We started talking one morning, and haven't stopped." A familiar tingle raced over her skin. "That's one of the things I like about him. We have fun hanging out doing nothing."

Vanessa's smile grew along with a knowing glint. "You two are perfect for each other. And you know what? When he sees you in that dress, he'll be speechless."

Warmth flooded her cheeks again. "Oh, I doubt that."

"Mark my words, kiddo," she said with a nod. "You're going to knock his socks off. I wish I could be there to see it. Now, we should talk about hair and makeup. That's Kiera's area of expertise, so how about we come over Saturday morning and get you gussied up?"

"Kiera?"

"She's the image consultant for GPS. She was a model for years so she knows hair and makeup. You'll love her. She's a riot."

"Oh, you guys don't need to do that." She couldn't pick out a dress, but she could manage her own hair.

"Of course we do. How fun will that be? And I'll even bring some breakfast treats." Vanessa's excitement mirrored the dance party in Marti's chest. Along with an actual date, she was getting actual girlfriends. The unexpected turns in her life lately left her speechless. Except for a whispered, *Thank you.*

– 32 –

Saturday afternoon, Marti perched on the couch, smoothing the silky fabric over her knees. Would he like it? Did he wish he hadn't asked her? She'd promised to run interference for him, so she'd do the best she could. *Don't let me embarrass him. Please.*

A car pulled into the driveway and her heart gave a goofy bump as she stood. She could do this. She was a big girl, and she'd faced a lot scarier things than this. As footsteps climbed the stairs, she checked her hair in the mirror. The soft curls Kiera had magically created were gathered at the back of her neck, secured with glittering clips and lots of hairspray.

The dress made her feel pretty, something she'd never felt before. From the halter neckline to the beading that sparkled, and the pleats that swayed when she walked, she felt like a princess. The bell rang and she gave a firm nod to the nervous girl in the mirror, then opened the door.

Sam's eyes went wide. "Whoa."

"Hi."

"You look…" A stunned smile filled his face. "Wow."

"Thank you." She tried to respond nonchalantly, despite the heat sliding up her neck. "You're very handsome yourself." Gorgeous in a charcoal suit. Her heart fluttered so hard she couldn't breathe. What if she fainted?

"Thanks, but you…whoa." He blinked several times. "So, are you prepared for Evans family overload?"

"You bet. Bring it on."

Chuckling, he held out his arm. She took it with a smile, trying to float down the steps beside him like she'd seen on TV. *More wobble than float in these shoes.* He opened the passenger door and she slid in with a casual air, pretending a man holding a door for her happened every day. It took three attempts for her shaking fingers to get the seatbelt buckled.

He climbed in and started the car, then paused, an uncertain lift to his brow. "Last chance to back out. You don't have to subject yourself to the inquisition."

"I never back down from a challenge," she countered. His relieved chuckle calmed her panic. "If we keep sitting here, we're going to be late, and I've heard that's very bad manners for wedding guests."

"Well, we don't want an angry bride, so let's go."

The ride to the church across the river in St. Paul passed quickly as Sam shared tidbits about his siblings. As the oldest, he had plenty of stories that made her laugh but also catch her breath at the obvious love he had for all of them. What would it be like to have someone like him in her corner, rooting for her? A big brother who would have her back and love her despite her long list of shortcomings?

She smiled and nodded as he chatted, unable to speak over the growing lump in her throat. Did he have a clue how blessed he was to have a family like that? Well, for tonight she'd pretend they were her family as well. They joined a crowd of people filing into the church, her fingers tucked securely in his arm. She could get used to this, having him at her side. *Don't go there, Cinderella.*

Moving toward the sanctuary doors, he squeezed her fingers and smiled. "You really do look amazing." As they followed an usher down the aisle, her feet barely touched the floor.

Sam watched Marti as she experienced her first wedding. Sitting up straight, hands in her lap, she followed every move, smiling through the songs, sighing at the candle ceremony. When the groom swept his bride into a kiss, she pressed her fingertips to her smiling mouth. Sam hadn't enjoyed his own wedding half as much.

Awaiting their turn to file out after the newlyweds, he whispered family descriptions as people went by. Aunt Bea, famous for her lasagna, and Uncle David, his woodworking mentor. Two more aunts and uncles. A few cousins.

"That grinning baboon is my youngest brother, Joey, and his girlfriend, Maxine. And behind them is my youngest sister Jessie. The man-bun guy is her boyfriend."

His siblings were anything but subtle as they passed, nodding at Marti, and grinning at him with pretend astonishment. He frowned at their antics, giving Joey the evil eye as he and Maxine strolled past.

More family filed by, including Mom who simply smiled at Marti as if it were no surprise to see her. Marti continued to nod and smile as he whispered their names. Lauren and her boyfriend. Lizzy and husband Rob. Ben and— Wow! *She* was Ben's co-worker? Ben did a double-take when he saw Marti. *What, he didn't think I could find a beautiful date too?*

When he and Marti finally filed out of the sanctuary, his family was ready. Too ready. The girls circled around, elbowing him out of the way as they introduced themselves, surrounding her with laughter.

Marti smiled and nodded, answering the barrage of questions, glancing only occasionally toward him. When he caught her gaze, he winked. She blushed. He loved that reaction. And the fact that his sisters hadn't overwhelmed her. Yet. He shared a smile with Lizzy who offered a subtle thumbs up. This promised to be a great evening.

– 33 –

Marti hoped the fairy tale never ended. From witnessing a heart-melting wedding, and meeting Sam's amazing family, to this beautiful reception, a delicious meal, and now gliding across the dance floor in Sam's arms, the evening sparkled.

"I had no idea you could dance," she said.

He raised an eyebrow, guiding her through the crowd. "I'll try not to be offended." He spun them in a quick circle, making her laugh, then settled back into the slower rhythm, looking rather pleased with himself.

"I got to talk to Lizzy. She's wonderful."

"Yeah, I lucked out in the twin department. She's the brains of the group, and she can out-sprint me any day." His smile had an impish edge. "But she could never keep up with me over long distances so she had to learn to run fast and disappear if she didn't want me to catch her."

"So I'd better polish up my sprinting if I want to stay ahead of you?"

His chuckle warmed her heart. She liked making him laugh. "Don't forget the disappearing part, if you don't want to get caught."

Their smiling gazes held as the song ended. Maybe getting caught would be okay.

"Don't run too fast," he said softly.

"Hey, Bro." Joey's voice cut between them. "My turn with the prettiest lady here. Aside from my own date, of course."

She turned toward him, hoping the heat in her cheeks wasn't glowing like a flare. "*You* can dance too?" She sounded silly and breathless.

Joey folded his arms and frowned, laughter in his dark eyes. "I think I should be offended by that."

Sam slapped a hand on his shoulder. "I got the same response, Joseph, but I didn't hear her complaining. Show her what you got."

The music started and Joey held out his arms. "We may look like Neanderthals, but all of the Evans men can dance. We like to surprise women. Keeps them on their toes."

She laughed and let him spin her around the crowded dance floor. Sam was certainly keeping her on her toes; charming and funny, smart but not condescending. She no longer felt like a complete idiot around him. She felt noticed. Pretty. Cinderella had lost her grip on reality, falling hard for the prince though she knew the story couldn't end well. Not when she still had to tell him who she was beneath the glitter and glam.

After a line dance, which she caught onto quickly, they joined Sam, Lizzy and her husband Robert at the long table reserved for the Evans clan. Marti plopped next to Sam, breathless and grinning. "Okay, I take it all back. You guys can definitely dance."

He slid a glass of ice water toward her, his mouth twitching. "And that's only scratching the surface."

They clinked their glasses in a toast, her insides a delightfully quivering mess. "I'm a little afraid of what else I'll find out about you."

"Oh, be afraid, Marti," Robert warned her. "Be very afraid. The Evans family is a complex bunch. I think they make stuff up to keep everyone off-balance."

"And you never quite know what's made up and what's not, do you, Roberto?" Sam's deep voice slid over her, blanketing her in a delicious warmth.

She took another sip of water, encountering Lizzy's perusal as she looked from Sam to her and back, a half-smile on her face. How could she possibly measure up to this family? *You can't, Cinderella, so get over yourself.* She turned to Joey, and asked the first question that popped into her head about his band. Soon they were engrossed in a conversation about guitars and future gigs, and

Lizzy's scrutiny faded. Now if only she could ignore Sam's arm across the back of her chair.

Moments later, Sam excused himself and led his mother onto the dance floor. What a wonderful picture they made, chatting and laughing together. If she'd had a real mother like that, maybe she wouldn't have messed up so badly.

"Hi, Marti."

She turned. "Hi, Ben." His smile and voice were so much like Sam's, but instead of the delightful tingle Sam evoked, Ben's more serious manner set her nerves on alert. Maybe it was the law enforcement vibe that made her want to hide.

"I haven't had a chance to talk with you tonight. How about getting some fresh air with me?"

She hesitated, then forced a smile. Spending time with a cop didn't seem wise, but how could she decline? "Fresh air sounds great. Is your date joining us?"

"She got called in to work, unfortunately. At least she got to eat before she left."

They wound around tables and people, and stepped out into a quiet, cool evening. She willed herself to ignore the abrupt chaos in her chest. They strolled in silence, that strange energy crawling under her skin. Hopefully Sam would come looking for her soon.

"You and Sam seem to be good friends," he said finally.

She smiled. "He's such a nice guy. I think I've been his community project for the past month or so."

"That's Sam," he agreed. "Always looking out for people."

"I was surprised to find out about his woodworking."

"Why's that?"

"I don't know." She shrugged as they rounded a corner of the building. "It wasn't what I imagined him doing. Silly, I know."

"I guess we all have things about us that would surprise other people," Ben said.

Her smile wobbled. "I suppose that's true."

"What would surprise him about you?"

Careful. "I'm not too complicated. I guess he was surprised to find out how much I like woodworking too."

His brow lifted. "Ahh. That would surprise me as well."

Marti smiled as Gramps's weathered face came to mind. "I had the best teacher." A police car zipped past, lights flashing and siren blaring. She crossed her arms tightly.

"Would Sam be surprised to know about Eddy?"

She stopped abruptly, the earlier chaos now a spinning tornado.

"I'm the cop who talked to you in the ER," he said quietly.

As they faced each other in the moonlight, images spun through her mind. Eddy's clients at her door. The knife coming at her. Black rage on Eddy's face.

"You look a lot better now," Ben said.

She wanted to plead her innocence, run away, pretend she didn't know what he was talking about. She stood in silence, blinking back burning tears. Eddy had warned her not to go to the police, and yet here she stood, talking to a cop out in the open. She glanced around, expecting to see him in the shadows.

"Eddy's in jail. We picked him up two days ago."

A hand over her pounding heart, she managed a nod. *Thank you.*

"He's named you as a primary member of his entourage."

She'd known this moment was coming since waking in the emergency room, been waiting for it since Eddy had found her at the Java Depot. She'd thought she was ready to face it, but the relief she'd expected was instead a blinding terror that shook every limb. *Oh, dear God. Help me.*

Ben took her arm. "Let's sit down over here."

Unable to speak, to breathe, she let him direct her to a bench where he helped her sit. She dropped her face into trembling hands as her heart cried words she couldn't form. Ben was silent beside her until she caught her breath. She sat up slowly.

"He showed us photos of you with his clients."

A tear slipped down her cheek, and she gave a stiff nod. She'd never see Katie again; Gloria would never bring her to the jail.

"I've also seen your sister."

She sucked in a sharp breath and raised a hand to stop his insinuation. "She had *nothing* to do with Eddy. She's totally innocent."

"I know." His tone was calm, his expression neutral as he studied her. "I've been looking for you since our ER chat. You're a hard one to track down."

"I wasn't hiding." Well, only from Eddy, and that didn't work so well. She watched the passing traffic. Would she even be able to see cars from her cell? Or smell fresh evening air?

"Marti, I'd like to hear your story. Eddy has had plenty to say, but I want to hear your side."

No one would believe her over Eddy's smooth and convincing version. She sighed heavily. "I met him at a restaurant. He seemed like a nice guy." *If you didn't have a brain in your head.* "We talked a lot about life. Mainly about mine, now that I think about it."

She lifted burning eyes to the stars twinkling overhead, hearing her grandmother's voice. *Grandy, I'm so sorry.* At least she'd go to jail having told someone the complete story. There was some relief in that. "When he mentioned he had a second business but no quiet place to work, I said he could use my apartment once in a while. I had a second job so I wasn't home much."

A truck rumbled past, people laughed in the distance. She'd miss the city noise.

"He didn't come all that often. I hardly noticed he'd been there at first. But then it was several times a week..." She rubbed her arms. "By the time I realized it wasn't my apartment anymore, it was too late."

"What did he tell you he was doing?"

"An online company where people ordered over-the-counter items." She shrank into the bench. "Yes, I'm that stupid. My mother always told me I was, and I proved her right. In a big way this time."

"Why did he try to kill you?"

She flinched. No one had said those words, yet she'd known if the neighbor hadn't broken down the door, she'd be dead. "The apartment manager sent a letter saying he had to get out." She felt Eddy's forearm cutting

THE COLOR OF TRUTH

off her air, saw the knife flying at her. "I told him if he left me alone I wouldn't call the cops. He didn't take it well."

"We can be thankful you have dependable neighbors next door."

"Had. The building wouldn't renew my lease because of Eddy." She rubbed her wrists, feeling the cold metal of handcuffs, smelling the stale cell, hearing the clanging of heavy doors.

"Here you two are." Sam's voice brought her head up. "I thought maybe my family had been too much for you."

Ben stood. "We needed some fresh air so we took a break."

Marti stared at him in surprise, then forced a smile for Sam. "You have very kind brothers."

"Yes, I do. And you'll always be safe with this guy around."

Safe and locked up. She'd miss Sam more than he'd ever suspect.

"I'm heading in for coffee," Ben said. "Either of you want any?"

"No, thanks," she whispered. At least he wasn't going to arrest her in front of Sam.

"None for me." Sam replaced Ben on the bench, settling close to Marti. "Let us know when they bring out the snacks, will you? Lauren said there'd be pizza."

Ben chuckled. "I'm sure you'll be able to smell it before it gets to the table, but yes, I'll let you know." He nodded at her. "Thanks for the chat, Marti. I'm looking forward to getting to know you better."

She managed to dip her head. That opportunity would happen soon, when he finally did arrest her.

As his brother strolled away, Sam stretched out his legs, locked his hands behind his head, and breathed in. "What a night."

"Mmhm." *With a surprise ending—your date gets hauled off to jail.* "The bride and groom look so happy."

"I like him. She's always had a bit of a wild side, but it sounds like he's had a calming effect on her. There was this one time when we were kids…"

A breeze sent his cologne past her as she listened to the comforting timbre of his voice. His strong hands gestured as a gentle breeze ruffled his hair. She needed to memorize these last hours of freedom, soak in the joy of sitting beside Sam, like a regular couple.

If they stayed out here chatting, maybe Ben would forget about her and go home. *When pigs fly.* No doubt he was very good at his job. There'd be no forgetting.

"And then there was this time at our family reunion when we were playing volleyball down at the lake…" Sam's anecdote faded beneath her pummeling thoughts.

She could take off, right now, and move away. Change her name. She could start a whole new life, maybe even fake her death so he wouldn't keep looking for her. Her throat tightened. How awful for Kat if she disappeared, but wouldn't having a sister in jail be worse? If she were "dead," Katie could go on with her life and have happy memories. And she'd be safe.

She shivered. No. She'd do what was best for everyone, and own up to her actions.

"Sorry," Sam said. "I'm talking and you're shivering. Here." He slid out of his suitcoat and wrapped it around her, snugging it close under her chin. His smile slid away as their gazes met, hers misty. "Hey, what's wrong? Do we need to go inside?"

"No." Anywhere but inside to face Ben. "This is perfect."

"But I made you cry."

"No, you didn't. Well, maybe." She offered a tremulous smile. "Giving me your jacket is the nicest thing anyone's ever done for me."

His frown relaxed. "You deserve far nicer things than that, Martina."

"Thank you," she whispered. She clutched his jacket closer and breathed deeply. What could be nicer than this?

A whistle interrupted. "Sam! Marti!" Joey waved from the doorway. "Pizza's here."

Sam waved back. Marti's stomach roiled. He stood and held out a hand. "I'm hungry!"

Returning to the party, still draped in the warmth of his coat and his grasp on her cold fingers, she tried to silence the death knell clanging in her head. For one lovely evening, she'd lived the life of her dreams.

— 34 —

Almost made it. Sam rolled his eyes as Lizzy hugged Marti, then whispered something that made her laugh. They'd almost made it out the door without going through a third round of goodbyes. Lauren and Jessie joined the female huddle. *Great. It could be another hour.*

Marti's presence beside him had changed the dynamics of the celebration, at least for him. She'd slipped so easily into his family; Lizzy had given him a thumbs up more than once. Lauren and Jess had repeatedly whisked her away for "girl talk." Joey had winked his approval after dancing with her.

He shifted his attention to the side of the room. Only Ben had kept his distance, studying Marti with that squinty-eyed focus he used on a case. They'd seemed to have a nice chat outside, and yet… Something had changed after that. Her joy, that had dazzled him throughout the evening, had faded. She had to be exhausted after an evening of interrogations.

"Excuse me, girls," he said, reaching between them to grasp Marti's wrist. He tugged her gently from the group. "This could go on all night, so I'm going to take Marti home before she falls down." The surprise in her doe-eyes made him want to pull her right into his arms.

Lauren pouted cheerfully. "I guess you should take her home. We'll see her again soon."

Sam cocked an eyebrow at Marti, still holding her wrist. "You might not want to get mixed up with this crazy group."

Her smile seemed forced. "They're wonderful."

"Well, don't say I didn't warn you."

The girls hooted with laughter as he led her out the door then reluctantly released his grip. He glanced at her as they strolled toward the parking ramp. She'd been amazing with his family, giving as good as she got from his brothers, making instant friends with his sisters. Even visiting with his mom for nearly half an hour. It had him feeling—

"So," he interrupted his thoughts, "now you've met the Evans clan. And survived."

"I deserve a T-shirt," she said with a tired smile, then added, "What a gift to have such great people in your life."

He chuckled. "And now they're in yours. Like a second skin, if I know my sisters."

She turned her head away, quickly swiping at her face. *Man, you did it again!* He pulled her to a stop and gently grasped her shoulders. "Hey. I didn't mean to scare you. They aren't that bad. Honest."

With a choked laugh, she shook her head, eyes glistening. "I know. I'm just tired. I haven't had this much fun in a long time. Thank you for a really wonderful evening. I'll never forget it."

The words had a ring of finality that made his heart clench. "There will be plenty more Evans events, if you're up to it. I know they'd love to see you again."

She stepped out of his grasp, her chin trembling as they stood in the glow of the street light. "I think running interference worked. You don't need me now."

Yes, I'm pretty sure I do. "But—"

"Would you mind taking me home? I'm more tired than I thought." Exhaustion rimmed her eyes, casting a dark shadow across her face.

Okay then. Getting the brush off. Disappointment formed a painful knot in his throat. "Sure. Of course."

"Sam, I—" She pressed her lips together and reached a hand toward him, then gave a sad little nod and turned away. "It has to be this way."

The last words were so soft, barely above a whisper, he wanted to believe he'd imagined them. He fell into step beside her. But he hadn't. *Ouch.*

Rubbing gritty eyes, Marti watched the morning sun tiptoe into her apartment. Still in her wedding attire, she'd been unable to move from the couch where she'd collapsed after Sam drove away. Her mother's smoke-tinged voice had grated against her heart, reminding her she'd messed things up yet again. She rested a wrist across her aching brow. *What's wrong with me? Why can't I get anything right?*

It wouldn't take long for Officer Ben to track her down here. Or at the Depot. She bolted upright and winced, waiting for her head to stop throbbing. If he arrested her here, it would humiliate Jason and Lorna. Or at the Depot, people might avoid Jason's shop because he employed people like her. She couldn't let that happen. Not to the people who had been so amazingly kind to her. She needed to end this fiasco with as little disruption to them as possible.

She hurried into the bedroom and peeled off the beautiful gown, refusing to admire it one last time. Brushing at a stray tear, she dressed in her old battered clothes, more appropriate for what she had to do, and dug out the memory card she'd hidden in Grandy's bag, tucking it into her jeans pockets. She straightened a few things in the tidy apartment, cleaned out the refrigerator, emptied the wastebaskets, and took the trash bag down to the garbage can.

At the kitchen table, she wrote several notes, jaw clenched as she finished the first few. When she got to Gloria's, she paused. What could Gloria possibly say to Katie to make the news easier? Nothing could soften the blow. She kept the note brief and ended with, "Tell her how much I love her, and that I'll miss her so very much."

She carefully arranged the evening dress on the couch, smoothing out wrinkles before propping a note for Vanessa against the gorgeous material. For a long moment, she stood, eyes closed, swaying as she felt Sam's strong arms around her while they danced. Then she saw his stricken expression when he thought she didn't want to see him again.

Pressing a fist against her chest, she struggled for breath. This was the hardest thing she'd ever done. She shook the memories away. He deserved far better than her. They all did. Leaving the apartment key on the counter, she pulled the door shut without looking back. Down the stairs and across the small yard, she quietly tucked a note for Jason and Lorna in their backdoor and hurried away.

The walk to Gloria's house in the silence of dawn took forever, her feet like heavy weights. As her heart screamed to see Kat, she stuck Gloria's note in the front door and hurried away, choking back tears until she reached the corner. She crossed the street and sobbed all the way across the park.

Wandering the quiet streets, the tears flowed. Grief made it impossible to breathe. She stopped atop the pedestrian bridge and stared blindly at the channel of water below. She loved everything about the lakes—listening to the gentle waves touch the shore, and the gulls that called as they floated lazily overhead. Watching the evening sunlight dance across the water. She'd loved it more with Sam.

She climbed onto the wall separating the sidewalk from the water, and lifted her face toward heaven. She would miss the breeze on her cheeks, the lake aroma. *God, can you make it go quickly? Don't let it drag out. I've done enough damage. I don't want to make it worse.*

"Hey! Lady, what're you doing up there?"

Sam paused, his hand on the bedroom doorknob, and squared his shoulders. He'd stayed hidden in Lizzy's guest room for most of the morning, not wanting to face his sister, but he desperately needed a run. He pulled the door open and narrowly missed colliding with Robert in the hallway.

"Well, well," his brother-in-law said. "We were wondering if we should make sure you were still breathing after your date."

"Still breathing," Sam said, moving on to the kitchen. He could hear Lizzy talking to the children. Great. An audience.

"Unca Sammeeee!" Griffin waved a spoon from his highchair.

"Hey, squirt. Whatcha eatin'?" Looking down at the green slime spread across the tray, he swallowed hard. His nephew's eating disasters had never made him queasy before.

"You look kinda sick, Uncle Sam," Victoria said, frowning up at him from her booster seat at the table. "Does your tummy hurt?"

He ruffled her blonde curls and forced a smile. "A little. Too much partying, I think, Princess."

Lizzy held out a glass of orange juice. "I'd say so. You okay?"

"Sure." He took a long drink.

Her cocked eyebrow said she wasn't buying his response, but she returned to slicing an apple. He'd need to make a quick escape to avoid the third degree about the evening. He drained the glass, and rinsed it out. "Thanks for the juice. I'm going out for a—"

"Not until you call Mom."

"When I get back."

"Sam."

Man, sometimes she sounded exactly like their mother. "What?"

She placed apple slices before each child, wiped her hands, and motioned him out of the kitchen. He rolled his eyes and trudged behind her.

"I assumed you'd be up and out early today to see your lovely date," she said, "but apparently it didn't end well last night."

He shrugged and took a paperweight from the shelf, rolling it around in his hand.

"We tried not to overwhelm her, but she was such fun to talk to. Even the guys thought so. Tell her we'll back off and—"

"It's not that, Lizzy."

"Was it Joey? He can come off pretty squirrelly. Should I call her? I'd be happy to."

"No need."

"But if we did something—"

"It's not you, okay?" he snapped. Her pinched expression made him flinch. "She had a great time with all of you, but she doesn't want to go out again. I wasn't expecting anything different so it's fine. Now, I'm heading out for a run. Tell Mom I'll call her later."

The slamming door was unintentional but satisfying. Without the usual warm up, he started down the block at a rapid pace. All of his siblings did better with dating than he did. He and Jillian met their freshman year at college. Getting married after graduation had seemed the logical next step, but that hadn't ended well. Now he couldn't even get a second date with Marti. Yup, he sure had a way with women.

He'd tossed and turned all night as the evening played nonstop through his mind. Her delight in the wedding ceremony, the surprise on her glowing face as they danced. The pretty blush that stole over her when he held her hand. He'd been as giddy as a kid with his first crush.

He slowed to a walk only halfway to the lake, a hand against the stitch in his side. Could he show his face at the Java Depot again or would that be too awkward? Were they even still friends? She'd looked ready to cry when he said goodnight. Maybe he scared her off by sounding desperate. He hadn't meant to. Suggesting another date seemed like a natural way to end the evening.

Something had changed for her during the evening. Had he said something stupid again? Danced too close? Made one too many bad jokes? Reaching the lakeshore, he stood quietly, hands on his hips. Whatever he'd done, her answer had been clear. Unexpected, but perfectly clear. His job now was to be a gentleman and respect that. He turned away from the lake and plodded back to Lizzy's.

– 35 –

"I'm sorry, but Detective Evans isn't in today. Is there something I can help you with?"

Marti kept her focus on the woman at the desk. *Breathe.* "Would it be possible to call him?"

"What would this be about?"

No going back. "I want to turn myself in." She willed the woman to take her seriously. *Please. Before I change my mind.*

"Have a seat while I call him."

Wobbling toward a bench, Marti sank down and knotted her fingers together. The thunder of her pulse muffled the woman's voice as she talked on the phone, and the footsteps of people walking by. The cold of the metal bench seeped into her skin, into her core. Shivering, she folded her arms tightly, closed her eyes and clenched her jaw, focused on her uneven breathing. In, out. *You have to do this.* In, out. *It's best for everyone.* In, out. *Sam was a wonderful surprise in your life but you know he deserves better.* In. *Come on, breathe in.*

She tried to remember the breeze on her face when she'd stood on the bridge. She hadn't meant to scare anyone; she'd only wanted to soak in her last breaths of freedom. Pretend it was just her and the lake on a normal day. But the fear on the young man's face had shattered the moment.

Warm fingers touched her arm and she jumped. The woman held out a cup of coffee. "I'll take you back to a room where you can wait. Detective Evans will be here shortly."

Marti accepted the cup and followed her to a square room with a single window to the outside. The woman indicated the bathroom down the hall and pulled the door closed behind her. Sipping the coffee, Marti paced, stood at the window, and paced again, forcing her mind to stay blank.

After what seemed like hours, the door opened and her heart stopped. Detective Ben Evans stepped into the room dressed in a starched white shirt and black pants. No longer the charming wedding guest but a man of authority. Who scared her to death.

"Good morning, Marti. Please, have a seat." He took the chair across from her. "I'm surprised to see you."

The unexpected kindness in his eyes brought Sam to mind. She pushed the image away. "I'm grateful that you didn't arrest me in front of everyone last night. It would have embarrassed Sam."

He leaned back in his chair, relaxed yet watchful. "I care too much about my brother to let that happen. Is that why you came in?"

"Yes. And I need to make sure Katie is safe. I'd hoped…" This room was a harsh reminder that anything she'd dreamed of didn't matter anymore.

"You'd hoped?"

She waved the thought away. "The only thing that matters is Katie."

"We found photos of your sister, with Eddy in the background."

She swallowed against a rush of nausea, as she had when she'd first seen them.

"He threatened to hurt her?" he asked.

She nodded. "He said awful things about her, what he'd do to her if I didn't cooperate."

"Is that why you didn't call the police?"

Lowering her head, she nodded again as tears dripped into her lap. "I put her in more danger when I didn't call."

A chair scraped the linoleum, and a moment later a tissue fluttered against her hands. She dried her face and straightened. Officer Ben stood at the window, hands in his pockets. His profile, so similar to Sam's, made her ache. *I'm so sorry, Sam.*

"I've spent some time with the prosecutor," Ben said, turning to face her.

"While Eddy provided a lot of incriminating evidence against you, we see extenuating circumstances."

He returned to the chair. "Here's the deal, Marti. We believe you have enough information to help us put him away for a long time. If you'll work with us, if you'll agree to testify, I think I can make sure no charges are brought against you."

What did that mean? She'd be free for now, but they'd put her away after the trial? "Do I still have to go to jail?"

"Not if you'll help us build the case against him."

"You aren't arresting me?" Hope breathed life into her lungs.

"Will you help us?"

She'd do anything to put Eddy where he belonged. But not if it put Katie in danger. "What if he goes after Katie?"

"We already have a detail on her. She'll be monitored 24/7. We know this guy, what he's capable of, so we're proceeding with great caution."

Hardly comforting. "He's evil. He always said he'd take me with him if he went down. He wouldn't think twice about getting to me through her."

"I agree. He's smart and ruthless. That's why it's taken us this long to build enough of a case to arrest him. With your testimony, I believe we can put him away for a very long time."

Their gazes held, Sam's words ringing through her. *You'll always be safe with Ben around.* She reached into her pocket for the memory card.

Marti stood in warm afternoon sunshine outside the police station, trying to blink sense into what had happened. She wasn't sitting in a jail cell. She wasn't even going to jail, because Ben had worked out a deal long before they met last night. *If you did this, God, thank you.*

She felt twenty years older than the girl Sam picked up for a date yesterday, than the girl who turned him away because she'd be doing jail time. She had a lot of explaining to do, to a lot of people. She shivered and rubbed her arms. She'd probably be homeless again, once she told Jason and Lorna the whole story.

Reality knocked her off-balance. No home meant Kat couldn't live with her. But her baby sister had grown up. It was time to tell her, and everyone, the truth. Kat had Tim to support her. And Gloria. She'd be okay.

A long sigh dropped her shoulders. Her stupidity had finally caught up with her, and now she'd lose everything that mattered. She might as well be in jail.

Trust me.

How? Her fingers curled into fists. *Everything is falling apart. By the time we put Eddy away, I'll have nothing left.*

A palpable warmth, like strong arms holding her tight, encircled her. She leaned into the sensation, breathing in strength and peace. At least she'd have told the truth, and done what she could to save future Andrews and Shareens. Putting one leaden foot in front of another, she turned toward Gloria's. She had a lot to do. Self-pity could wait until tonight on a cot in the shelter.

When the door swung open, Gloria's scowl hit her like a physical slap. Without a word, she stepped back to let Marti step inside.

"Did Katie see the note?"

"Since my name was on it, she handed it to me before going off with Tim, followed by the cop who watches us constantly."

Thank you, Ben. "That's a relief. I found out last night that Eddy is in jail, and he's named me as an accomplice."

"Which you are."

The harsh words stung. "I went to the police station this morning fully expecting to be arrested, but they're more interested in working *with* me to make sure he gets put away for good than putting me in jail."

"Lucky break."

More like a God break. "I'm grateful for how things have turned out."

"What's important is that Katie is safe. I take it the cop will be with us until this is over?"

"Yes. We don't want Eddy to try to get to me through her, so there will be security of some kind around the clock."

"Obviously, while this is going on, there won't be any discussion about Katie moving out."

202

Marti flinched. "Right."

From Gloria's, she made her way slowly to Jason and Lorna's. Even if they hadn't seen her note, she would still come clean. From nearly a block away she could see them sitting in the rocking chairs on the front porch. The urge to run away pulsed through her until her heart pounded crazily against her ribs. *What do I say, God?*

Lorna leaped from her chair, and hurried down the steps before Marti reached the front walk, arms outstretched. "You're home!"

The welcome released the control she'd clung to; she cried as Lorna whispered soothing words and held her tightly.

"All right, now. Let's sit down and you can tell us everything," she said finally, leading Marti up the steps and into the chair beside Jason.

"Hey, kid." He handed her a box of tissues.

Marti mopped her face, unable to stop the short, hiccupping breaths as her heart finally slowed.

Lorna handed her a glass of ice water before pulling another chair close. "Now, tell us what happened, and we'll figure out what to do."

Marti wrestled back another rush of tears, and took a long sip of water. Praying for the right words, she started from the beginning.

An hour later, Jason leaned back and rocked thoughtfully for a moment. "I've known Ben Evans since he started on the force. He's honest, fair, and the hardest working cop I've ever met. You're in good hands with him, Marti."

It was comforting to hear Sam's sentiment echoed by Jason. She twisted the tissue in her hands. "I am so sorry I brought this mess to your doorstep. I don't want my stupid mistakes reflecting badly on you."

"We raised five kids, four of them boys," Lorna said. "We've dealt with greater messes than this."

Doubtful.

"You need time to rest after such a scare," she added, patting Marti's arm. "Why don't you go lie down for a bit. We'll call you for dinner."

Jason held out her apartment key. "You'll need this."

Gratitude swelled against her ribs as she remained in place.

"You heard the boss," he added gruffly. "Go on up and take a nap. You look like death warmed over."

She took the key, but when she opened her mouth, he waved her off. "Go. Now. We'll talk more at dinner."

The stairs seemed a mile long as she returned to the apartment she'd never expected to see again. The sense of having dodged a bullet made her weak, but facing Eddy in a trial set her nerves screaming. Yet worse than all of that was what she had to do tomorrow. She had to tell Sam.

– 36 –

After two long days away from the Depot, and Marti, Sam finished moping. If he didn't want to lose her completely, he needed to go back and act like nothing had changed. Because really, nothing had. Except they'd had a date better than he could ever have imagined. And he'd realized how much he wanted her in his life, even after she rejected him.

Approaching the familiar shop, his steps slowed as he rehearsed how he wanted to act, what he should say. What he shouldn't say. A few feet from the door, he stopped short. Sunlight pouring in the windows highlighted Marti's gleaming dark hair where she sat at his usual table. With Ben.

He sidled back, hoping she hadn't seen him, although her focus was centered on his brother. His sneaky, back-stabbing brother. She spoke earnestly, hands spread wide then clasped on the table. Her shoulders drooped as she shook her head.

Ben spoke and she shrugged, tipping her head the way she did when they studied the Bible together, eyes narrowed as she bit her lip.

The world pounded in rhythm to his pulse. Had she known Ben before the wedding? Was *he* the reason she didn't want to be more than friends? He blinked hard against the haze filling his vision, his thoughts running rampant. Maybe that's why Ben had stayed away from her for most of the evening, so nobody would suspect. Especially him. But that made no sense. None of this did.

Marti and Ben stood. She wiped her face and nodded to something he said. When he put a hand on her shoulder, she smiled weakly. She closed her eyes briefly before setting her shoulders and nodding more firmly.

Spinning away, Sam sprinted down the block, then down another, dodging cars as he crossed busy streets. Ben had moved in on the only woman to catch his attention since the divorce. The woman he'd thought he'd come to know. Lungs burning, he ran from the coffee shop, and Marti. And his lousy brother who'd always seemed above that sort of thing. And his stupid, lonely life.

Finally, unable to pull in a solid breath, he stopped, bent over as he panted. He wasn't the only one who saw how special she was. They'd had one real date. That's all. He was simply a friend who visited the coffee shop.

Approaching his townhouse, he stopped. Jillian and her daughter played in the yard, chasing bubbles that sparkled and danced around them. It should have been his family. Jill threw her head back in a familiar way as she laughed. Her daughter's dark curls mimicked her mother's, chubby arms spread wide as she squealed and raced unsteadily after the bubbles.

Lungs still burning, he continued toward them. He'd known Jill would be a good mother, despite her bad choices. The little one seemed happy and healthy, throwing herself into her mother's arms in a fit of giggles. Ryan, the idiot, had given them up.

When Jillian saw him, she stopped tickling her daughter, waiting for him. Her gaze narrowed. "You okay?"

"Rough morning."

Getting to her feet, she hoisted her daughter in her arms. "Adrienne, you remember my…friend, Sam. Can you say hello to him?"

She leaned into her mother's shoulder and stuck a thumb in her mouth. Sam forced a smile at the beautiful child. "Hello, Adrienne."

When she buried her face in Jillian's neck, Jillian tickled her gently. "That's not polite, sweetheart."

"She's wise not to be too accepting of strange men."

"You're hardly strange."

"Up for debate. I need to grab a few things from the house. You guys keep playing." He jogged up the front steps and felt oddly intrusive entering his own home. He'd grab some T-shirts and— The framed photo on the bookshelf stopped him. Unable to resist, he picked it up. Marti's face glowed, those big brown eyes sparkling at him. Not the expression of someone seeing his brother.

"I'll bet you two had fun at the wedding." Jillian's voice came from the entryway.

He nodded and continued to the bedroom where he stuffed the picture frame and clean clothes into a duffle bag. He'd rather leave the photo here but Jillian would immediately have questions.

She and Adrienne were in the kitchen when he emerged. "That's it for me. You two have everything you need?"

"We're great. Thanks." She looked over her daughter's head, biting the corner of her lip. "I have three interviews set up next week. I'm hoping I can be out of here soon."

He slung the bag over his shoulder. "No rush. There's plenty of room at Lizzy's." And plenty of chaos to keep him from dwelling on Marti and Ben. "I'll pray that the interviews go great. Keep me posted."

"I will. Thank you."

Striding down the walk, a pained breath escaped. "Two strikes, Lord. Not interested in trying again anytime soon."

No need to swing and miss a third time.

Marti wiped down the table where she and Ben had talked this morning. Where Sam always sat. He hadn't been in to the Depot since their date, and probably wouldn't be back. She flinched at the stab in her heart. She might as well have cut off her arm. Sam had become her best friend, her safe place. The reason she'd learned to smile again.

She forced herself to move to the next table. Ben's visit had been a chilling reminder that her life wasn't her own anymore. But really, it hadn't been since Eddy appeared. As long as she gave the police what they wanted, Katie stayed safe, and she stayed out of jail. Ben had been silent as they looked at each photo on the memory card, while she'd prayed it was enough. When he left the room with the card, he took her last defense against Eddy. What if it weren't enough? Even his kindness when he returned with a fresh cup of coffee hadn't stopped the tremor that even now shook her core.

So she would meet with him, the prosecutor, and anyone else who wanted information from her, until they finally went to trial. Whenever they summoned, she'd have to go. Whatever they asked, she'd better have an answer. No, her life was no longer her own.

She retrieved her trusty broom and dustpan from the storeroom, and a corner of her mouth lifted when Sam's voice came to mind. "You handle that broom like a pro." Stunned that someone so handsome would talk to her, she'd probably sounded like an idiot in her response. Her smile deepened then faded. The start of an amazing, and far too short, friendship.

Sweeping every corner of the nearly empty shop, she replayed this morning's unexpected conversation with Ben. Details he needed about Eddy's contacts, descriptions of how he'd run the business. A request for her to look at mug shots.

"Have you told Sam yet?" he'd asked.

Shaking her head, she'd asked Ben not to tell him yet and he'd agreed. Sort of.

"I won't tell him, Marti, but if he asks, I'll be honest."

She'd stood looking at him through tears, her heart breaking as she nodded. She couldn't expect him to lie to his own brother.

His gentle hand on her shoulder had brought little comfort. "You can trust him, Marti."

To hate her forever. He'd never understand her involvement with the very people he despised most. Never. Ben had urged her to do it soon, even providing Sam's address on a slip of paper. She'd slipped it into her apron and nodded.

Returning the broom to the storeroom, she stood still for a long moment, her palm against the scribbled connection to Sam. If she listened hard, she could hear the remnants of her life crashing down around her. A wrong step and so many people would suffer. She needed a sane voice in this craziness.

A face came to mind, flooding her with hope. Yes. That's who she needed.

Elbows resting on his knees, Sam propped his chin on his knotted hands and sighed. He'd finished the cradle this morning, to Jimmy's delight, accepted the team's accolades with nodded thanks, then escaped the shop for a walk. He hadn't planned to stop by Faith Church, but here he sat in the empty sanctuary.

Two days after seeing Ben and Marti, and he was still angry. At them. At life. At everything. Coming here seemed useless. He hadn't been through the doors since the trial. Glad to be back on speaking terms with God, he could thank Marti for getting him back into the Bible, but he'd avoided returning to church. The bitter confusion that muddied his thoughts should have kept him away, yet here he sat.

"Sam Evans." Pastor Joel settled into the pew ahead of him. "Good to see you."

Sam shook his hand. "You too."

"What brings you by on such a beautiful morning?"

"I was out for a walk and thought I'd stop in."

"Have time for coffee in my office? I have nothing on my calendar for the next hour. Love to get caught up."

Conversation sounded exhausting, and he was lousy company. "Sure." Joel had touched base occasionally over the past year. He'd been grateful for the persistence.

Over cups of church coffee, they shared thoughts on how the Minnesota Twins were playing, and their picks for the upcoming football season. Joel asked about his siblings, but not about Jillian. Sam didn't bring her up. Very soon she'd be out of his house, and his life, and he could pretend the strange event never happened.

Sitting in the familiar office, where he'd spent hours working through the pain of the divorce, Sam sidestepped discussing his personal life, but Joel gently persisted with open-ended questions that diffused the simmering anger.

"I'm glad you attended Heather's wedding. What did you enjoy most?"

Dancing, talking, laughing. With Marti. "It was great having the family all together."

"I can imagine the grief you got from your brothers about bringing a date."

He tasted the flare of anger. "Doesn't matter. Especially since my date is now dating my brother."

Joel's eyebrows flew up. "Really? That seems out of character for your family."

"I would have agreed until I saw it myself."

A gentle knock at the door interrupted, then the secretary popped her head in. "Joel, your eleven o'clock is here."

He nodded at her, then returned his attention to Sam. "Sorry. How about we continue this conversation tomorrow?"

Sam stood, needing a run. More conversation would only create more anger. "Let me get back to you."

The gentle perception behind Joel's wire-rimmed glasses said he wasn't fooled. In the open doorway, Sam extended his hand. "Thanks for your time, Joel. It was great to reconnect."

Joel's firm handshake lingered a moment, requiring Sam to meet his gaze. "It certainly was. I hope we can talk again soon." He released his grip and grinned. "Sorry for the bad coffee."

Sam chuckled. "Nothing beats the Java Depot dark roast. I'll bring some in."

"Now that's coffee I can get excited about." Joel looked past Sam and smiled. "Speaking of the Java Depot."

Sam turned and encountered the somber doe-eyes that had haunted his dreams.

"Hello, Sam," Marti said quietly.

− 37 −

Her mouth desert dry, Marti wasn't sure how she formed the greeting.

"Hey." Sam's eyes were frosty.

It broke her heart that she'd hurt him. She stiffened her legs against the tremble, and turned to Joel. "Am I interrupting?"

"Not at all. Sam and I were getting caught up after far too long."

"Well, I'll let you get to it," Sam said. "Thanks again, Joel."

She stared numbly after him as her heart slowed its pounding.

"Come on in, Marti," Joel invited. She followed on wooden legs and settled at the table. He took a seat across from her. "I'm glad to see you."

She cleared her throat. "Thanks for seeing me so quickly."

"My pleasure." He offered a gentle smile. "That seemed a bit uncomfortable with Sam."

Humiliating. Sam couldn't get away fast enough. She clasped her hands in her lap and deflated. "That's why I'm here."

"I see."

Lips pursed, she prayed for the right words. "Remember when I told you I was a drug dealer?"

He nodded.

"Now I'm the main witness for the prosecution. But I don't know if I can do it." She wanted to wake up from this nightmare. "I'm scared."

"Are you being threatened?"

"Not since they put him in jail. I'm afraid something will happen to Katie

211

if I testify. If something happens to me, where does that leave her? What if they go after all the people who've been so kind to me?" The lump in her throat choked her. "I couldn't stand it if more people got hurt because of me."

"What does Sam have to say about it?"

She bit her lip. "I haven't told him. Any of it. He wouldn't understand. After what happened to Andrew, he hates drug dealers and everyone associated with them."

"You don't think he'd want to help?"

Sam's declaration to rid the neighborhood of people like Eddy, his anger and agitation, had all made his intentions perfectly, painfully clear. "No," she whispered. "I don't."

"That doesn't sound like the Sam Evans I know. I hope you'll change your mind and let him make this journey with you, Marti. In the meantime, I'll do everything I can to help you."

"But if you get involved…"

He leaned back with a smile. "Our God is far more powerful than any drug dealer or defense lawyer. God and I will be right beside you every step of the way. We'll do this together, okay?"

The calm assurance, the warmth of his expression relaxed her shoulders. "Thank you." *Thank you, God.*

With the dress draped neatly over her arm, Marti stepped into GPS and greeted Tiffani, listening for Sam's voice. Desire and fear of seeing him played tug-of-war inside.

"Hey, Marti! Great to see you." Tiffani came around the desk and hugged her. "What's in the bag?"

"My dress from the wedding. Is Vanessa here?"

Tiffani's charcoal-lined eyes went wide. "You can't give it away! It was made for you."

"I'll never have another place to wear it, so I might as well let someone else enjoy it." Keeping it would only serve as a reminder of the night she'd been exposed as the fraud she was.

Kiera came down the stairs, arms loaded with colored folders. "Marti! How nice to see you." As she approached, she wiggled perfect brows. "I hear the wedding was amazing."

"It was lovely, but now that Cinderella's back in the real world, she wants someone else to have the chance to wear this."

"You're sure you want to part with it?"

"That's what I said," Tiffani said, returning to her chair. "It won't look half as good on anyone else."

Marti smoothed a crease from the bag. She didn't want to part with it, but she didn't need a painful reminder of what could have been, in a different life. She needed to forget any of it happened. She cleared her throat. "Thank you for all your help. I couldn't have pulled it off without all of you."

"You're more than welcome. We had a blast, didn't we?" Kiera set the folders on the corner of Tiffani's desk, wrapped an arm around Marti's shoulders, and directed her toward the stairs. "Come on. I want to show you where we keep consignment items for the women using our services. Your dress will make someone shine like it did you."

She led Marti up the staircase and along a short hallway. In a brightly lit room at the end, she waved her hand toward several round racks of clothing. "Welcome to the GPS Boutique."

Signage atop one round rack stated "Business Casual," another "Professional." A third rack in the back held dresses, skirts, blouses, and jackets. Mirrors placed around the room reflected bright colors and patterns. Men's clothing lined one side—dark suits, white and pastel shirts, a rack of ties.

"Wow. This is better than the thrift store."

"Many of the women who come here have never owned a suit, or any clothing appropriate for an interview. This way they can wear something that gives them confidence and makes them look great without costing anything."

Kiera took the dress and urged Marti to browse. Arms now strangely empty, she wandered the room, admiring the like-new clothing. She fingered a turquoise necklace on the backwall. Maybe wearing something more presentable would have helped when she was job hunting.

Get over yourself. A new outfit won't make you any smarter. And it won't make you different from who you are. She turned toward Kiera. "I think this is a great idea. Your program offers so many amazing services."

The redhead smiled as she attached a tag to Marti's beautiful dress. "Thanks. God is using us to change the lives of His people in this community. It's super exciting." She hung the dress on the rack. "Marti, one thing I've learned is that who we think we are is often very different from who we really are. We let other people speak untruth over us, and eventually we accept it as actual truth."

The beautiful dress hadn't made her worthy of Sam or his family. The real Marti had been hiding beneath yards of beautiful material. Makeup only masked the ugliness of her past. "For some of us, it *is* the truth," she managed. "I've got to run. Thanks again for all your help."

Without waiting for a response, she hurried out of the room, down the stairs and out the front door. God loved her. That would have to be enough. The truth followed her all the way home.

"Who is it?" Jimmy's question came from behind him.

Sam glanced over his shoulder, sanding block paused on the board. "Who's what?"

"It's got to be a female that has you this out of sorts."

"I'm not out of sorts." The scraping of sandpaper filled the silence.

Jimmy settled against the workbench, arms folded. "I'm not leaving until I know what's going on."

Sam inspected the front of the drawer, then set it down with a thump. "It's nothing you need to worry about."

"Ah. So if it's a secret, it must be a female and it must be serious."

"We only spent infrequent time together." Every day for lunch. And Sunday morning walks. And dancing.

Jimmy huffed. "Nice plan, Mr. Smooth. Wouldn't want her to think you're interested."

He'd tried to make his interest clear. He stared blindly at the drawer. She'd been so beautiful at the wedding, and he'd thought he was the luckiest guy there.

"Hello?"

He snapped back to the present. "What?"

"You're mooning over her like it's your first crush." His eyes narrowed. "If I had to guess, which apparently I do, I'd say we're talking about Gus."

Lips pressed in a firm line, he shrugged. "Her real name is Marti. And she's interested in someone else now."

"How do you know that?"

"I saw them together." He worked the clench from his jaw, and made a few halfhearted strokes with the block. "The other day."

Jimmy crossed one ankle over the other. "What aren't you telling me, Sammy?"

The image of Ben with his hand on Marti's shoulder had burned into his brain. "The other guy is Ben."

Jimmy released a loud snort of disbelief. "You think *Ben* moved in on her?"

"So it seems."

"No way. That's the dumbest thing I've ever heard. Of everyone I know, Ben is the last person who would do that. Especially to his own brother." He frowned. "Unless he didn't know you were into her?"

"Oh, he knew." He'd turned his back and Ben swept Marti away to charm her outside on a star-lit night. A man in uniform, even while not wearing it, always won the girl.

Jimmy silently studied Sam into a squirm. "That's nuts. We both know that's not how he works."

He'd never considered that Ben would do that, but Marti was special enough to catch anyone's interest. "I know it doesn't make sense," he admitted, rubbing the back of his neck roughly, "but I saw it. And she was clear in telling me she wasn't interested."

"Then there's another explanation. Either you misunderstood her *or* what you saw. You need to talk to Ben, and to her too. And I need you to stop wrecking products and get your head on straight, or I'll start docking you for all the boards we have to toss."

Jimmy was right. One way or another, he needed to resolve this. Sulking hadn't accomplished anything. "Fine. I'll talk to him."

"Sooner rather than later, okay? I need you focused so we can get the Meyer order done on time."

"Got it." He needed to start pulling his weight again. While he might feel like *dead* weight, he owed it to Jimmy not to act like it, and he owed it to himself to have it out with Ben so he could move on. With or without Martina.

Marti stood on the sidewalk, the slip of paper rattling in her grasp. She could do this. She had to. Sam deserved the truth. Shoulders set, she went to the front door, missing the doorbell on her first try. *I can do this. God help me do this.*

The door swung open and she blinked in surprise. A pretty woman smiled back at her, an adorable toddler on her hip.

"Hi. Can I help you?"

"Oh. I, uh…I thought Sam Evans lived here." She backed away. "I must have the wrong address. Sorry."

The woman stepped out onto the step. "This is Sam's home. I'm Jillian Evans."

Marti's mouth opened and closed before she forced a smile. "Hi. I'm Marti. Gustafson. A friend of Sam's. Is he home?"

"Not at the moment. I expect him back soon. Oh, there's my phone." She thrust the child into Marti's arms. "Could you hold her a moment. I need to grab that call."

Digging the cell phone out of her pocket, she turned away to answer, leaving the towhead with Marti. The child was beautiful, with thick hair and green eyes. Chewing on the plastic giraffe, she paused long enough to smile at Marti and reveal perfect tiny teeth.

Sam had a child. And a woman, his wife, living with him. Marti swayed against the railing, tightening her arms so she wouldn't drop the toddler. But hadn't he said he was divorced? She searched their conversations. So he'd gotten back with his ex and never mentioned it? Or that he had a *child*?

The woman returned her phone to her pocket and reached for the baby.

"Thank you. I've been waiting for a call about a potential job." She smiled. "Turns out it was Sam."

Marti nodded dumbly.

"Is there a message I can give him?"

"No." She moved backwards down the steps. Nothing appropriate. "I just stopped by to say hi. Nice to meet you." She hurried away, fighting angry tears. She came to reveal her secret, and met his face-to-face. That changed everything.

– 38 –

"Hey, bro. Where've you been?" Ben waited at the concession stand. His quizzical expression held no twinge of guilt.

"Busy." Sam focused on stretching. Why hadn't he cancelled the run?

"Too busy to return calls? If Lizzy hadn't said you're still alive, I'd have an APB out on you. You don't usually drop out of sight like that."

"A lot going on." Maybe once they were moving, he'd relax. "Let's go."

They ran in silence for the first half mile. Never one for small talk, it was impossible to read anything into Ben's calm demeanor.

"What do you hear about Lauren's job?" Sam asked finally.

"She still likes it," Ben said. "She said she didn't realize how much the office politics were affecting her until she left."

Another half mile in silence. "So, still seeing that girl you brought to the wedding?"

Ben glanced sideways. "She's my partner's sister. Gorgeous but has a boyfriend."

That explained him moving in on Marti. "Ahh." *Ask him.* "Anything new at work?" he asked instead.

"Crazy busy getting ready for trial. I told you we brought Eddy in, didn't I? The elusive Eduardo Victor Pantino."

Sam stopped. "You did? When?"

"A few days before the wedding. Sorry. I thought I told you. We're building one heck of a case against him, thanks to our star witness."

He grabbed Ben in a hug. "Man, that's the best news ever! Great job, Detective Evans."

"Thanks." Ben stepped back. He'd never accepted accolades well. "But I can't celebrate until he's put away permanently."

"How'd you track down your witness?"

Ben started walking. "She sort of fell into my lap."

"Can't argue with that." His feet itched to run or dance, celebrate somehow. "She's got enough on him for a conviction?"

"Plenty."

He made a sound of disgust. "She must have been in pretty deep to have that kind of info. You'll put her away too, right?"

"We gave her immunity."

"What? Every single one of them needs to go down, Ben."

"There are extenuating circum—"

Sam waved a hand sharply. "Don't bother. She might not have run the outfit, but if she's got enough to put him away, she's as guilty as he is."

Ben focused straight ahead. "I know that's how it sounds, Sam, but it's more complicated."

Whatever. Her sob story didn't matter. Anybody with that kind of inside information had to be as guilty as Eddy for Andrew and Shareen's deaths.

"Don't go soft, Ben," he ordered. "We have to get these people off the streets. Away from our kids. Let me help. I'll talk to Andrew's parents, kids at school, whatever you need." He stopped. "Now's your chance, Benjamin. Throw everything you've got at all of them."

Ben walked a few steps ahead, then turned slowly, torment clouding his face.

"Ben? What's the matter?"

His stoic brother set his hands on his hips and he kicked at a rock. Finally he lifted his head. "You need to know something, Sammy. About the witness."

Sam held his hands up to stop him. "Don't want to hear it. The less I know, the better. I'm not sure I can be trusted with how I'd react if I saw her."

"Sam…"

Gazes locked, a knot formed in his gut, icy cold, edged with fear. "It's not...not one of...us, right? I mean, it can't be Jessie or Lauren. And I know it's not Lizzy." He shook his head again. *What a stupid thought.* "That leaves Joey, and despite some of the crowd he hangs with, I'd stake my life on—"

"It's Marti."

After a pause, he burst out laughing. "Oh, right. Marti! She's no more part of Eddy's world than I am. The poor kid's too busy trying to keep her head above water." His laughter died when Ben didn't react. "C'mon, man. Marti isn't the type to get involved with someone like that."

Ben turned away and Sam blinked quickly to stop the sudden spinning in his head. His brother wasn't much of a joker. But if it wasn't a joke... "She can't be your witness, Ben. That doesn't make sense."

"She is. She was involved—accidentally, but involved."

"That's ridiculous!" He stalked a few feet away and then returned, ready to pound his brother for the accusation. "You are way off-base, pal."

Jaw clenched, Ben's gaze remained steady. "I'm sorry, Sam. When you first introduced us at the wedding, I knew immediately. Remember me saying I'd talked to a witness in the ER who disappeared? She was in such tough shape then, we only talked for a few minutes."

Nausea surged. He swallowed hard. "What happened to her?"

"Eddy beat her to within an inch of her life. If the neighbor hadn't broken down the door, she'd be dead."

An image flashed before him—her attempts to cover up the bruises on her face, the bandage on her arm. Blood pounded loudly in his ears. This made no sense. She was no more a drug dealer than him. She couldn't have hidden that fact all this time.

"She wanted to tell you herself, Sammy. She asked me not to, and I said I wouldn't, but that I also wouldn't lie to you. Go talk to her, Sam. Hear her out."

"You bet I'll talk to her." He jabbed a finger at his brother. "You'd better be ready to apologize when I come back."

Ben's revelation chased him back to his car. There had to be a decent explanation behind this. Marti wasn't a drug dealer. His stomach churned at the thought of her frail body taking a beating. He'd kill the scumbag himself if he got within reach.

His car lurched to a stop in Jason's driveway off the alley. *God, give me the right words.* Trudging up the stairs to her apartment, he focused on slowing his racing heart. She'd laugh at such an absurd accusation, and then they'd go see Ben for that apology.

The door swung open before he could knock. Still in her Java Depot apron, there were dark circles under her eyes, her face pale and drawn. Her silence scared him more than Ben's words. She stepped back to let him in, then moved into the kitchen area. Behind the counter.

Hers wasn't the face of a criminal. He couldn't fall for someone who ruined lives. So why couldn't he form words to repeat Ben's accusation? "Why did you say no to a date after the wedding?"

Her brow lifted, as if she'd expected a different question. "Because I'm not your type."

"What's my type?"

Her chin trembled. "Beautiful and smart and worthy of someone like you."

"That describes you."

"No," she said, sadness in that one word.

At one time he'd thought *he* wasn't good enough. "Ben told me about the case he's built against that drug lord, Eddy."

She stood silent and still, head down.

"He said the strangest thing today, that they've built a really strong case based on their star witness. You." He gave a brittle laugh. "I told him that was ridiculous. You'd have told me if it were true."

In the oppressive silence, hope shattered at his feet.

"I said there's no way you'd ever know someone like Eddy. And if you did, you'd have said something after hearing me talk about the kids he killed." He was babbling, to stave off her response. "You're not the kind of person who'd get involved with scum like him." *Please tell me I'm wrong.*

Leaning heavily against the counter, she deflated. "Not intentionally," she said finally.

Fire surged through his veins. Years of fighting to put the man behind bars, of watching his drugs pick off some of the brightest kids. Of clawing his way out of his own addiction. And right under his nose— What an idiot! Anchoring his feet, he crossed his arms.

"I've wanted to tell you, to explain—"

He stopped her pitiful words. "You've had plenty of chances." The tears in her eyes fueled his anger and stabbed his heart. "There's nothing you could say that would bring Andrew or Shareen back. What about all the other kids hooked on your drugs? The ones that won't beat their addiction? How many other families have to suffer because of the greed of people like you?"

He paced, his chest constricting. "How do you sleep at night, *Gus*? Don't you hear the agony of what your drugs are doing to these kids? To our neighborhoods?"

Face creased with pain, large tears streamed down her cheeks.

"I could have been another casualty except I had a dad who dragged me to treatment. I'm one of many whose lives have been ruined by people like Eddy. Like *you*. But so long as you people get your money, you don't care."

He was such a rotten judge of character, he hadn't recognized a drug dealer shared his life. He spun away, pinching the bridge of his nose to calm the roiling emotions. Questions swirled in a chaotic mess. Why hadn't she told him? Why hadn't Ben? She'd pretended to be someone she wasn't, and hooked in almost every member of his family. What was he supposed to do now?

"I've been meeting with Ben. I'm going to testify."

He spun back and jabbed a finger at her. "You got that right. And you'd better not try to protect him."

She jerked back, horror on her white face. "I would never protect him. I want him to rot in hell." She turned away, fingers pressed to her mouth. "It's where we both belong."

Sam's heart lurched at her words. How could this have happened? Who was she? *God, what do I do now?* He strode to the door and shut it firmly behind him, then stood for a long moment on the landing, breathing deeply through his nose. The elation he'd felt at Ben's initial news had morphed into such chaos he didn't know what to do, how to respond.

Her muffled sobs tore at him, and he reached for the doorknob, then yanked his hand back and charged down the steps. Closed in his car, he cradled his head in his hands, tears in his eyes. Images burned—her shy smile when they'd first met, excitement when she read the Bible, laughter over dripping ice cream. Her slender frame in an orange jumpsuit behind bars.

He started the car and drove away, his heart in splinters.

Marti spent the first hour after Sam slammed out of her life emptying her despair into the toilet. Then she cried until the sun set, snuffing the light out of her life. She could only hope the searing pain in her chest would make her heart stop beating.

If only Eddy had succeeded in killing her. She curled on her side, fists pressed over her heart. How could she live with this guilt? Knowing her silence allowed his empire to flourish at her own kitchen table? Seeing Sam's grief even now about the kids he thought he should have saved. He'd been one of them too. All because she kept quiet when she should have run to the police the moment she knew the truth.

She ground her knuckles against her eyes. Knowing how much Sam hated the people responsible for Andrew and Shareen's death, she'd been terrified to own up to what she'd done. If she had, he might still have walked away, but it wouldn't have been after stomping on her heart. The angry betrayal in his words had seared into her like a bolt of lightning.

Even the beating from Eddy hadn't hurt like this. She buried her face in her pillow. She'd have preferred Sam threw a punch; she would recover from that. She never would from this.

− 39 −

Marti dragged herself into work the next morning, bleary-eyed and broken-hearted. If Sam didn't believe her story, why would a jury? If someone who knew her couldn't see the truth, strangers wouldn't be able to either. Testifying would be a waste of time, and then Eddy would kill her.

"Whoa. You look awful," Ibrahim commented as she trudged past.

If it were even half as bad as she felt, it must be ugly. She slipped the apron strap over her head. "Rough night."

"I know you don't drink, so it's not a hangover."

"It's a life hangover."

"Huh?"

"Never mind." The after-effects of terrible choices.

"You and Sam get in a fight?"

His name made her flinch. "He found out the truth about me. It didn't sit well."

"He's not good enough for you, Marti."

Dear Ibrahim. He was a true friend, even knowing her story. "You're sweet. Okay, I need to think about something else for a while."

"Can you fix the lock on the back door? It's so loose, it wouldn't take much to kick it in."

"Sure. Anything else need fixing?"

He grinned from his post behind the beverage station. "I'll bet we can come up with a few things. Make the ol' boss man happy."

The list of fixit items kept her mind occupied and her hands busy throughout the morning. She knew Sam wouldn't step foot in the Depot again, but she couldn't help looking up every time the bells jangled, nor could she stop the drop of her heart when it wasn't him. Each time, she'd set her shoulders and focus her thoughts elsewhere. Anywhere but on Sam Evans.

The days dragged on until finally Saturday arrived. She desperately needed to spend time at church.

"Marti!" Vanessa's voice rang out across the crowded Faith Church lobby. She weaved through the people, her tummy leading the way. "It's great to see you."

Marti mustered a smile that felt foreign. Days of slogging through life since Sam stormed out had left her exhausted. If spending time in worship didn't revive her, nothing would. "Hi. You here alone?"

"Kurt will be here soon. He met a couple of kids for an early supper. Come sit with me. I want to get caught up."

Unable to muster the energy to refuse, Marti followed. They settled in a back pew where Vanessa chattered about River House, and the new classes starting at GPS.

"I'm thrilled that they asked you to lead the carpentry class with Sam." She pressed a hand to Marti's arm, blonde eyebrows lifted. "Things must be going well with you two?"

Marti shook her head. "I won't be helping with the class."

"Oh, no. What happened?"

She blinked against the burn of regret. "My life."

The worship leader's voice broke between them. "Hey, everyone. Great to see you tonight. How about we do some worshipping together?"

"Come on." Vanessa took her hand and pulled her from the sanctuary, leading her to a quiet corner in the lobby. "Tell me what happened."

Marti's mouth went dry. Though she'd promised herself to be upfront with everyone, losing Vanessa's friendship would be the ultimate blow. Mustering courage from her depleted resources, she started at the beginning.

"I never figured someone like Sam would come into my life," she admitted when she finished. "Not someone so good and kind. I should have told him right away, but I couldn't find the words."

"When did he find out?"

"A couple days ago. Not from me, unfortunately. I went to his house to tell him, but apparently he's living with his ex." Something he never bothered to share. If she weren't so exhausted, she'd be angry.

Vanessa sat back, wide-eyed. "That's news to me. Are you sure?"

"Very. Then, when I saw him coming up the stairs to my apartment, I knew Ben had told him."

"He didn't take it well?"

"Not that I expected him to." She wiped a stray tear. "I'm everything he hates. I'm one of 'them.' He still hurts so much over Andrew and Shareen."

Vanessa sat quietly for a moment. "Richard told me Sam took responsibility for their deaths and can't let go, no matter what others have told him. He blames himself as much as he blames Eddy."

She reached for Marti's hands. "You say you were too stupid to see who Eddy really was, but how could you? I wouldn't have either. We trust people, Marti. That's not a bad thing. Sometimes they take advantage of us, but you know what?" She squeezed Marti's fingers. "I'd rather endure that on occasion than close myself off to the people God places in my path that maybe I can help, or who can help me."

Marti soaked in the earnest words, turning them over in her heart. All her life, every time she'd trusted someone, it blew up in her face. Except lately—Jason, Vanessa, Kiera. Even Sam. Maybe she'd trusted the wrong people.

"I get why you were afraid to tell Sam. I didn't tell Kurt for a long time that I was partly responsible for the accident that took my sister and brother." She sighed. "After I told him, I realized that by hiding from the truth, I'd wasted a lot of time that could have been spent working through things together."

"It's too late for Sam," Marti said. "He can't get past this."

"It's never too late for God. Oh, there's Kurt. Can we share your story with him? He knows a lot of people in the community who would be very happy to help put Eddy away."

Marti watched him approach. She trusted Vanessa, so she would risk trusting her husband. As she told her story again, the burden on her heart seemed to lighten. Maybe she didn't have to make this journey alone after all.

Climbing the stairs to her apartment, Marti managed a tired smiled. The hours spent with Vanessa and Kurt had loosened the band around her throat that had formed when Sam walked out of her life. Their prayer over her had reminded her where to put her focus. Sam would never forgive her, but she could learn to forgive herself. Both Kurt and Vanessa had assured her God would show her how. Even so, she would grieve Sam's absence from her life.

As she slid her key into the lock, nearly transparent letters on the window caught her eye, and her breath caught.

DON'T TESTIFY

It seemed to be written with soap, subtle but there. She scanned the yard, the alley, Jason's house. No movement, nothing out of place. She scurried into the apartment, and slammed and locked the door behind her. Heart pounding, she grabbed a kitchen knife and checked the closets and under her bed, closing the blinds on every window as she moved through the apartment. Returning to the living room, she pushed the couch in front of the door.

She perched on a kitchen stool and set the knife nearby. How long had the message been there? She shivered. Which of Eddy's 'associates' had written it? How did they know where she lived?

Don't testify. She fought a surge of hysteria. Eddy knew where Katie lived. Did they leave a message there too? She pulled out her phone. No, Gloria would call the minute something like that happened. She dialed Ben's cell phone.

"Don't touch it," he instructed. "I'll be over shortly. Keep the door locked. I'll call you when I get there so you can let me in."

Marti paced, thoughts tumbling in a panicked mess. Ben had the information they needed to put Eddy away. She didn't have to be at the trial. She wouldn't be if it put Katie in more danger, but then she'd go to jail for not cooperating. She'd do that if it kept Katie safe.

The ring of her phone made her jump. Ben had arrived. He snapped photos of the warning before joining her at the counter. "To be honest, we've been waiting for him to do something like this."

Her mouth dropped open. "You could have warned me."

"We've had people watching you," he said.

She blinked, unnerved. She'd been clueless. "Well, that didn't stop Eddy's people from finding me."

"You haven't exactly been in hiding, although that might be worth considering now."

"No! Not unless Katie comes with me." No way would she hide and leave her sister in plain sight.

"I don't think it's necessary," he said, "yet. I'll make sure Eddy and his attorney know we'll add witness tampering if either of you are threatened again. I'll also remind them we already have the photos and your taped testimony in hand. Hurting you or Katie will only strengthen our case."

Comforting. Sort of. "Focus on keeping Katie safe. I can take care of myself."

Ben raised an eyebrow.

She flushed. If she were prepared. Maybe.

"You've talked to Sam, I take it," he said.

More like Sam talked at me. Loudly. "Sort of. I wish I'd been brave enough to tell him sooner. Sorry it put you in an awkward situation."

"Goes with the job."

She drooped. "He'll hate me forever over this."

"He'll be angry for a while," Ben conceded, "but he'll get over it."

"Not in my lifetime."

Marti cleared off the table, grateful the morning rush had ended. She barely had the energy to be upright let alone keep pace with so many customers. When the line had grown to eight, Jason emerged from the back to help her ring. Afraid she'd burst into tears if she looked at him, she'd nodded her thanks.

On the next table sat a full mug of coffee beside a clean napkin. Huh. Maybe the customer had been called away before getting to enjoy their drink. Beneath the cup sat a folded slip of paper. She carried the cup toward the back to dump it out, unfolding the note as she went. She barely heard the cup hit the tile, or felt the liquid that splashed against her legs as she stared at the words.

WE KNOW WHAT YOU DID TO KATY.

"Marti? What happened?"

She lifted her head slowly and encountered Jason's frown. "What?"

"You're white as a sheet. And you're wet." Jason's words came in slow motion.

"Oh." What was that strange buzzing? "I dropped... I'll clean..."

"Ibrahim, can you get this? I'm taking Marti to the office."

He propelled her through the swinging doors and settled her at his desk, pushing her head down. "Stay like that," he ordered, then left the room, returning with a bottle of water. "Better?"

The buzzing had stopped, but her head felt heavy, her thoughts thick.

"Drink this."

She obeyed, her fingers numb. He helped her for the first few sips, then dragged a chair over and sat in front of her. Elbows on his knees, he leaned toward her. "What's going on?"

What *was* going on? She couldn't feel her own body.

Jason pried open her left hand and took the crumpled piece of paper. He read it, frowning. "What does this mean? What happened to Katie?"

Feeling rushed back like a summer storm, thoughts and emotions crashing in chaos. Someone knew what happened with Katie. Who? How?

"Marti!"

Her attention snapped to Jason and she put a hand to her mouth. "Sick..." He thrust the waste-basket in front of her, and she released what little she had inside. Other people cried or yelled when they got a shock like this. She threw up. It was getting old. Dropping back in the chair, she lifted the water bottle with a shaking hand, spilling some in her lap.

"What happened to Katie?"

Did she really have to share every rotten detail of her life with the world? Katie didn't know she hadn't always been this way.

It is well.

No, it's not! Make this stop. "I can't...talk about it."

"Who gave you this note?"

She shook her head, trying to picture every face that had come through the line. She hadn't paid attention; she'd been so focused on making it through the morning. "It was under a cup of coffee that nobody drank." The staccato pattern in her chest made it hard to breathe.

"Did you know anyone who came through? Anyone who looked like they might be working for Eddy?"

"No, no one." She put a hand to her forehead, face scrunched against the burgeoning headache. "But I didn't really look."

"Okay. It might come to you later. I'm going to call a cab and send you home—"

"No. I'm fine." She straightened. The last thing she wanted was to be alone with her thoughts. "Let's forget it."

Jason grunted. "That won't happen. Do you want to show this to Ben or should I?"

Neither, if it meant she'd have to explain. She put her hand out. "I will."

He set the note on her palm. "I'll check with him to make sure you do. This can't be ignored, Marti. They're threatening you. That's illegal."

Yes, they were. With the one thing she'd never wanted anyone to know, especially Katie. "I'll show it to Ben. I promise."

"Okay." He stood and motioned to her. "C'mere."

She went into his open arms, burrowing into his strength and acceptance. She didn't deserve the wonderful people God had put in her life, but she would be eternally grateful.

— 40 —

Sam ignored Ben's repeated calls, stayed to himself at the woodshop, and politely but firmly told Lizzy to forget he occupied space in her home. No, he didn't need meals or someone to talk to, he'd snapped when she protested. He needed space. The hurt on her face compounded his guilt and anger. He ran every evening to exhaustion, but even sleep didn't allow a reprieve from rampaging thoughts and images.

Finishing a run the third night, he swung by his townhouse for a few books. He knocked quietly.

Jillian opened the door with a smile that disappeared. "You okay?"

"Fine. Just finished a run." He stepped in. "Sorry if I stink. I want to grab a few books."

"You don't stink, and you don't have to whisper. Adrienne can sleep through the smoke alarm."

"That's good. I think." At the bookshelf, he pulled two books and searched for a third. "How's the job hunt going?"

"Great. I have a third interview tomorrow. I'm pretty sure I'll get an offer, so hopefully I can be out of here by the end of the week."

He glanced toward where she'd settled on the couch. "I'm sure you'll be glad to get settled in your own place."

"Definitely. I've got daycare lined up for Addy, assuming the job comes through, and a hold on an apartment not far from the hospital. And I've got every digit crossed that it all works out."

Pulling the third book from a pile, he faced her. "Keep me posted."

"I will. Sam, before you go, can we talk for a minute?"

He hesitated. "Sure." He sat in his favorite chair and raised his eyebrows. "Anything specific?"

"Yes." Sitting cross-legged on the couch, she twirled a long strand of hair. "I'm not sure how to start."

"The beginning is usually the best place."

She gave a half-smile. "You know the beginning. Two crazy college kids met in the cafeteria and fell in love playing on the same intramural volleyball team."

Great. A rehashing of his biggest failure. *God, I could use a break here.* He managed a single nod.

"It was good in the beginning, wasn't it? Our marriage?"

"I thought so." *But I thought everything was great with Marti too.*

"I really was happy," she said, as if reassuring him.

He nodded.

"Were you?"

He pulled in an irritated breath. "Where is this going, Jill?"

Color filled her cheeks and she twisted her fingers in her lap. "I…I want you to know that the divorce was hard for me too."

He bit down on his tongue and looked away.

"I never meant for any of that to happen. I don't think our problems were any worse than anyone else's, but instead of working on them, I took the easy way out. Not that it was easy for any of us."

"True."

"I never dreamed I wouldn't be building a family with you."

"Life has a way of surprising us," he said.

"Ryan wasn't—" She blew out a short breath. "He wasn't supposed to replace you. I was being stupid and selfish, and it messed up a bunch of lives."

"Yeah, it did."

She searched his face. "You've changed."

"I suppose I have." Who wouldn't after the past few years he'd endured? Not to mention falling in love with a drug dealer. *Don't go there.* "Haven't you?"

"I guess. I understand the value of relationships now, when before I took them for granted. I took *you* for granted."

"I think we all take the people in our lives for granted until we realize how fragile life is. How fragile connections are." How important truth is. He sighed. "I took you for granted by spending so much time at the Teen Center. I assumed you were doing fine because you were always independent and driven. You didn't seem to need me, but I never thought to ask if that were true."

"Oh, I needed you," she said, "but I wouldn't admit that even to myself. So you could have asked, and I'd probably have told you everything was fine."

"Maybe. I should at least have asked." Wow. He'd never expected to have a civil conversation with Jillian.

"Thank you for that." Her smile tugged downward. "I wish we had a do-over. Life would be a whole lot different, wouldn't it?"

He nodded slowly. Her regret had a strangely quieting effect, like the night casting its blanket on the end of a day. In this case, on the end of an era. The anger he'd clung to faded into stillness. Their marriage hardly seemed real anymore.

He was suddenly, completely worn out, exhausted from days of running in anger, and trying to breathe with a battered heart. From years of bitterness, fear, and self-incrimination. *God, I'm so tired of myself.* He pushed to his feet. "Time for me to head home."

She met him in the middle of the room. "This is your home, Sam. You belong here. We've grown and learned from our mistakes. We could build a new relationship, be a family again."

In the back of his mind, he'd expected this. Richard had been right. But he'd tasted something sweet and life-giving with Marti. Even after her betrayal, he wouldn't want to go back to what he'd had with Jillian.

With gentle hands, he grasped her shoulders. "We gave it our best shot, Jill, but it didn't work. Let's not put ourselves through that again." She started to speak and he shook his head. "I'm in love with someone else."

She deflated. "The girl in the picture."

He dropped his hands. "You'll be fine, Jillian. You've got a new job and a fresh start. You're a great mother, and you'll be a great wife someday. Thanks for this conversation. I'm glad we can part on friendly terms."

As tears filled her eyes, he pressed a kiss to her forehead. "I'll be praying for everything to fall into place for you. Let me know when you're ready to move out and I'll round up some help."

He left her standing in the middle of his living room and let himself out, books under his arm. There was a strange, unexpected lightness in his heart. A sense of overwhelming relief. It was time to leave his failed marriage behind, permanently. Move forward without regret, even though the future blurred into a question mark. He needed the counsel of a wise friend to help him sort things out. He'd call Joel in the morning.

— 41 —

Marti sat on the steps at the front of the sanctuary, looking at the cross that hung overhead. *God? If Katie finds out the truth about me, she'll hate me forever. And that will kill me.* She pressed a fist against the pain in her chest. *I can't testify. I can't!*

She folded her arms and hung her head. *Keep me from making things worse. Don't let Katie be hurt anymore.*

"Marti?" Ben's voice, not God's. He stood at the bottom of the steps.

"Thanks for coming," she managed, with only a slight tremble in her voice. "I need to show you something." She pulled the notes from her hoodie pocket and held them out.

Ben sorted through them as he sat down. "When did you get these?"

"The first one a few days ago at the Java Depot. Someone left it under a cup of coffee. The second one that afternoon, in my front door. The last one yesterday morning in Jason and Lorna's mailbox. Gloria called and said a note had been left in her door too, saying pretty much the same thing."

Ben released a long breath through his nose. "Apparently Eddy didn't think I meant what I said. What are the notes referring to?"

She pressed her lips tight for a long moment, then opened the last door to her past. "I pretty much raised Katie from the time she was born. I changed her diaper, fed her, played with her. I stayed up with her at night, got her dressed in the morning. I was her mom."

"How old were you?"

235

"Nine."

He frowned. "Were there any adults there with you?"

"Our mother was physically there most of the time, but usually drunk." Memories rose like ghosts. "I didn't do everything right, but it seemed okay most of the time." She'd never forget that day. Katie's flushed face and listless behavior. So hot her blonde curls stuck to her forehead, sweat dripping down her face as she whimpered.

"When Katie was two, she got really sick. She had a fever for days, and this rash," she motioned across her chest, "that kept getting worse. I don't think I slept that whole time. She wasn't getting better so I...I..."

She'd heard on a TV show that a bath could bring down a fever. Katie loved taking a bath. "It worked on TV."

"What did?"

"Taking a bath to bring down a fever. So I put her in there with a few toys, and ran to get a clean towel." She squeezed her eyes shut. "I was only gone a minute, maybe two. When I came back—" She clenched shaking hands together, forcing herself to face the memory. "She was underwater. Just...laying there." Blonde hair splayed out, eyes closed. Dead.

"I pulled her out, and pounded on her, and she started coughing. Our mother came in and freaked out, so I called 9-1-1. They took Katie to the hospital. She was never the same," she whispered.

"Do you remember what hospital?"

"No. I suppose either the big one downtown or maybe North Memorial." She'd crouched dripping and shaking against the wall as two men in white shirts hurried in, scooped Katie up, and rushed away. Her hysterical mother left with them.

"Marti," Ben said, his hand on her arm, "you were a child. You did the best you could."

She shrank from his compassion. "I ruined her life."

He squeezed gently and let go. "She's grown up to be a delightful young woman—happy, content, and secure in your love."

He didn't understand. After the incident, Katie was never like other children. She struggled in school. She didn't have the sense not to trust people. It wasn't always apparent, but Katie was different. Disabled. Because her older sister, the one person who could protect her, messed up.

"I never told her what happened." Now someone else would and she'd lose the only reason she had to keep breathing.

"Let me check into a few things before you talk to her. I have a suspicion…Well, let me make a few calls first. Wait until I get back to you. Okay?"

She nodded dully. It wouldn't change anything, but she needed time to find the courage to face Kat. "Okay."

It is well.

Stop saying that. It's even worse now.

Sam stood outside the sanctuary listening to Marti's story. He'd left Joel's office calmer than he went in, ready for a run to clear his head. Hearing Ben and Marti's voices had stopped him at the door. Had anything good *ever* happened in her life? Maybe her lousy childhood explained her getting mixed up with Eddy. That wouldn't make it okay, but at least it provided a reason she'd gone down that path.

As she and Ben emerged from the sanctuary, he slipped out of sight and waited for her to leave the building while Ben made a call. Sam's heart squeezed as he watched her walk out, shoulders slumped.

The anger that had fueled him since confronting her had cooled after praying with Joel. Though he tried to hold onto his outrage, hearing her pain-laced words now dampened it more. But he didn't want to feel sorry for her. He didn't want to feel anything for her.

He approached his brother as the call ended. "Ben."

"Sam! What are you doing here?"

"Meeting with Joel."

"You just missed Marti, although," his gaze narrowed, "I suppose that's fine with you."

Sam ignored the jab. "I heard what she told you."

"Ah. More ammunition for you. Attempted murder or maybe negligence?"

The uncharacteristic sarcasm pinched. "I'm not out to get her, Ben." He sighed. "Your news wasn't what I expected. I've needed time to process it."

"Did you give her a chance to tell her side?"

Not exactly. He didn't like seeing himself through Ben's words.

"I didn't think so. Maybe you should. It's a lot more complicated than girl meets drug dealer and becomes one herself. Much as you'd like it to be, the world isn't always black and white."

The edge in Ben's voice, the accusation in his eyes, were a punch to his gut. "Sounds like you've lost your professional perspective, Detective."

Ben stepped close, nostrils flared as he jabbed a finger into Sam's chest. "When it comes to you, yes, I have. You're an idiot, Sam. That girl is braver than anyone I've encountered in all my years on the force. She's put everything on the line to help us lock Eddy up. She had nothing to do with Andrew or Shareen, but you've decided she was personally responsible.

"You know what, big brother? You might consider whether your self-righteous attitude is helping or hindering this case. Marti was scared to death to tell you about her involvement because, God knows why, she cares for you. Instead of throwing her a life-preserver, you left her to flounder."

Muttering an oath, he stalked toward the door, then paused to glare back at Sam. "Maybe, once you get over yourself, you could help us find more evidence against Eddy. Marti isn't the enemy, Sam. But *you* might be if she ends up too afraid to testify."

Sam stood in stunned silence as Ben flung open the door and stormed out. *I'm* the enemy? But she... He blinked. He didn't actually know what part she'd played in the whole mess.

Ben had said it was complicated. There were extenuating circumstances. They'd given her immunity. His brother was the most thorough, dedicated professional he knew. He wouldn't let her get off without punishment unless he thought it best. Ben never let his emotions make decisions.

Unlike me. Sam dropped his head. He'd walked out on her without hearing her out first. He would never have done that to the kids he worked with, no matter how big of a mess they were in. But he'd done it to Marti, and sliced off a piece of his heart in the process.

Time to grow up, Evans, and do the right thing.

— 42 —

Dreading the silence of her apartment, Marti left the meeting with Ben and detoured to GPS. She needed to stay busy, talk to people, anything but listen to her own thoughts. When she opened the screen door, the handle wiggled in her grip. She should fix that before she left.

"Hey, Tiffani."

"Marti! What are you doing here on a Saturday?"

"What about you? Don't you get a day off?"

"Nope, never. My boss is a slave driver." She laughed. "I'm filling in for the weekend gal who's off having her baby. Speaking of babies, Vanessa is at the hospital right now too!"

"The baby's coming?" She clasped her hands. Wonderful news amidst the mess of her life.

"Sure hope so. Kurt took her in right after lunch, so we're all waiting by the phone. Make sure to check the website for updates."

"I will. And I'll be praying everything goes smoothly." *Bring that baby into this world safely, Lord. And protect my sweet friend.*

"So how come you're here?"

Marti shrugged, fingering the plant on Tiffani's desk. "I'm a little restless, so I'm looking for something to do. I'm handy with tools and stuff, so after I fix that screen door handle, maybe there's other stuff I could fix?"

Tiffani's mouth hung open. "Are you serious?"

Oh. Stupid idea. Got it. "I'm sure it sounds a little weird but I like doing that kind of stuff. Unless you've got someone who does it. Which you probably do. In that case, never mind." She took a step backward. "I'll get out of your—"

"Slow down!" Tiffani said with a laugh. "I was surprised because we've been talking about needing a maintenance person. So if you're willing to step in for the day and fix stuff, that would literally be an answer to prayer."

"Really?" Excitement bloomed.

Tiffani dug through the papers on her desk, pulling a sheet out with a triumphant cheer. "Here are some of the things we'd like done. Simple stuff, really, but nobody has time to do it."

Looking over the list, a strange sensation seeped through her. This might be a place where she fit in, where she was needed. She smiled at Tiffani. "Point me to the tools."

Within minutes, she'd fixed the screen door handle. Then she tightened every doorknob in the house, changed four light bulbs, and emptied the garbage from each room. She didn't know a thing about plumbing, but slid under the bathroom sink and figured out how to fix the leak. She didn't even mind getting squirted a few times.

She washed windows on the first floor, cleaned marks off walls, and swept the kitchen floor. As the sun rested on the horizon, she dusted the main living area.

"Okay, girlfriend," Tiffani said, hands on her hips. "Time to close up shop. You are absolutely amazing."

"Thanks for letting me help out." Marti put the toolbox and rags back in the closet, and washed her hands. She handed the list back to Tiffani. "Is it okay if I come back another time to paint the porch rail?"

Tiffani grinned. "You've already done more than half of the list, but if you want to do more, it's fine with us. Let me lock up, and we can head out together." She struggled with the deadbolt on the backdoor until it fell into place. "Dang thing," she muttered.

Marti laughed. "We'll add it to the list."

Outside on the porch, Tiffani sighed. "I'm starving. Hey!" She nudged Marti. "Wanna grab something to eat at Millie's Cafe? Or do you have to be somewhere?"

"No! I mean, yes, I'd like to and no, I don't have to be somewhere. I didn't eat lunch so I'm hungry too."

Tiffani hooked their arms together and tugged. "Great! Let's go."

Marti held back tears as they walked the four blocks to the cafe. Two friends hanging out for the evening. Having dinner. Like people did. *Thank you.*

Sam waited outside the Java Depot until a line formed at the register where Marti stood, then slipped in and sat at his usual table in the corner. It seemed a lifetime ago that he'd last sat here, impatient for a chance to talk to the brown-eyed beauty who flipped his stomach with her shy smile. The impatience had been replaced with dread as he rehearsed what he needed to say. *Okay, God. I'm ready. I think. Give me the right words.*

He took his place at the end of the line, staying out of her sight as he shuffled closer. Heart in his throat, he stepped up to the register and waited.

She handed the customer their order, then turned back to the register. Her eyes went wide, and she swallowed before asking, "What can I get you?"

He cleared his throat. "Ten minutes of your time when you have a break."

"Anything else?" Her chin trembled.

"A large dark roast."

She rang his order, filled a cup with steaming coffee, and gave a tiny nod as she handed it to him, then turned her attention to the next person. Returning to his table, his heart slowed to normal. He pulled out the curriculum and forced his focus to the papers. So far so good.

An hour later, a presence paused beside his table. Marti waited, wariness clouding her expression. He gestured across the table. "Have a seat."

She perched on the chair and sipped her ice water, silent.

"So. I, uh… How are you?"

"Fine."

"I heard from Ben that they've got both you and Katie under surveillance until the trial."

She pursed her lips and nodded. No doubt she hated the idea, at least for herself.

Sam rubbed the back of his neck. *Help, God. What do I say?* He drew a breath and leaned forward. "Marti, I need to apologize. Again."

Her eyebrows jumped up.

"I way overreacted. I was so happy when Ben said they'd brought Eddy in and charged him, but when he told me you were the main witness," he lifted his hands, "I lost it. I didn't want it to be true. And then, when he told me about what Eddy did to you, that made me even crazier. There were so many thoughts and emotions hitting, I freaked out. At you. You didn't deserve that. I'm really sorry."

She blinked quickly, her dark eyes shiny.

"I'd like to hear your story, if you'd tell me. It's what I should have done right away, but I let my emotions take over and did everything wrong. Would you tell me what happened?"

She wiped the condensation from her cup with even strokes of her thumb, her forehead creased. Finally, she spoke. "There isn't enough time now. I have to get back to work."

"How about over lunch? Unless you have plans. Or another day?"

"I think my break is at 1:30."

He nodded at the papers strewn across his table. "I've got plenty to keep me busy."

"Okay." She offered a half-smile and returned to the front counter. He relaxed into the chair, thankful she hadn't totally shut him out. Or kicked him out. *Help me not mess this up, Lord.*

Toward the end of the lunch rush, Sam asked Ibrahim to make sandwiches for him and Marti, the response a terse yes. When he brought the bag to Sam's table a few minutes later, he kept hold when Sam reached for it. "Watch your step with her, Evans," he said.

Did everybody know how bad he messed up? "I plan to," he assured the young man. "I'm hoping to fix things starting right now."

Marti appeared at Ibrahim's side. "Did you make our lunch?" She hugged his arm. "You rock. Thanks."

He smiled at her, then sent a warning glare toward Sam before returning to the counter. She raised an eyebrow.

"Let's say you've got plenty of people protecting you," he said. "How about we head down to the lake?"

Silence blanketed the short walk, reminding Sam how much he missed being with her. Talking and walking, and laughing. They settled on a bench and ate, conversation polite and strained. After he cleaned up, she clasped her hands in her lap and faced the lake. The story she revealed broke his heart, made him furious, and magnified his guilt.

"So the latest threat is that they'll tell Katie what happened." Her face drooped with exhaustion. "I waited too long to tell you. I don't want to make that mistake with her, so we're getting together tomorrow."

Ben had been right. The extenuating circumstances made a huge difference. How could anyone go through so much and still be determined to provide for someone else? Her remarkable strength shamed him. "I am so sorry I didn't ask you to tell me this before going off like a cannon. I've been a real idiot around you." Heat filled his face. "I hope maybe someday you can forgive me?"

Her profile crumpled. "Of course. I'm sorry I wasn't brave enough to tell you everything at the start." She brushed a stray tear away. "You'd been so hurt by what happened to the kids, I couldn't hurt you more. But it wasn't right to keep it from you."

"What's hurt me the most is my own stupid behavior. After my tirade, I realized I'd ruined the best thing that's ever happened to me." He brushed his fingers against her cheek.

Doubt shadowed her face and she shifted slightly away. "I went to your house last week, to tell you the whole story."

"You did? If I'd been there, we wouldn't have had to go through all this."

She studied him with a strange expression. "You weren't there," she acknowledged, "but your wife and baby were."

"I don't have— Oh. You met Jillian." Anger flared. Jill had conveniently forgotten to mention it.

"Why didn't you tell me you have a child, Sam?"

"I don't! That's what broke up my marriage. Jill got pregnant with another guy. The baby isn't mine."

Her eyebrows pinched upward together, then plummeted. "She cheated on you?!"

Lord, don't let this change her opinion of me now. "Yup. Pretty humiliating."

"Then why is she living in your house?"

"She showed up one day a few weeks ago and needed a place to live. I let her move in until she could find a job, and I moved to Lizzy's, where I still am. Jill told me she thinks she got a job so she should be out in the next week or so."

Marti touched his arm lightly. "I'm sorry. That must have been a terrible thing to go through."

"I lived." He shrugged. "Anyway, it led me to you."

A smile wavered at the corners of her mouth. "Maybe, when this is all over, we could try being friends again?"

"No." He reached for her hand. "Martina, I can't wait that long. I want to be right beside you when you testify. You can put this guy away once and for all, but I don't want you doing it alone."

Her mouth opened but there was no response.

Uh oh. Overkill. He shifted his weight. "Unless you don't want me around after I was such a jerk."

"I thought you hated me."

"No way. That will never happen." Putting a finger under her chin, he leaned forward and kissed her gently. It took heroic effort not to pull her into his arms. When he sat back, he lifted an eyebrow. "See?" Could she see his heart pounding under his shirt?

A smile crept onto her flushed face, then her phone chimed and she blinked. "I have to get back."

He pulled her to her feet and into a hug. After a heartbeat, she leaned against him. "We have all the time in the world, Martina."

They were halfway back to the Java Depot when they saw Ben hurrying toward them. Marti's stomach lurched, and she tightened her fingers within Sam's.

"Marti, glad I found you."

His smile loosened the talons of fear.

"Sam," he acknowledged, then turned his attention back to her. "Marti, I've done some digging into what happened to Katie."

She swayed, and Sam put an arm around her shoulders. Now she *would* go to jail.

"I checked her medical history, and found details about the hospital stay. First off, that whole rash and fever thing? Scarlet fever. The antibiotics they gave her in the hospital got rid of it, and there were no after-effects."

"But—"

He held up his hand. "None. You caught it early enough that the antibiotics worked great."

"I did? They did?"

"And the records said she wasn't under water long enough for that to affect her in any way. You need to hear this. The records also said she has a very mild form of fetal alcohol syndrome from your mother drinking during her pregnancy. Katie's developmental delays came from that, not the bath. The syndrome affects her cognitive processing, but not severely.

"Marti, *you* were the one who protected and cared for her. The County stepped in to put Katie in a safe environment once your mother wouldn't let you back into the apartment."

Marti feared if she blinked, the whole amazing story would pop like a balloon. Katie's issues weren't her fault? "Are they sure?" After all this time?

"It's in black and white in her medical records, which I got to comb through with a subpoena. Only a brief mention of a bathing incident. Nothing about a drop on the head either."

"You dropped her on her head?" Sam asked.

"Hey, I was nine," she shot back. "She wiggled a lot, right out of my arms one time. She landed on the carpet, not exactly on her head."

He chuckled and squeezed her shoulders. She desperately needed this news. "Thanks for digging into it, Ben. This is great."

"The judge was out of town so it took an extra day to get the subpoena, but it worked out."

"What made you check her records?" Sam asked.

"It seemed there had to be a better explanation for Katie's delays than a dunking in the tub."

"Wow." Marti put a shaking hand to her forehead. "I don't know what to think."

"Right now you need to think about getting back to work before you get fired," Sam said.

Marti smiled all the way back to the coffee shop, one hand tucked in his, the other looping onto Ben's arm. Right where she belonged.

– 43 –

As the bells jangled, Marti looked up from the register. "Well, good morning, Jimmy."

He approached with a cheerful swagger. "'Morning, Marti."

"What can I get for you?"

"Actually, I didn't come for a beverage, but that coffee smells amazing, I'll have a cup of your light roast."

"Coming right up." Filling it to the brim, she snapped a lid on the cup and handed it to him. "On the house." She'd pay for it later, the least she could do for someone who had been so kind to her.

"Really? Thanks!" He glanced behind him. "Since no one's waiting..." He pulled folded papers from his back pocket. "These are for you to look over."

She unfolded them slowly. A job application. A short letter stating a starting salary, blank lines at the bottom for a signature and a start date. Stunned, she met his raised eyebrow. Much as she wanted to immediately scratch her name on the line, she had to be upfront.

"Marti, go take a break," Ibrahim said. He winked. "I'll holler if I need you."

She moved around the counter on jellied legs and followed Jimmy to a table.

"So what do you think?" he asked. "Ready to join us?"

Regret reared its head again. Would her past ever stop hounding her? She lifted her chin. Only if she made the right decisions going forward. "I'll consider it," she said, "but there's something you need to know about me first."

"Okay." He leaned back in his chair and took a sip. "Lay it on me."

As she'd done so many times already, she cleared her throat and started from the beginning. The part where Eddy stepped into her life was the hardest to share.

"The day he beat me up was the best day of my life. Now I'm working with the police to put him away. But that doesn't change the fact that I didn't stop him when I could. Nothing I ever do will make up for that. So, you might want to reconsider your offer. I'm a felon without the conviction."

Jimmy's expression was unreadable. "Thanks for sharing your story, Marti. I appreciate your openness and honesty. Sounds like you've had a pretty rough time."

She shook her head. "Lots of people have it tougher. I made things so much worse when I didn't go straight to the police."

"Hindsight is a great teacher."

Tears burned up her throat at his understanding. She'd have loved working with him.

"I'm all about second chances. And third and fourth. What matters to me is that you're doing the right thing now. So, my offer stands. Will you sign the offer letter and join the team?"

She couldn't speak over the lump in her throat, so she accepted the pen he held out.

Jason took the news with his usual blunt kindness. "Well, it's about time."

He wasn't even a little sad? "You could have fired me, if I'm that bad."

His rumble of laughter startled her. "Marti, Marti. I meant it's about time you went for a job that you're suited for. You've been great to have here, but I know this isn't where your heart is. Jimmy talked to me last week. He wanted to be upfront about trying to steal you away from me. I told him to go for it."

"You did?"

"You've got to use your God-given talents, kid, and as much as I appreciate your sweeping expertise, this place isn't where you'll use them. Lorna and I plan to cheer you on as you make a name for yourself. We might even start charging you rent."

A smile broke through. She'd be thrilled to pay her own way again. "Well, I might pay it." He chuckled and her phone buzzed in her pocket. "It's Gloria."

Jason waved her off and turned to the paperwork on his desk.

Marti answered as she headed out the back door. "Hello?"

"They left another note for Katie," Gloria said. "She saw it this time, and freaked out."

Marti stopped short and the door slammed behind her. "What does it say?"

"That she'd better convince you to not testify or something bad will happen. She locked herself in her room. You need to come over here and fix this."

The only way to fix it was not to testify, but even that might not stop the threats. She paced like the caged animal she'd become. "Can you get her to talk to me?"

Muffled knocking, then Gloria's voice followed by Katie's at an unnaturally high pitch.

"She won't open the door," Gloria said.

"Tell her I'll be right there."

"Make it fast. In the meantime, I'm going to check flights to get us out of here until this mess is over. Maybe DisneyWorld or a quiet beach somewhere."

Marti called Ben as she raced to Gloria's. He said he'd meet her there. She left a brief message for Sam.

Gloria held the door open as Marti approached, a dark frown on her face. "This has gotten totally out of hand, Martha. Your poor decisions have put this whole family in jeopardy."

"I'm aware of that. I can keep apologizing but that won't change anything." At Katie's bedroom door, she knocked lightly. "Kat? It's me, hon. Can I come in?"

The door flung open and Katie yanked her into the room, then slammed it shut and locked it. Marti held her shaking sister firmly, praying for wisdom and words and calm, and whatever else God might want to throw at them.

"Okay, shh. Let's sit on the bed for a minute." She brushed blonde strands from her sister's wet cheek as they settled. "You're safe, Kat. I'm here, and there's a police officer right outside protecting us. Nobody's going to hurt either of us, okay?"

"H-how do you k-know?" Katie hiccupped. "The note s-said something bad would h-happen if you testify."

"They're just making noise, sweetie. Big talk to keep me from telling the truth about a very bad man. I'm not worried." Maybe a little.

Red-rimmed eyes filled her sister's pale face. "You're n-not?"

"Nope." She forced bravado into her voice. "We have a lot of wonderful people watching out for us. Like Officer Ben, and Sam, and Gloria, and Jason and Lorna."

"But why are there people who want to hurt us?"

Marti held Katie close and rocked. "Because they're bad people who don't want anyone to stop them from doing more bad things. If I don't speak up to stop them, they'll keep doing it. Does that make sense?"

Katie's breath was still choppy as she nodded. "I g-guess so. But can't someone else do it?"

"I'm the one who knows the most about this bad person."

"Are you afraid?"

Terrified. "I'm not afraid to tell the truth. That's what God expects us to do. So even when we're scared, He helps us be brave enough to do the right thing."

A knock at the door made Katie jump. "Go away!"

"Katie, it's Officer Ben. Can I talk with you and your sister?"

The reassuring voice calmed the tremors in Marti's stomach. Katie turned to her, eyebrows raised. When Marti nodded, Katie opened the door.

"Hi, ladies." He smiled. "Can I join you?"

"Come on in, Officer Ben," Marti said. "We're talking about bad people. You must meet lots of them in your job."

He closed the door gently behind him and leaned against it. "More than I care to."

"Aren't you scared of them?" Katie had returned to her spot on the bed, glued to Marti's side.

"Sure. Everybody gets scared sometimes. My job is to put those bad people in jail where they can't hurt anyone, so that's what I focus on. Your sister is helping me with an especially bad man, so that makes my job easier."

"Marti is helping you?" She sat up a little straighter. "Really?"

"Really," he said. "I wouldn't be able to do my job half as well without her help. She's the bravest person I know."

The fear in Katie's eyes receded, replaced with shining pride. "That's so cool. But…" The pride dimmed. "Someone wrote a note saying something bad would happen if she testifies. What if they hurt her?"

Marti caught Ben's glance.

In the reassuring smile he gave Katie, Marti saw a flash of Sam. "That's another thing the police do, Katie—protect people. So we're doing everything we can to keep her, and you, and Gloria, and everyone else safe."

When Katie rested her head against Marti's shoulder, she wrapped her arms around her tightly. She'd do anything for her little sister. "Officer Ben is very good at his job, Kat."

"I'd be so sad if something bad happened to you."

"Well, I would be too," Marti said, "so we're not going to let it, okay?" *God willing.* It was time to tell Katie the whole story. The truth would protect them.

– 44 –

Sam shifted on the bus bench next to Ben, squinting across the street at the Java Depot. "I'm beginning to feel like a stalker."

Ben chuckled at the muttered comment. "Because you are," he said. "But I won't press charges since it's obvious she doesn't mind. Good thing she starts working with you next week. I'm sure Jimmy will appreciate you being back on the job."

"He agreed with me about keeping an eye on her. *My* eyes." He folded his arms, focused on the Depot door as people came and went. "I'm glad Jason insisted she live in the house with them, instead of the garage apartment. Man, she can be stubborn."

Now Ben laughed aloud. "You two are going to be interesting to watch in the coming years. Not sure who's the stubbornest."

"That's not even a word." He stood as Marti emerged from the Depot, his heart doing a goofy jump when she waved.

She crossed the street and joined them with a bright smile. "Wow. I have two bodyguards now?"

"Ma'am, I saw this man sitting here staring at the coffee shop," Ben said, flashing his badge. "Fits the stalker profile to a T. Would you like to press charges? I can lock him up right now."

Marti laughed, pink dusting her cheeks as she took Sam's arm. "No, thank you. I appreciate the company *everywhere* I go." Her smile twinkled up at him. "It's sweet, like a boy carrying my books home from school."

"Ready to beat up any bullies that might wander by," he agreed. *Any bullies.* "Thanks for the ringing endorsement, Ben."

His brother winked at her. "I think you're in safe hands, Marti. I'll see you tomorrow morning at 8:00 to go over more trial stuff, right?"

"I'll be there." As he walked away, Marti sighed. "Have I mentioned I love your brother?"

He frowned. "Define love."

"As in I wish I'd had an older brother like him." She batted her eyes at him. "Could we walk over to say goodbye to Katie? Please?"

He wound his fingers around hers, doubting he'd ever be able to say no to her. "Anything you want, Princess. How about we get her a treat for the plane?"

Marti's face lit. "Peanut brittle!"

At the ice cream store, Sam asked the clerk to put the treat in two bags. On their way to Gloria's, he handed a bag to her. She offered a piece to him, then savored hers with a blissful smile. When they reached the house, they were busily licking their sticky fingers.

Katie opened the door and squealed with delight. "You brought Sam!"

"What am I? Yesterday's leftovers?"

Sam returned Katie's hug. "I'm the appetizer," he assured Marti, "you're the entrée, and Katie's the dessert."

"Speaking of dessert," Marti handed the bag to her sister, "here's a gift from Sam. For your plane ride tomorrow."

"Peanut brittle!" She clutched the bag in both hands, a pleading lift to her brow. "Can't I have a piece now? I'll die if I have to wait."

Sam and Marti exchanged smiles. "Okay, just one," she said.

Settled on the front step in the afternoon sun, Katie ate the biggest piece she could find while Marti talked about the repair work she'd done at GPS, and interesting customers at the coffee shop. When the conversation moved to Katie's vacation, her demeanor drooped into a pout.

"Don't you want to go?" Sam asked.

"Not really. I mean, it will be fun since I haven't been there, but Gloria wouldn't let Tim come, and I'm really going to miss him." Lips pursed, she folded her arms and frowned at the ground, the treat bag forgotten beside her.

Marti scooted closer to her. "Hon, Tim isn't going anywhere. He'll probably be on this front step waiting for you a week from now."

"But what if he's not?"

She hugged her. "He will be. Trust me."

Sam nodded. If he wasn't, he'd have some explaining to do. Nobody hurt one of his sisters.

Marti emerged from her morning shower humming a worship song she'd heard at Faith. Even the rumble of thunder couldn't dampen her spirits. This morning Katie would head off on an adventure to Florida, away from the worry about the upcoming trial, safe with Gloria and Buster. Far from Eddy.

She wiped the foggy mirror. Eddy had said he'd picked her because she was stupid and easily manipulated. The reflection smiled at her. He hadn't counted on how God would change her through the people He put in her life. She'd take on Eddy and then take him out, with Ben and Sam beside her.

The phone rang. Gloria. Katie probably forgot something.

"Good morning, Gloria. Ready for—"

"Katie's gone."

Marti froze. "What?"

There was a sharp inhale. "We got everything packed last night and she went to bed. I went in there a few minutes ago to see if she was up, but she's gone. Her bed doesn't look slept in."

"Wait. Not slept in?" Marti tried to blink sense into Gloria's frightening words. "Where is she?"

"I don't know! She's not answering her phone, and her small suitcase is gone."

Marti darted into the bedroom and yanked a shirt out of the drawer. "Have you looked for her?"

"Of course! Buster is driving around right now."

"Did you call Tim?" She struggled to pull jeans on with shaking hands. Thunder rumbled a warning.

"He's not answering either."

She had to be with him. "I'll call Ben on my way over. Stay there in case she comes back. Maybe she and Tim are saying goodbye. I'll be there as fast as I can."

She disconnected the call and sank to her knees, face in her hands. "God, help us. Keep her safe. Show us where she is. Please."

It is well.

"If it's not, I won't survive it." She finished dressing, and dialed Ben's number as she grabbed a raincoat, and raced down the stairs. The call went to voicemail. "Ben, Katie's missing! I'm going to Gloria's. Call me!"

She left a similar message for Sam, then ran the rest of the way, arriving breathless, frantic, and wet from a sprinkling rain. Bursting through the front door, she called, "Katie? Katie!"

Gloria came out of the kitchen, her pale eyes red and puffy. "She hasn't come back yet."

Marti stood in the living room, swallowing against a rush of fear. "Was there any kind of note? From her or...anyone?"

"Nothing. I've checked her room, the mailbox, everywhere." She tried to light a cigarette, then tossed it aside with a curse. "Why would she run away? She said she *wanted* to go to Florida. I know she was mad that Tim couldn't come, but that's no reason to run away."

Katie didn't think the way most people did, but running away was extreme even for her. Unless— Marti's heart pounded so hard she dropped onto the couch. Did Eddy find a way to grab her? The doorbell rang and she flew off the couch to fling open the door. Not Katie, but Ben. He hugged her firmly, then led her to the couch, inviting Gloria to join them. Marti listened to Gloria recount everything that happened after she and Sam left late yesterday afternoon. Nothing out of the ordinary, no indication she wasn't getting on the plane in the morning.

"What if..." She couldn't form the words.

He squeezed her hand. "We've already got people talking to him. I don't think he'd do something this stupid, but they'll put the pressure on him to make sure."

She pulled in a steadying breath and stood. "I have to get out there."

"We have an APB out on both her and Tim, so the beat cops are watching for them," he said. "We've also got someone watching his house as well as Jason's. Got your phone? Call if you find her, or if you think of a place we should look."

She fled the house with no clue where to go first. Much as she wanted to give in to the growing hysteria, there wasn't time. Two hours later, she rested on a bench by the lake, head in her hands. Raindrops plunked against her hood and slipped off to splatter on the grass. Had she really thought she'd find them sitting at a coffee shop or strolling along the path, jumping in puddles? If Kat ran away with Tim, she wouldn't want to be found. If Eddy did something—

"Marti!"

She jerked upright, then was on her feet, flying into his arms. "Sam!" The tears she'd held in check since Gloria's call flooded over. "If Eddy took her, I won't testify. Not if he's going to hurt her. I can't!"

Arms wrapped tightly around her, his warmth and calm seeped into her. "We'll find her, Martina," he promised. "Shh, honey. We'll find her."

"I can't lose her," she hiccupped. "She's all I have."

He leaned back and lifted her chin. "So what am I, yesterday's leftovers?"

She managed a trembling smile.

"You've got me, and Ben, and the whole police department looking for her. We'll find her." His serious expression reflected the conviction in his words. "Okay?" he prompted.

She wiped her face and nodded. *Pull it together. You're no good to Kat if you fall apart.* "Okay. Thank you."

"Let's go see Ben."

At the police department, they were given cups of coffee and ushered into a small room, assured that Ben would be with them soon. Wet and shivering, Marti perched on the edge of a chair, cradling the cup as she stared at the floor. Sam's heart ached at the pain etched on her face.

"Sweetheart, we're going to find her, and she's going to be fine." The reassurance sounded hollow in his own ears. *Right, God?*

She gave a slight nod. Sam resumed pacing. When the door opened, Marti jumped, unmindful of the coffee that splashed on her. Kurt and Richard entered.

"We want to be part of the plan," Richard said, taking the chair next to Marti. He wrapped an arm around her. "We'll find her, Marti. If she and Tim are together, they can't have gotten far."

Her chin quivered. "They could have if they left last night."

Ben came into the room, acknowledging Richard and Kurt with a nod before turning to her. "We're tracing their cell phones and bank accounts, checking transportation."

"Which won't matter if Eddy's people took her."

"Marti, we don't—" Sam said.

Ben cut him off with a shake of his head. "We're checking that angle very carefully. He said, of course, he hadn't orchestrated any of it, but he's not known for his honesty."

Sam curled his fingers, his arms stiff at his sides to rein in his frustration.

Kurt squatted in front of Marti, and took her hand. "We've got feelers out all over town, Marti. And the prayer warriors are doing their thing." He offered an encouraging smile. "We're going to find her."

She thanked him quietly, then her eyebrows lifted. "Oh! Did Vanessa have the baby?"

His face lit with a wide grin. "She did. Angelique Elizabeth Wagner. Seven pounds, lots of dark hair."

"She's a beauty," Richard added.

Marti clutched his hand. "Oh, I'm so glad, Kurt. And Vanessa's okay?"

"Doing great." The pride on his face squeezed Sam's heart. "You can bring Katie to see them both very soon."

"We'd love that."

Sam watched the exchange, shamed. How did she manage to think of someone else in the middle of her own crisis? He had a lot to learn from her.

She looked to Ben. "So, what's the plan now?"

"We're covering the city again in quadrants. Can you think of any place she might go to hide? Any place particularly special to her?"

"Not really." She shook her head slowly, focused on the window as if looking through places they'd been. "We went to the Falls a while ago, but she wouldn't know how to get there. She didn't go anywhere by herself."

"Okay. Keep thinking on that." He pushed to his feet. "I'll go get an update and be right back." He glanced at Sam and motioned with his head.

Sam followed. The door shut behind them, and Ben urged him down the hall. Obviously it wasn't something Marti should hear. His heart did a drum roll.

"I just learned something that may or may not change our search."

"About?"

"Tim." Their gazes held. "Sam, he's Eddy's stepbrother."

— 45 —

Marti paced the confines of the small room. Kurt and Richard had left, promising to stay in touch. Sam and Ben hadn't returned. Her wet clothes made the room damp and stuffy, sweat dribbling down her back. She spun toward the door. "I can't stand this."

The hallway was empty. Looking for Sam or Ben would waste time. She left the air-conditioned building, the muggy air slapping her like a wet towel. The rain had stopped, but the clouds hanging low overhead promised more. She turned at the corner and ran.

Jason greeted her from behind the register in the nearly empty coffee shop. His smile faded as she approached. "Marti, you're soaked."

"Katie's missing."

"What? When?"

She rubbed her face. "Last night or this morning. They were leaving for Florida this morning, but when Gloria went in to wake her up, she was gone." She blinked quickly. "Ben is checking to see if Eddy is involved."

Jason's bushy brow lowered. "Is that what they think happened?"

"We don't know. Maybe you could pray that we find her soon?"

His bear hug was tighter than usual. "Of course we'll be praying. And I'll put it out there for everyone I know to be looking for her." He kissed her forehead. "God will help us find her, kid. Stay focused on that."

She nodded and left the shop, wanting to believe that with every ounce of fading faith. She knew from experience God didn't answer every prayer, at least not the way people wanted. Walking the streets until the sun set and lights flickered on, she continued to leave messages on Katie's phone. Sam called, offering to walk with her. She asked him to stay with Ben in case Katie was brought to the station.

He agreed reluctantly. "Martina, there's something you should know. We don't know how or if it affects anything."

She clutched the phone.

"Sweetheart, Tim is Eddy's step-brother. I know that may seem like bad news, but Ben hasn't found any connection between them other than that, so I don't think we need to panic."

Eyes closed, she released a long breath. She'd suspected this since meeting Tim at Gloria's. Aside from a similar first name, there'd been no other connection that made sense. And she'd refused to let her thoughts go there. She hadn't considered step-brothers.

"Marti?"

"I'm here. I've expected it, in a way."

"You have? Why?"

She explained the conversation in Gloria's backyard. He asked why she hadn't shared her concern at least with Ben. Katie's description of Eddy hadn't matched the man she knew, so she'd let it go. Seeing him with his hair cut short, she should have made the connection but she'd been too terrified to think straight.

She trudged back to her apartment as they talked, her phone battery beeping a warning. Promising she'd try to sleep for a bit, they hung up. Her leaden legs barely made it up the stairs. She plugged her phone in, changed into dry clothes, then curled up on the bed and stared into the darkness.

Sam drove the streets of Uptown into the evening, pleading with God and calling Marti. More driving, more pleading. He'd never felt this helpless, even after Andrew and Shareen died. Marti's pain resonated inside him; the fear in her eyes seared into his heart. He was more scared than he'd ever been.

He wanted to find Katie, to make everything better for Marti, to erase the years of neglect for both of them. Hours of thinking had brought the realization home—he couldn't. It wasn't his job nor did he have the ability.

He parked near the lake and walked in quiet darkness to the bench he and Marti often shared. He'd struggled against life's injustices, staggered under his father's relentless badgering. Railed against losing everything. His life, and his heart, had been in constant turmoil. Now the chaos quieted, replaced by a longing so intense it stole his breath.

"God?" His voice echoed in the silence. "I can't fix this for Marti. I can't save Katie. I couldn't save Andrew or Shareen. I've demanded to know why terrible things happen to people who don't deserve it, and I've been mad that you wouldn't explain."

He leaned forward, elbows on his knees, and lowered his head. "But you don't owe me an explanation. You don't owe me anything. It's me who owes you."

Time and again, people had intersected his path with the right words at the right time, including Marti. Her quiet presence had challenged and strengthened him to leave his past failings behind and be the man God called him to be. Now here he sat, unable to save the day for her, yet strangely at peace with his helplessness. He'd do what he could, knowing God would take care of things His way, not Sam Evans' way. Releasing the last of his resistance, he let tears roll. *Thank you.*

Hours later, his phone woke him where he'd dozed off on the bench. He squinted against the early morning light and checked the ID. Ben. "You find her?"

"No. And Marti's not answering her phone."

Unable to sleep, Marti returned to Gloria's at first light. Dark clouds hung so low they seemed determined to block her way. Thunder pounded. She huddled deeper into her jacket against spritzing rain.

Gloria's house sat quiet and dark, shades drawn. Obviously, Katie hadn't returned. She passed it and stood at the edge of the park now shrouded in gray fog. Playground equipment looked like tombstones in a cemetery. The light shower changed to heavy drops. A swing drifted in the breeze, water gleaming on the black rubber seat. Katie had always loved to swing. Rivulets raced down the molded slide, gushing over the edge. The emptiness of the park weighed on her like a heavy hand of judgment.

Air left Marti's lungs in a pained sigh. She'd spent so many years trying to get it right, to make amends for robbing Katie of a normal life, she hadn't fully enjoyed their time together. The towhead with adorable dimples and blonde curls had become a lovely young woman, and she'd missed it. She'd learned the truth too late. And now Katie had to pay for her mistakes, her ineptness. Her stupidity.

Lifting her face, she let the rain pound her. "This is all my fault. *My* fault, not hers." Water pelted her face, poured inside her jacket. The sky grumbled. "Take me! I'll pay for my mistake. Let her be okay."

If Tim hurt Katie, she'd never get over it. If Katie was dead, she wanted to be too.

"She never did anything wrong," she shouted at the clouds, at God. "This isn't fair. She doesn't deserve this. She deserves a happy life without me messing things up. Please! Let her come home."

She lowered her head. "Please. Show me what to do. Help me," she finished in a choked whisper. Raindrops slapped against the blacktop, dancing around her in glee. Thunder rolled long and deep. The pain in her heart burned like a lightning strike but still she stood here, alive. Alone.

"Marti!"

She looked heavenward, trembling. God called her to judgment and she was ready.

"Marti!"

The voice grew louder, as if God stood behind her. She turned. Sam was running toward her. She raised a hand and he stopped. He couldn't be anywhere near her as God gave her punishment. His blond hair was darkened by the rain, his clothes plastered to him.

"Stay away," she called. "You shouldn't be here. I don't want you caught in the middle of this."

His hands lifted. "Middle of what?"

"My punishment." She was so tired of being strong, of holding herself together. It hadn't made a difference. "It's my fault Katie's gone. I told God to take me, not her."

"Marti—" He took a step closer and she slid back.

"I mean it, Sam." She lifted her face and raised her voice, spreading her arms wide. "I deserve whatever you want to give me!"

"Martina, this isn't your fault." He shouted over the thunder. "*I* screwed things up. I didn't listen to you. If it's anyone's fault, it's mine."

Such a dear man. She had never deserved him. "This has nothing to do with you, Sam."

"Marti, Katie is—" A loud crack of thunder blotted out his words.

"No!" She dropped to her knees and covered her face. She couldn't breathe. *Don't let her be dead. Please!*

Strong arms came around her, his voice near her ear. "Katie's safe, sweetheart. She and Tim turned up at the Depot."

She leaned back and stared at him, blinking against the rain pouring over them.

"She's safe!" he repeated. "And she's waiting for you."

"Are you sure?" She grasped his shirt. "She's alive?"

"Alive and well. Honest."

She sagged against him. *Thank you, God. Thank you, thank you.*

His arms tightened and he rocked gently. "She's okay, sweetheart. It's over. You're both safe. I won't let anyone hurt you."

Katie's alive. Sam's here. God didn't strike me down. She loosened her grip. "Does God," she hiccupped, "give second chances?"

"Every day." He gently wiped her cheeks. "And every time we mess up, He forgives us yet again. He paid too high of a price not to."

Unexpected, peaceful certainty covered her like an umbrella. She touched his face. "I'm glad."

"Me too." He grasped her fingers and pressed a kiss to the tips, then helped her to her feet. "C'mon. Let's go see your sister." With an arm wrapped tightly around her, he directed her out of the park.

<hr/>

Marti leaped from the car as Sam pulled up in front of the Java Depot. She was two steps into the coffee shop when Katie barreled into her, sobbing.

"I'm s-so s-sorry, Marti. We didn't kn-know what to do."

Marti clutched her close, soothing her sister through her own tears. "Shh, Kat. It's okay. You're here now. You're safe." Katie's tear-streaked face was the most wonderful sight ever. They clung together as they cried. "It's okay, sweetie. Let's sit down and you can tell me all about it."

"Two hot cocoas coming right up." Jason's eyes were wet.

Settled close together, with Sam beside her, Marti drew the story out piece by piece.

"We weren't planning on running away," Katie said. "Honest. I believed what you and Sam said, that Tim would be waiting when we got back. He was going to come over in the morning to say goodbye."

Jason set two mugs before them, whipped cream piled high with chocolate drizzled over the top. He winked at Marti when she thanked him.

"This looks so yummy!" Katie declared, her distress momentarily forgotten.

Marti allowed her a moment to enjoy the treat before directing her back to the story. "So, what happened during the night?"

"I was getting ready for bed when he called. He was really freaked out. His step-brother had called and said some really weird things about me, and you, and even Tim. I thought he was such a nice guy when he bought us all that stuff, but he's not." Her eyebrows pinched together. "He told Tim he had to help him get out of jail."

"How?"

"Take me away and hide me so you wouldn't testify."

With Katie's wide blue eyes focused on her, Marti kept her expression calm as her heart recoiled. "So," she managed eventually, "is that what Tim did?"

"No! He was really scared. He told Eddy he'd think about it. Then he called me and we decided we had to hide in case Eddy sent someone else to do it."

Marti put a hand to Katie's sweet face. "You were so brave, Kat. Where did you go?"

"We went to his math teacher's house and hid in the garage."

"All night?"

Nodding, Katie wrapped her arms around herself. "It was so cold, and there were scary noises. When his teacher found us in the morning, we asked him to bring us here."

"Why didn't you call me? Or answer your phone?"

"Tim said his brother would track our phones, so we threw them in a garbage can."

Marti pulled Katie into a hug, thanking God once again. "You are amazing, you know that? I'm so proud of you."

"Really? I thought you'd be mad."

"I wish you'd called me or Sam or Officer Ben, but you two did what you thought was safest, and that took a lot of courage. I'm so thankful you're back, and you're both okay."

"Me too. I was scared, and I just wanted to be with you."

"We're together now. And someone has a big birthday coming up very soon that means we can be together all the time."

Katie's face lit up. "I can't wait!" She leaned close and whispered, "But right now I have to go to the bathroom."

Marti laughed and shooed her toward the back of the shop. As Katie hurried away, Marti leaned against Sam, exhausted and content. "Where's Tim?"

"At the station with Ben, giving a statement. He's a good kid, Marti."

"I think you're right."

He tucked her hair behind her ear, a tender smile on his face. "You've been amazing through this whole ordeal, Martina. It's going to take a lifetime to get to know you."

Her heart turned over. A lifetime. That sounded about right.

– 46 –

When the guilty verdict was pronounced, Marti took her first full breath since meeting Eddy. After months of preparation, they'd done it. Guilty on all counts. She met his seething gaze as he was led from the courtroom, chin up despite the aura of evil that chilled her when he passed. She'd started each day with a prayer for courage, and prayed through her hours of testimony. Each night she'd fallen into bed exhausted from facing him again, yet filled with gratitude for being carried through another day in court.

She could finally go forward with her life. The idea made her dizzy.

"We have to celebrate," she declared to Sam as they left the courthouse, her hand tucked securely in his.

"I agree. How about we head over to GPS to share the news?"

"Perfect!"

The short ride from downtown Minneapolis was filled with laughter. Once parked in front of the familiar house, Sam opened her door and held out a hand, which she accepted with a blush. She would never get used to being treated like a princess.

He pulled her into his arms. "Have I told you how proud I am of you?"

"Yes." She smiled. "But you can tell me again."

He gathered her close. "Martha Joy Gustafson, you are the most amazing woman I've ever met. You are brave, focused, and loyal to your bones. You managed to bring down the empire of a guy the police have been after for years."

"Not on my own," she protested.

"No, but this case would have fallen apart without you." He rested his forehead against hers. "You were the one on the witness stand facing a man who'd threatened you and your sister, who'd tried to kill you, and who kept the pressure on right up to the guilty verdict, but you stood your ground." He lifted his head and grinned. "Remind me to never be on your bad side."

Laughter, pure and toe tingling, burst from where it had hidden for most of her life. "Well, you keep that in mind, buster. I'm not someone you want to tangle with."

"Oh, I'll remember," he chuckled. His smile softened as he traced a finger along her cheekbone. "And you need to remember that you are amazing, talented, smart, and so beautiful it makes me act like an idiot around you."

"You might have to remind me," she whispered before he leaned in for a kiss.

When he pulled back, he tapped her nose. "We'd better go in now or we might not make it at all."

Her cheeks flamed as he steered her up the walk. "Good plan," she managed.

Opening the front door, he stepped back. "Ladies first."

She giggled and stepped into the entry. "Well, aren't you—"

"Surprise!" The shout sent her stumbling backwards into Sam. Smiling faces, balloons, and streamers crowded the room. "What in the world?"

"You wanted a celebration." He propelled her into the well-wishers.

Marti moved through the group from one hug to the next, sharing laughter and tears with the people who had come to mean so much. The beloved GPS staff. Kurt and Vanessa holding their four-month-old daughter. Dear Pastor Joel.

She was swarmed by Sam's sisters, hugged by his brothers, and squeezed by his mother, which made her cry harder. Ben winked as he held out more tissues. Jimmy, Jason, and Lorna stood with Katie and Tim in the kitchen. Katie alternated between hugging Marti and crying. Gloria and Buster nodded at Marti from the other side of the island.

"Can I have everyone's attention?" Sam's voice rang out over the conversation and laughter. "Where's Marti? Oh, there you are. Come up here, please."

She weaved through the crowd and stepped up on a makeshift stage of cement blocks and plywood. Grinning, he pulled her close. "This might get a little uncomfortable," he whispered. "People are going to say nice things about you, so smile and nod."

"Nooo—" When she tried to move away, he held her tight against him.

She fidgeted as one person after another told her how proud they were, how she'd impacted their life as well as the community, how important she was.

"I now know what grace under fire looks like," Ben said. "What a whole police force hadn't been able to do, you did with brains and determination." He raised a glass. "Anytime you want to consider becoming a cop, Marti, you let me know."

"Thanks, but no thanks." Her swift response drew laughter and applause.

"Marti, my dear." Mrs. Evans stood beside Ben. "You've brought so much joy to our family in such a short time." She blew a kiss and Marti managed a teary smile.

Finally, Sam drew the accolades to a close and asked Joel to pray over the food that covered the kitchen counters. As people moved toward the kitchen, Marti wrapped her arms around Sam.

"Thank you," she said.

"Don't thank me. I didn't tell them what to say."

"No, thank you for making them stop." Although she would cherish their kindness forever.

He laughed. "Maybe I'll get them going again once you start eating."

"Don't you dare." She started to step down from the platform.

"Hey." He pulled her back. "There's something I want to show you tomorrow. I'll pick you up at eight and we'll have breakfast on the way."

"Eight?"

"It's an all-day affair. Trust me, you won't want to miss a minute."

She hesitated, then nodded. "I hope I won't regret trusting you, Sam Evans."

"Never, Miss Gustafson."

Marti opened the blinds and smiled. Sam leaned against the side of his car in the driveway, holding two Java Depot cups. She waved, then raced through the rest of her morning prep. Although it had taken a while to unwind after the unexpected celebration, she'd had the most restful sleep ever. She scribbled a note and slid it under Katie's bedroom door, then grabbed a sweater and skipped down the stairs of their garage apartment. Sam greeted her with a kiss that rocked her down to her toes.

"Wow," she said with a breathless laugh, "that was the best good morning I've ever received."

He wiggled his eyebrows. "I think I can do better."

She pushed him away when he leaned in for another. "Doubtful. I'm starved, and dying of curiosity, so don't try to distract me."

Releasing a dramatic sigh, he opened the passenger door. "Fine. In you go."

She responded with a sparkling smile. "Thank you. Mmm. Something smells delicious in here."

He slid into the driver's seat and slapped her hand as she reached toward the picnic basket. "Hang on a minute. I want to say something first."

She feigned a pout that didn't hold.

"I've been thinking about what you said last night, about trusting me." He took her hands. "I can't promise I'll never mess up, but I want you to know that I will always tell you the truth, and you will *always* be able to trust me to be beside you through whatever life throws at you."

"I'm hoping life is done throwing stuff at me, at least for a while," she said, then squeezed his fingers. It still snatched her breath to think this amazing man had chosen her. "I never thought I'd have someone like you in my life. I thank God for you every day."

He leaned forward and kissed her gently, and all thoughts of breakfast faded. When he sat back, she opened her eyes slowly, toes curled.

He winked. "See? Told you I could do better."

Her face heated. "I'm impressed."

"Let's pray and get moving."

She smiled through his simple blessing, silently adding her own thanks, and asking for whatever she would need to be a blessing in his life.

"Breakfast is served."

Chatter filled the next hour before Sam turned off the highway onto a county road. Another twenty minutes, then Marti straightened in her seat. "This looks familiar." She watched farm fields go by. "Like I've been here before. Maybe in a dream or something."

Sam nodded. "Farmland can look pretty much the same when you're driving past one after another."

They rode another mile in silence. "Wait...I know that place." She turned to look fully out her window as they passed the farm. "It is! That's the McCarty farm." She spun toward him, eyes wide. "The farm next to my grandparents'."

She sucked in her breath, and pointed. "There! Oh, Sam! That's the farm. Our farm."

He turned onto the winding gravel driveway and parked near the two-story farmhouse. She sat still, a trembling hand to her mouth as she stared, waiting for Grandy to come out of the house. The pounding in her chest filled her with bittersweet joy. "How did you know?"

"Did a little digging. Then I called the owners and they invited us for lunch. There they are now."

"We can get out?"

"That's the reason we're here, sweetheart."

She struggled to find her breath, wanting to laugh, needing to cry. When Sam opened her door, she grasped his hand with a white-knuckled grip. A collie went racing past, chasing after two children who ran with bubbles floating behind. A horse neighed in the field.

"Welcome!" A middle-aged couple approached with wide smiles. "We've been so excited to meet you. You must be Martha. We're Jerry and Stephanie Johnson."

She shook their hands, unable to speak. If she opened her mouth, she'd lose the tiny shred of control holding her together. Chickens clucked nearby, pecking at the ground. The rooster called from his perch on the henhouse.

"Thanks for having us out," Sam said. "This farm meant a lot to Marti and her sister as they were growing up."

"We bought this place from your grandmother," Jerry told Marti.

"Wonderful, solid farm folk. We're honored to carry on their legacy."

Stephanie put an arm around Marti's shoulders. "Come see the house. I'm dying to hear your story."

This is a dream. It has to be. An amazing, happy dream that she never, ever wanted to wake up from. There were new appliances in the kitchen, blinds instead of curtains on the windows, but it smelled the same—something yummy baking in the oven, coffee perking on the counter, a vase overflowing with wildflowers on the table.

Marti closed her eyes and drew a deep breath. "Grandy loved to bake. My younger sister spent hours and hours in here with her while Gramps and I were either out in the field, or doing woodworking in the barn."

"The best room in a farmhouse is the kitchen, don't you think? Let's go see the rest." Stephanie led her into the living room. "I hope you can excuse the mess. With four kids, three of them boys, it's a never-ending battle to get them to pick up after themselves."

Marti walked through the beloved farmhouse, seeing it as an adult but with a child's heart. So much love here; laughter, singing, prayer. Freedom. She'd been such a burden to her mother, why wasn't she sent out here to live? No, they'd have had to drag her kicking and screaming away from Katie. Their mother hadn't cared for Marti, but she would never have let go of her baby.

When the tour finished, they joined Sam and Jerry in the yard. "Ready to see the barn?" Jerry asked.

Marti nodded. "Yes." *No.* What if the way she remembered spending time there with Gramps was more imagination than reality? What if she'd dreamed it all up?

Sam took her hand as they approached the familiar building that gleamed under a fresh coat of red paint. The door hinges no longer squeaked, the windows had been replaced. She followed Jerry. It smelled the same—weathered wood, sawdust, animals, and leather.

Her attention jumped to the corner and her breath hitched. Gramps's large, paint-splattered workbench had been replaced with newer, smaller benches of pine and plywood, dotted with color, nicks, and scratches.

Memories engulfed her. Gramps's humming, the scrape of sandpaper, the whine of the saws. The aroma of paint and poly, and the thrill of seeing her finished project. She strained to hear Gramps's deep, raspy encouragement, the meow of barn cats, the clang of the dinner bell.

Her smile was bittersweet relief. Time spent here had been the best of her life. Her memories were clear and true.

"I added a workroom and storage back here." Jerry led them to an addition, and stepped aside to let Marti enter.

She stepped through the doorway and stopped abruptly, hands pressed over her heart. There it was—her grandfather's workbench. She crossed the room slowly and ran her fingers across the battered, paint-spattered plywood.

"Martha Joy, what do you think of this color?" Gramps's voice. "Here, let me show you an easier way to hold it. You're a natural with tools, you know that? Makes a grandpa proud."

She longed to lay her head on the familiar wood and cry. He'd never once said she was stupid, never raised his voice at her. No, she'd made him *proud*. She turned to Sam standing nearby, suddenly conscious of the quiet around her. She managed a wobbly smile as he took her hand, and looked to their hosts. "I'm so glad you still have it."

"We are too," Jerry said.

"Some of the items that were left were too beautiful to part with." Stephanie gestured toward a back room. "We put them in here, hoping family would come to claim them at some point."

Heart pounding, Marti followed her through a doorway to a storage area. "Oh…"

The dresser Gramps had been finishing for her bedroom, one side waiting for stain. An inlaid chess set sat on top. And the rocking horse he'd restored; she'd been mesmerized as he added the final colors. How Katie had loved it. Oh! There was the larger version of the box she'd tucked the memory card into. She smiled through her tears. These lovely people had preserved Gramps's legacy.

Stephanie moved around her and took a file folder from the box. "We found this tucked in here. It seemed like something you'd want."

Sam stood close as she looked through the papers. Legal stuff. Words she'd never be able to pronounce. She lifted a frown to him, her breath catching at the tears in his eyes.

"It's a petition for custody, Martina," he said, his tone husky. "Your grandparents were trying to get custody of you and Katie."

What? "When?"

He thumbed through the papers. "About ten years ago."

A tear spilled over. "Right when Gramps died." *They fought for us!* That explained why her mother cut off communication.

"They wanted you here, sweetheart."

She nodded, unable to speak. Joy pulsed through her. It hadn't been her imagination. She and Katie had belonged here.

"We're glad all these things will have a new home," Jerry said, from where he and Stephanie stood off to the side, tears trickling down Stephanie's cheeks.

Hope leapt within as she looked at Sam.

He grinned and nodded. "Jimmy agreed that you need to work on your grandpa's workbench."

"At the shop?"

"Yup. And we'll be taking the rest of the items home."

Marti burrowed against him, her heart throbbing. God was fitting the broken pieces of her life together. So amazing. So…God.

After a lively lunch with the Johnson clan, Sam and Jerry loaded what they could into Sam's car. Then Marti and Sam strolled out to the fields.

"This has been the most wonderful surprise of my life," she told the amazing man beside her. "Thank you."

He pulled her close and dropped a kiss on her nose. "You're welcome. I feel like I've gotten to know your grandparents a little after being here with you."

"They feel alive to me again." And still loving her.

In the glow of the setting sun, she stood at the edge of the golden field, and spread her arms wide. The truth she'd sought had been hers the whole time. With all her flaws and shortcomings, she'd been loved by her grandparents, was adored by her sister, and eternally treasured by God. She'd done good things and bad, been knocked down but gotten back up. She wasn't perfect, and yet she was. Perfect in God's eyes.

Strong arms came around her and she pressed back against him, safe in his embrace. Sam had seen her potential long before she had. He'd witnessed her failures and successes, encouraged her, and loved her before she'd learned to love herself.

The future, as bright as the sunshine pouring over them, beckoned. She couldn't wait to leap in.

And we know that in all things God works for the good of those who love Him, who have been called according to his purpose.
Romans 8:28

If God is for us, who can be against us? He who did not spare His own Son, but gave Him up for us all—how will He not also, along with Him, graciously give us all things?
Romans 8:31-32

Dearest Reader,

Thank you for reading *The Color of Truth*! I hope you enjoyed Marti and Sam's story as much as I enjoyed writing it. If so, would you **please consider writing a brief review** on the site where you purchased this book? One of the best ways to spread the news about a book you've enjoyed is to write a few sentences sharing your thoughts. **Reviews are gold to an author**, and so often give us the encouragement we need to keep writing stories for our readers. The other way is, of course, to **tell your friends and family!**

My ultimate goal as I write is two-fold: to glorify the mighty God I serve, and to share inspiring, encouraging stories that point people to the Source of all goodness, the One who can and does redeem everyone who seeks Him.

May the Creator of all that is good, bless you and keep you until we meet again!
Stacy

Gratitude Beyond Words

As always, one of the most amazing parts of my writing journey has been encountering the people God puts in my life along the way. Here are just a few who have helped make this third book possible.

My heartfelt thanks to...

God Almighty who leads me into truth and away from my own foolishness (daily, it seems!), who has called me to write for His Kingdom, and who provides just what I need exactly when I need it.

Mike—steady as a rock, funny as ever. Thanks for 35+ years.
Camry and Nate, Aaron and Rosanna—pizza, games, unending encouragement. Love you!
Kaira Mae, Miles, and Baby C—your unfiltered and unfailing trust inspires me.
My extended family—thanks for always checking on my progress. Over and over and over...

Brenda Anderson—my Caribou companion and unflagging cheerleader.
Sharon Hinck—your gentleness and faith have kept me going.
Noelle Epp—enduring patience in the face of change. We figured it out!
Polgarus Studios—professional, personal, and fun. Thank you!

Nina Engen—Marti & Sam, Eleanor & Excelsior, and us.
Forever Friends—love each one of you, girlfriends.

My Beta readers—Nina, Brenda, Beverly S., Robin W., Esther M., Ann G., and Jennifer S. Eagle eyes, every one!
My readers—for sharing the fun and saying such nice things!

And as always to...
All of the wonderful, talented writerly people God has put in my life. Critique partners, ACFW MN-NICE, retreat buddies, chapter-mates, brainstormers, chocolate lovers, dedicated servants of Christ. What a joy to create alongside every one of you!

Thank you, Sweet Jesus, for the privilege of serving you through writing.

About the Author

Stacy Monson is the award-winning author of The Chain of Lakes series, including "Shattered Image," "Dance of Grace," and "The Color of Truth." Her stories reveal an extraordinary God at work in ordinary life. A member of ACFW (American Christian Fiction Writers), Stacy is the past president of MN-NICE, as well as the area coordinator for ACFW in Minnesota. Residing in the Twin Cities, she is the wife of a juggling, unicycling physical education teacher, mom to two amazing kids and two wonderful in-law kids, and a very proud grandma of 2.5 grands.

Let's Connect!

For news about upcoming books, contests, and other fun stuff – stop by my website at www.stacymonson.com

Facebook: https://www.facebook.com/stacymmonson/
Twitter: https://twitter.com/StacyMonson
Instragram: https://www.instagram.com/stacy_monson
Pinterest: https://www.pinterest.com/stacymonson/

The Chain of Lakes series:

Shattered Image

Available on Amazon and other fine online retailers

Dance of Grace

Available on Amazon and other fine online retailers

The Color of Truth

Available on Amazon and other fine online retailers

Made in the USA
Lexington, KY
10 June 2017